MY LADY LIPSTICK

Karin Kallmaker

BELLA BOOKS

2018

Bella Books, Inc.
P.O. Box 10543
Tallahassee, FL 32302

Printed in the United States of America on acid-free paper.

First Bella Books Edition 2018

Editor: Katherine V. Forrest
Cover Designer: Judith Fellows

ISBN: 978-1-59493-568-8

Other Bella Books by Karin Kallmaker

From the Author

One person births a book, but it takes many to create the delivery room. Friends, family, readers, booksellers, librarians, musicians, artists, writers, editors, publishers, bloggers and chocolatiers, who, along with Derry, Dingle, Kinsale, Juneau, Skagway, Seattle, Banff, Calgary, Albuquerque, Santa Fe and the Navajo Nation, all played a part in the creation of this one. Honorable mention to my daughter Lee who brought *Zelda* and *Overwatch* into my world, making me nearly, almost, kinda cool.

If Lisa the bartender rings a bell, you first met her in *Warming Trend* and again in the short story "Good Morning." Frankly, she's a bit upset that you had to be reminded.

I consulted websites, personal blogs, medical journals, and individuals about living with anxiety disorder and other issues that keep company with it. Any mistakes in this portrayal are my own.

About the Author

Karin Kallmaker has been exclusively devoted to lesbian fiction since the publication of her first novel in 1989. As an author published by the storied Naiad Press, she worked with Barbara Grier and Donna McBride, and has been fortunate to be mentored by a number of editors, including Katherine V. Forrest.

In addition to multiple Lambda Literary Awards, she has been featured as a Stonewall Library and Archives Distinguished Author. Other accolades include the Ann Bannon Popular Choice and other awards for her writing, as well as the selection as a Trailblazer by the Golden Crown Literary Society. She is best known for novels such as *Painted Moon*, *Substitute for Love*, *Captain of Industry*, *Maybe Next Time* and *The Kiss that Counted*.

The California native is the mother of two and blogs at kallmaker.com. Write to her at karin@kallmaker.com or search for "Kallmaker" on social media—there's only one.

A complete list of books by this author available from Bella Books can be found at www.bellabooks.com.

When you purchase from the publisher more of your dollars reach the women who write and produce the books you love. Karin thanks you for your support of books for and about lesbians!

Twenty-Eight, the same number as my age when I completed my first novel. Or a perfect cribbage score, sans a one-eyed Jack.

"We know what we are but know not what we may be."
-Hamlet, IV.5.43-44

CHAPTER ONE

Paris Ellison was so angry she made a seven-layer English Trifle and two large pans of double cocoa brownies.

She even dribbled water over the letter from Reynard House, Proud Member of the Reynard Media Group. But the ink refused to smear and the words continued to taunt her.

She'd said no once, and now the nerve—the nerve! To offer her first-class tickets, reservations at a Fifth Avenue hotel, and the assurance of box seats to *Hamilton*—how rude!

She whipped ganache into submission and drizzled it on the first pan of still warm brownies. She'd slice them later before taking them to Lisa's tomorrow. The second pan of brownies went into the oven, and only then did she pause in her fever of anger-fueled anxiety baking to read the infuriating letter again.

Anita Topaz did *not* make personal appearances. Paris had been perfectly clear about that from the get go. But with the merger the new people at Reynard House preferred not to notice that little detail.

A scratch and yowl at the door made her look at the clock. Right on time, Hobbit sidled in to offer mid-morning greetings by way of gracing Paris's jeans with orange tabby tomcat fur.

"You're not fooling anyone, you know. I'm just Second Breakfast to you." Yielding to the cat's single-minded agenda, she dropped a small scoop of crunchy dry food into the dish next to the door. Hobbit promptly abandoned his adoration of Paris's ankles and dug in.

"Just because Reynard House is the new owner, that doesn't mean my contract is revised. Not yet at least." Hobbit ignored the bowl of fresh water Paris set down next to the dry food. "They can't make me, so there. I owe them four books in the next two years, and on schedule. Not one thing more."

The oven timer beeped and she left Hobbit to his loud snacking. She turned the pan in the oven and reset the timer. The custard was cool enough now to assemble the trifle, and she devoted herself to carefully lining the bottom of her only clear glass bowl with fresh sponge cake and splashing it with sherry. Apricots and silky vanilla custard followed, then she repeated the layers until the glass bowl was nearly full.

At least the Misses Lambeth and Richards upstairs would love the treat. She'd take it up after supper and check on the progress of the colds that had kept her usually gregarious and active landlords in "little old lady" mode, as they called it. They did like a drop of sherry now and again, and nobody could feel out of sorts with a dessert like this one.

Except her, maybe. Her day had begun as peacefully and predictably as any other since the day she'd hunkered down in this haven. Then the mail had arrived this morning, again bringing demands.

Hobbit finished up Second Breakfast and padded across the faded linoleum to the soft brown carpet of the living room. He stretched and flexed, then sauntered to the sunny window seat, lord of all.

Paris ignored the loud, disapproving sniff at the layer of cat hair on the cushion. "What do you think this is, some swanky New York hotel?" She prodded the top of the brownies in the oven with a fingertip and judged them as needing one more minute. "Speaking of which, look at this letter."

She carried the offending paper to the window seat and showed it to Hobbit. Hobbit let out a grudging purr, and granted access to his belly while Paris read the letter aloud with renewed outrage.

"Looking forward to finalizing all the details, sincerely, *blah blah blah*," Paris finished. "See? They're trying to bribe me into going, and you know why I won't." Hobbit had heard all about why Paris had moved three thousand miles from her last job. "Anita Topaz isn't going to this meeting. She's not going to do a TED Talk or whatever Reynard Media calls it for any—" She whirled to face the kitchen. "Foul word!"

She dashed across the living room toward the ominous you're-too-late scent of overcooked brownie. Her socks slipped on the linoleum, catapulting her through the kitchen door. She yanked the pan out of the oven, burning her wrist on the door. The pan slipped out of her grasp. She lunged to save it and whacked her head on the counter so hard that the world went dark for a moment.

The dancing stars in her vision went away finally as she Jackie-Chan rubbed the dent in her skull. At least it felt like a dent.

Hobbit coiled into view from around the corner of the kitchen island, tail kinked with annoyance that the clatter and cursing had disturbed his morning nap and petting. Rightly presuming that the fallen brownies were not anything he would want to eat, he pointedly began cleaning a paw.

"I'm not leaking brain matter," she told the cat's back. "Thanks for asking."

At least the brownies had landed face up. The edges were hard and tasted burnt, even for people who loved that part. Increasingly foul-tempered about the whole world, she set to using a melon baller to scoop out the still moist and edible interior. Chocolate, sugar, and butter in any form was edible, right? Brownie Curls… Lisa might still be able to use them.

Now that was an idea. Why wait until tomorrow? Getting out of the house would probably make her feel better. It had been three…four days? Her last brownie delivery to Mona Lisa's as a matter of fact. Not for the first time she was happy to have found a way not to eat her bouts of anxiety-baking all by herself, and it even involved exercise. If Lisa didn't think anyone would buy the salvaged brownies, they could certainly eat a few themselves. It was that kind of day.

Five minutes effort with little plastic bags and ribbons to tie them closed went without major mishaps. Two dark, moist curls of brownie in each. Paris thought they looked appetizing, but Lisa would have to agree. She shoved the letter into her back pocket, thinking she'd ask Lisa's advice about it.

Hobbit gave a discontented *moof* as she dumped him on the front porch.

"Go find Elevenses wherever it is you spend the rest of your time. I know it's early, but I'm getting some fresh air."

Hobbit slithered under the hedge with a parting yowl.

"Yeah, yeah, yeah. I've been called worse."

She pulled on her coat, grabbed up the basket with her wares, and let herself out into the blustery blue day. Lisa wasn't expecting Paris to show up with baked goodies until tomorrow. Still, as Lisa had said in the past, there really was no limit to how many brownies a bar full of sports fans could consume.

Tipping her face to the sunshine, she zipped up her hoodie. The sharp wind off Massachusetts Bay shouted winter, but the sun was seductively whispering spring. San Francisco was never this extreme. She pushed away the pang of longing for Gorilla Barbecue and the pale, sandy beach at Pacifica.

She'd grown to like this town of Revere and nearby Boston, but in the nearly five years she'd lived here it hadn't turned into home.

It was hard to stay angry on such a glorious day. The blue sky refreshed her eyes and the sun warmed the tip of her nose. It was as if the long, frozen, wet, dirty, slushy, slogging New England winter was over. But she knew that was a lie. As her landlords had warned her, March coaxed you out of your jacket, then dumped a foot of snow down your back. Much like life itself.

The only aspect about her apartment she didn't like was its position near the bottom of a hill even San Franciscans would call steep. It did mean that her landlords had a great view toward the harbor and that Paris's rental space was light and airy. But the location was a challenge to someone without a car.

She took a deep breath and set off up the hill with steady, long strides. Steep roads aside, renting the basement flat of the Lambeth/Richards house was still an ideal arrangement. The ladies had cash to help with their bills and repairs, and Paris had sunny windows, a solidly constructed kitchen that allowed her to bake off her anxieties, and an oversized bedroom with a big bay window where her desk was turned to face the flower and vegetable garden.

Her name appeared nowhere on a lease or utility bill. Exactly the way she wanted it.

That Anita Topaz's meteoric success meant Paris could afford more—a lot more—didn't make a bit of difference. Anita Topaz was not online, didn't Tweet or chat, and she did *not* do personal appearances!

In danger of losing her recovering good spirits, she paused halfway up the hill. There was plenty of mud and slush lurking in the gaps between squares of sidewalk. Fortunately, her Doc Martens were perfect Adventuring Gear for New England winters. Snow and mud never slowed her down. Once she made it to the top of the hill, it was only two more minutes to a frequently scheduled bus that was only two short stops from the T—and from there all of Boston was within reach. It was also only three minutes to a grocery and five minutes to Mona Lisa's. Her living quarters were as close to the rest of the world as she wanted them to be.

With her hoodie pulled up and zipped to her chin, jacket flapping in the wind and wrinkled jeans scruffy at the knees, she might have been any of the local youths walking home from the high school for lunch. True, none of them carried a picnic basket right out of Little Red Riding Hood swinging from one hand.

At the top of the block she paused to inhale deeply and smiled in spite of herself. There was a finch chirping in the distance. Spring was indeed coming. The last of her anger seeped away, leaving behind cautious contentment paired, as always, with the tickle of anxiety.

No news there. She'd known all along that her Berserker Baking Blitz was rooted in her hyperactive flight-or-fight instinct.

The flashing Sam Adams Lager sign over Mona Lisa's familiar green door was a welcome sight. The flutters and shivers that had tightened her chest eased. *Note to self—fresh air is good for you*. It wasn't the first time she'd told herself that. It wouldn't be the last.

The steamy, golden air inside the bar was also good for her, she decided, even if her sunglasses immediately fogged up. The familiar sharp aromas of beer, furniture polish, and tangy tomato soup were immediately comforting. She shucked her coat and unzipped the hoodie. Her word count could wait. She'd clearly needed this break.

Mona Lisa herself was working the front of the house, and that was always a beautiful thing. It was just past noon and customers were scarce. By five o'clock there wouldn't be an empty seat at the gleaming oak bar, especially if Lisa was still working it. Paris didn't know where Lisa had picked up her mad skills, but she made filling a beer mug as eye-catching as a striptease. It certainly helped that she had a mane of sun-streaked yellow hair and a figure that filled out a Shetland sweater and Levi's in all the best ways.

Paris sent a chin nod Lisa's way, hoisted the basket into view and got a nod in return. Her usual cushioned chair in the corner near the front window suited her just fine, especially with her face to the sun and back to the TVs. At the moment the muted televisions were replaying a broadcast of a baseball game so ancient it was in black and white. It still roused a cheer from a die-hard Red Sox fan at the far end of the bar. Next month, on opening day, the place would be packed.

"What did you bring me?" Lisa put a cup of coffee on the table in front of Paris and dropped into the opposite chair. "I made that a couple of hours ago. Up to you if you drink it."

Paris sipped. Contrary to Lisa's description, the coffee was hot and fresh. "What every growing girl needs. Can you use some brownies? I know I'm early. I'll have the usual tomorrow."

Lisa made a *hmm* sound that Paris had learned meant that the calculator in Lisa's brain was adding up the potential profit. Pity the fool who thought the tanned, blond surfer girl exterior meant there was no business sense on the inside. "It's going to be a slow night."

"I had an anxiety incident."

"Sorry to hear that. All better?"

"Mostly."

"They look awesome." With a Betty Boop coo in her voice and shimmering tears in her eyes, Lisa asked, "Would fifteen be okay?"

It was tempting to say yes to anything Lisa suggested, but they'd played this game before. With a Spock eyebrow lift, Paris corrected, "I think twenty. And the cup of coffee."

The corner of Lisa's mouth twitched. "Spoilsport."

"Does that big blue eye thing ever work?"

"Oh honey, you'd be surprised." Lisa was peering into a baggie. "Why are they shaped liked that? What went wrong?"

"I got distracted. Sorry they don't look so great."

"They look like a Stoli White Russian with a chocolate chaser to me."

Paris appreciated Lisa's creativity. "That does sounds delicious. What cute name will you give that concoction?"

"The 'Adulting So Hard.'" Lisa flashed her a brilliant smile. "I know it's the first of the month, but I haven't picked a March special yet. Bring me more next week, just in a box is fine. No need to wrap them for single sale."

"Sure." Paris's attention was caught by a new arrival. Small and pale skinned, she looked like a recent arrival from the Emerald Isle itself. If the saffron and green pleated skirt wasn't proof of heritage, there was a tweed flat cap holding down the abundant, wildly tangled orange-red curls.

"You have a customer."

Lisa was already rising to her feet. "She's been a regular for the past couple of weeks. There's a new production rehearsing at the Ferley Playhouse she's in. It's always the same order—soup and a half pint."

"Lunch of champions."

She watched Lisa chat amiably with the newcomer about how wonderful it was at last to see the sun. Paris had heard often enough that former Floridian Lisa didn't like the bitter Boston winters, but Lisa always added that her Alaskan-born wife knew how to keep her warm, wink-wink.

The most important fact Paris knew about Lisa was that she'd been a whistleblower against a large hotel chain in a dispute on union pay for waitstaff. She'd pointed out they were not paying wages for required prep time. They'd fired her. She'd sued. The quick settlement had bought the bar.

Good thing, since Paris was sure Lisa would never get work in a hotel again, not in New England, anyway. When a woman stuck her head above the weeds, there was no shortage of people willing to throw bricks at it. And if she interfered with profits, they never forgot her name.

She sipped the coffee and quelled the prickles of tension that threatened again. When a shadow fell over the table she jumped.

The redhead was holding out a folded piece of paper. "The bartender said this belonged to you. I found it on the floor inside the door." The lilt in her voice confirmed she wasn't a native New Englander.

"Crap!" Paris snatched the letter out of the woman's hand. "I can't believe I dropped it."

"I thought it was trash and unfolded it to make sure. *Hamilton* tickets, sounds grand."

Paris didn't hide her annoyance that the woman had read it. "It's really none of your—"

"I know. I'm a speed reader. Helps with auditions and acting. Anyway, I hope you have a great trip."

"Sorry. I didn't mean to be rude."

The full lips split into a broad smile. "Yes you did. I couldn't help but absorb the whole thing, but it was still rude of me. So now we're even."

Hoping her nervous swallow didn't show, Paris held out her hand. "I'm Paris."

"Diana."

Though the handshake was brief, it had the surprising effect of abating Paris's anxiety completely. Impressions rushed in— light freckles dusted Diana's cheeks. Her eyes were insanely green. The lipstick was winter-ripe cranberry and the fingers that had brushed her palm were exquisitely manicured and tipped with the same red. The tweed peacoat fit the slim figure perfectly and its large buttons were covered with the same suede piping that outlined the collar. Classy buttons meant couture, as Paris had found out doing research for her high-fashion thriller, *Hands Off the Merchandise.*

Diana had that…that…*thing*. That same whatever it was that Lisa had. That *thing* that made a plain woolen scarf sing with casual elegance.

"So you're Anita Topaz?" Diana's puzzlement was plain on her face. "The writer?"

Double crap, Paris thought. "It's a pen name. And I would really prefer no one else know Paris Ellison is the real person behind the name."

Her *hmm* sounded a lot like Lisa's, as if they were sisters from different mothers. Luckily, Diana seemed only mildly intrigued. "Good for you. You're not what I would have pictured for the Queen of the Bodice Rippers, and that's probably shame on me thinking writers look like their characters."

The more Paris heard her voice, the more aware she was that Diana's accent was unusual. Definitely not American, and not Canadian either. It didn't sound quite English or Welsh, or have the inflections of Irish cadence her landladies still had. Maybe a mix of all of those with something else?

Intrigued against her will, Paris temporarily abandoned her plan for a quick goodbye and heading home at full speed. "It's true. I'm not personally a heaving bosoms kind of woman.

On book covers, I mean." She didn't add how annoying it was that since Reynard had assumed control the covers had become increasingly pink, the gowns even more low-cut, with the woman dwarfed by a man who looked like he could snap her in two. Her first three books had been taglined, "A Smart Bodice Ripper." Under Reynard the word "smart" had disappeared, as well as the nuance that the phrase was ironic—her books didn't have bodices and clothing was only ripped when the person wearing them thought it a dandy idea.

She added truthfully, "The covers are chosen by marketing pros, and they seem to know what people want to see."

"When people see what they expect to see it makes them comfortable." Diana pulled on supple leather gloves. "I have to get back to rehearsal. Could you tell me where the nearest postal box is?"

Surprised Diana hadn't seen the building that lay between Mona Lisa's and the Playhouse, she began, "The post office is a few blocks—"

"A drop box is fine."

"It's pretty well hidden from the street by the hedges, but I know they pick up from it at three. It's not on your way."

"I like diversions."

It might have been the whack on the head earlier that made it hard to focus on anything but those impossibly green eyes. Paris heard her own voice offering, "I'll show you."

"That's perfect." Diana cinched up her scarf and declared, "Master, go on, and I will follow thee."

"To the last gasp with truth and loyalty?"

Diana blinked in surprise. "Have I found someone who likes Shakespeare as much as I do?"

"I don't know how much you like Shakespeare, but my mother loved *Romeo and Juliet*."

"Hence, Paris for your name?"

"That and *Casablanca*."

"We'll always have Paris," Diana mused as they left the bar. "She sounds interesting, your mother."

"She was." Forestalling an automatic expression of sympathy that would flick at a nerve that would always be raw, Paris quickly added, "I'm no Juliet, and I'm also glad not to have gone through life as Romeo either. Turn right at the corner."

Paris had caught a broadly mimed wink of approval from Lisa as they had gone out the door. She hoped Diana hadn't seen it. Paris had never picked up women in Lisa's bar, or even wanted to. Hell, Lisa would want all the details on the next visit.

It wasn't as if Diana pinged what little gaydar Paris had ever had. It had been a matter of high humor among Paris's former colleagues that she had said, "No way!" when informed that Jodie Foster was gay. She was definitely going to blame leaving with Diana on the konk on the head. It was now throbbing for real.

"It's a block over." Paris pressed for the pedestrian light when they reached the corner, then scrambled to keep up as Diana jaywalked. They skirted cars waiting for the light to turn and reached the other side without mishap. "So what play are you rehearsing?"

"An adaptation of *Tartuffe*. The director is hopeful that with some backing there'll be money for off-Broadway. It's very political and given the times there could be interest."

"But you have your doubts?"

Diana seemed startled at the question. "Was I that obvious? I'll have to work on that."

"You seemed hesitant is all."

"If it does make it to New York, it won't be with this cast. We're good enough for working out the bugs, but that's about it."

"Turn in to the parking lot here." Paris led the way around the high hedges that surrounded the small drugstore. "They hid it well."

"I'd have never seen it. Thank you." Diana pulled a small, thickly padded envelope from a surprisingly capacious inner coat pocket.

Paris caught sight of an address in Utah before the package disappeared. It was so light it almost didn't make a sound as it landed on the mail already in the box. "Hope it gets there safely."

"Me too. Well thank you. I really do have to hurry. Do you go to Mona Lisa's often?"

"Twice a week."

"Then maybe I'll see you there again."

"Maybe," Paris echoed. And she stood there rubbing the bump on her head and watching the petite figure make its way to the corner and then out of sight.

CHAPTER TWO

Diana Beckinsale put two blocks between herself and the helpful but unsettling Paris before she paused in her brisk pace to savor the moment. The wind snatched at her cap but the bobby pins held. She imagined her package whisked away instead, carried over the green expanse of the ridiculously large American continent until it floated to a gentle rest on the desk of the one person she was certain would recognize the contents.

As soon as she could confirm that it had arrived she'd trash the burner cell phone, bow out of playing Dorine and be home in plenty of time for her brother William's wedding ballyhoo. It was a shame—*Tartuffe* was heaps of fun, and choosing to set a play about avarice behind fake piety inside the West Wing of the White House was brilliant. But, as much as she adored performing, Diana wasn't looking for that kind of notoriety.

The only oddity of the whole Boston job was that woman, Paris. Diana really hadn't had any intention of prying, but once opened it was impossible for her not to take in the contents of the letter she'd found. Queen of the Bodice Rippers Anita Topaz was actually a tatty, hoodie-clad twenty-something? Okay, she might be thirty—her taut, light brown skin would resist wrinkles for years. Not that Diana had ever seen a photo of the writer for comparison, but it was surprising nonetheless. When she'd first entered Mona Lisa's and assessed the occupants, she'd mistaken the figure for an underaged boy hiding his face in a bar.

When Lisa had pointed her that way to return the letter, Diana had been gobsmacked. As she'd approached the huddled figure she'd realized for starters that her presumption of gender had been wrong. She also hadn't expected large, deep brown eyes greeting her not with gratitude but open suspicion. The instant snarl in those eyes left Diana with the impression of a formerly gentle dog that had been kicked so often it growled a constant warning at the world to keep its distance.

In the chaos of her reactions she'd mistakenly given the woman her real first name. Not that it mattered, she assured herself—they were unlikely to meet again.

What mattered on this brilliant, wonderful day was that her feet hardly touched the ground, so elated was she by a job well done and now completed. The beautiful day had burst into pure glory as the package had slipped from her hand.

She came to the mud-filled gap in the sidewalk she'd been going around for the last several weeks. Between the sun and her exhilaration she decided it was time to show it who was boss. With one running step for momentum, she jumped it cleanly. And laughed at herself for putting her arms up as if seeking a perfect score for the dismount.

"Nice move!"

Diana turned to find Jeremy, who played the titular Tartuffe, applauding her. "Thank you kind sir."

He gallantly tucked Diana's hand under his arm as they crossed the street to the theater. With decades in local theater and a love of performance for its own sake, Jeremy had no illusions about the scope of his abilities. He made rehearsals lively and wasn't fond of behind-the-scenes drama. Of all the small, local productions Diana had crashed for cover, this one had been among the most pleasant.

As she shed her coat off stage and found her curled and ragged script where she'd left it before the lunch break, Diana flashed again on the puzzle of Paris's surprising identity. The woman had been dressed like someone one paycheck from homelessness. Diana didn't know much about publishing, but a writer with a name she recognized from supermarket shelves, well, wouldn't she be more like a Meryl Streep in *She-Devil*? With a mansion on pristine headlands, diamonds glittering from a hat pin? More like Diana's own relatives for that matter, with casual wealth dripping from every spa-tightened pore?

She wondered about the incongruity of the Paris Ellison-Anita Topaz puzzle until the smell of old dusty seats and stage floor varnish pushed all thoughts but the production out of her head. She did like the play and the players. It would be hard to walk away this time.

* * *

Hours later Diana's back was the only thought in her head. As she climbed the steep, linoleum-covered stairs to her attic apartment, every step was accompanied by a pulse of tear-inducing pain. Her ebullient mood had masked the warning signs. The Nurofen tablets she'd hastily swallowed before leaving the theater had helped, but the annoyed and loudly complaining vertebrae hated the stairs. Well, it was only for a few more days. The privacy and week-to-week cash rental were exactly what she had required.

Her first stop was the bottle of Tylenol-3 she kept in the cupboard next to the fridge. The milk was a little iffy, but she didn't want to wait until she'd heated a tin of soup to take the medication. It would blunt the edge. Getting off her feet plus a good night's sleep would do the rest. She made a mental note to wear flats or trainers tomorrow.

The rock-slab of a chair at the tiny dinette table gave her immediate relief and for a moment she closed her eyes and willed the pain to subside. She'd had years on the gymnastics circuit to learn how to play hurt. Ten years after her last competition she was still playing hurt.

When the pain had faded from a hot red to a tolerable yellow on her personal meter, she eased the wig off with the help of a cotton swab and baby oil, and set it carefully on its pedestal. The windy day meant she had new snarls to brush out later. Feeling better by the minute, she wrestled her way out of her boots and carried them to the closet alcove. Her Irish lass attire fell onto the laundry pile alongside last night's perfect costume she'd worn for an off-stage performance only she would remember.

Last night, she thought. Pure joy. All of it.

A wig of short black hair, a ubiquitous button-up white shirt, black slacks, and apron, and carrying a tray—presto! She had become part of the wallpaper in a busy restaurant. Entering the kitchen unchallenged was a simple matter of confidence. In a hotel the kitchen linked to everywhere and security was limited. Nobody noticed room service waiters. Tray lifted to block her face from the security camera, a quick knock, a few moments with her treasured *Sissone* pressed against the electronic lock and she'd entered the room. The object of her desire hadn't even been in the hotel safe, just tucked in a jewelry case with other far more precious items. The case had been in the top dresser drawer, right on top.

One of the easiest jobs she'd ever done.

Happy to relax into warm yoga pants and her faded red Arsenal sweatshirt, she filled a saucepan with tinned mushroom soup and put it on the larger of the ancient stove's burners. It would take a while before it reached tepid, let alone truly hot. Even though their ubiquity was a Yankee mystery, she was happy to spot a packet of oyster crackers in the jumble on the table. They would hold her over while she took off her makeup.

The dinette table was only big enough for her makeup mirror and supplies. Witch hazel and cold cream worked wonders. The Irish lass her own family wouldn't recognize disappeared in minutes.

Color contacts out and the heavy makeup off at last, she became the brown-eyed towhead that Evelyn, Countess Weald, would acknowledge as the product of her first marriage. They loved each other, to be sure, but Diana's frequent and lengthy absences helped hearts grow fonder.

Naked of all artifice and the last of the cold cream wiped away, she switched off the mirror. She'd worn so many masks for so much of the last few years that sometimes the real self she was looking at seemed a stranger, and it unsettled her.

Feeling much lighter and aware that the codeine was moving the pain from yellow to green, Diana plucked a sepia-toned photograph from its anchor point in the corner of the mirror. She studied the high forehead and long plaits of black hair that framed the woman's somber face. At the neck of what was probably a deerskin ceremonial dress was a small brooch of ordinary stones and turquoise beads strung and twisted to clasp a small dark feather. The faded coloration of the very old photograph had turned the beads a uniform dusty brown.

She allowed herself a grin as she fished out the photo album she kept in the smallest of her half-unpacked suitcases. Flipping it open to the ribbon she used as a bookmark, she slid the photo into its original sleeve and used the mirror's lighting to study the brooch one last time. It might have been an indication of rank or merely ornamental. It could have been a gift from a suitor who showed devotion by supplying fresh feathers, or a fetish the native woman had made for herself.

Diana now knew the beads were clay red stone and beautifully variegated turquoise. The combination had looked gorgeous in the palm of her gloved hand.

She sipped her soup from the least chipped of the mugs the landlord provided while ensconced in the apartment's only other chair. The recliner worked, albeit with a screech like a banshee, and the floor lamp next to it put good light on her treasured photographs. Turning the pages was a happy journey of past successes and future endeavors. Obsidian earrings, a carved leather choker, a delicate glazed black and white bowl. An elaborately carved wooden fish hook, unpolished diamonds set into an unfired ceremonial goblet—so many pretty things. Some of them she'd touched, but for most she was still waiting for that moment.

After William's wedding she'd pick something new and start the whole process over again.

All the adrenaline of the past month slowly drained out of her until she was too limp to move. It didn't matter. The recliner was no worse for her back than the Murphy bed. The thump of her landlord arriving home for the night was the last thing she remembered.

She woke cold and stiff and mightily wished she'd grabbed a blanket. At least her back had stopped aching. The photo album tumbled to the floor as she dragged herself upright. Groggy and yawning, she got the Murphy bed lowered without the usual conk on the head. It was no sooner in place than she realized the album was now out of reach underneath. She could leave it until morning, after she tucked the bed into the wall again. But the knowledge that something so precious to her was on the floor would likely keep her awake, so she slithered under the bed and emerged with the album. There were advantages to being small and nimble.

About to switch off the overhead light for good, she found herself standing stock-still with one hand on the light switch and the other holding the album. It had fallen open to the third page, displaying one of the first photos she'd collected. It featured a burly man at a podium, about to strike an elegant, curved gavel to the wood.

Her sleepy brain slowly called up the object's data. The delicate handle was carved from highly polished, partially petrified ram's bone. The head was a stunning single piece of faceted obsidian laboriously bored to allow the handle to fit through it. A thin disc of rose gold was inset over the eye where the two pieces joined. In spite of disputed provenance, at its last auction the artifact had fetched over two thousand pounds. The winning bidder and current so-called owner was the American tycoon in the photograph. A man with fingers in entertainment—television, tabloid news, films. And publishing.

Her drowsiness fled. She closed her eyes to recall the fallen letter. Anita Topaz's letter. Signed by Ronald Keynes Reynard himself.

CHAPTER THREE

"Dang it," Paris muttered. She spread the letter out on her desk, cursing that she'd forgotten to have Lisa share and commiserate with her about the heavy-handed tactics. That woman, Diana, had walked in and then everything had gone off track.

Lisa knew that Paris obsessively guarded her privacy, and she knew why. After Lisa had blown the whistle on hotels underpaying waitstaff she'd gotten all sorts of nasty threats. But Lisa had ultimately been protected by the law, and the people she'd turned in had real names and had committed defined crimes.

Paris had criticized a game. Her entire life had gone up in flames. No more video game story design, no more launch parties, no more sparring about user engagement stats with nerds from other, better funded companies.

All gone, and there was nothing anyone could do about it. No way anyone could turn her life back to the way it had been.

In the matter of a dispute with her publisher, though, she had some recourse to the law because of her contract. In her previous life she'd watched high-level negotiations over rights to color schemes, art, names, story lines, music, and even phrases, so she knew the value of consulting a lawyer who understood the nuances of rights management. It wasn't too late to call hers.

Finn's brusque manner suited her. He always took her calls and skipped over the flattery. "What can I help you with, Paris?"

"Reynard House wants me to meet in person to discuss being a featured speaker at their big annual Ronald Reynard Conference—that event they call RonCon. I have told them no twice, but they're pestering me to go. I don't have to do this, right?"

Finn's tone was reassuring. "Without looking up your contract, my recollection is that you don't. You are not required to do any publicity work at all. That's the status quo until renewal next year."

Her wave of relief was immediately squelched by his next words.

"If they balk then I would recommend approaching another publisher. You've made Anita Topaz reliably valuable."

"I'd rather not change publishers. Though it feels like I already have with the new staff they brought in." Paris bit her lip. Generating extra curiosity about Anita Topaz by dumping publishers was a risk she could do without. And there was no promise a new publisher wouldn't be just as curious and eager to exploit the shadowy persona behind the books. "The people who handled my account, did the editing, sent me proofs, they've all left. My new editor was effusive and all that, but either I've suddenly outgrown all my bad habits or she wasn't particularly engaged. The people I hear from all the time now are from marketing. They keep sending me articles about how I'm a mystery woman and the world is dying to know who I am. I think they're the ones placing the articles."

Finn tsk'd. "Do you have any proof of that? If you did, I could lean on them about good faith."

"No, not really. I just—I know the way the world works. It's simple to place articles like this as native advertising. But nothing's changed. Neither Anita nor I do Facebook or Twitter or Hangouts or Chat. No online Q-and-A, no puff-piece interviews, not even by email. None of it. Frankly, if there's some sort of viral fever to learn all about Anita Topaz I'd rather not know." Thinking about it stirred the panic she'd felt when she realized her blog was going viral in so many bad, bad places.

"There's a massive flux in the industry," Finn said. "I wish I could tell you that their lack of investment in editors and bringing on a large staff of marketing interns was unique to Reynard House. Media groups want stars and that means live performance. Writers who play the part of superstars on reality TV, web series, and talk shows. When you first signed you were a nobody they were taking a chance on who happened to win a contest. Now that Anita is a success, they want to level up that investment."

"Can't I leave being famous to people who want to be famous? Kardashians can have it. Reynard Media Group buys my publisher and suddenly there's a stream of articles about how everyone wants to know more about me? It sounds suspiciously like the beginning of a marketing campaign."

"Well, remember when we went over the contract and their proposal, even the old company was taken with Anita Topaz's first-time-novelist-nobody-to-star story. Wins contest, gets published and that story only gets better with every new bestseller you release. It lures other writers to sign with them."

"I know they want performing bears. It's not me. Why can't I be an exception? Why can't I write books and be left alone?"

Finn made a noise she thought meant he was processing. Her previous lawyer had sent over a summary of past issues, but she didn't know if Finn recalled any of it. It wasn't really relevant, except it explained in full detail why she feared public scrutiny. Did he think she was irrational?

"Of course you get to say what you do and don't undertake on behalf of promotion of your brand. You own Anita Topaz, not them." Though his words were heartening, his tone held hesitation. "If you did decide to take your next contract elsewhere, it's possible the bidders will have a little more curiosity over the fact that you want no personal contact at all. Five years ago that wasn't as big a deal, but lately the large contracts I've negotiated, well, it seems as if the industry's focus is entirely live media driven now."

"They want their writers to be TV stars?"

"Media darlings, to have vibrant buzz-worthy personalities," he clarified. "Personally, I don't see that this works except for those authors-turned-celebrities who are good at personal appearances and thrive on it. Plenty of successful writers don't want to be performers, and there are plenty who really ought to stay far away from live appearances. It's not in their wheelhouse and actually damages their brand. Secrecy and mystery can be a selling point too. But I have to tell you the truth. My saying so isn't going to change any minds."

"So at renewal, they might be really antsy over something that doesn't have anything to do with the books." Paris realized she was rocking on her feet. The soft blues and greens of the curtains had gone brown, a sure sign that this morning's elevated anxiety was rising again. She had to end the call soon or she risked a full-scale panic attack, and she was never, ever having one of those again. Ever. "Or my sales."

"I have to renew my advice to you to get an agent. I can only speak to contracts as they are offered. An agent is proactive, and you're a proven commodity now. Please think about it."

"I will."

"Meanwhile, let's not borrow trouble. This business is mercurial. That's two years and four books from now. All you need to know is that they have no current contractual leverage to make you do anything you don't want to do."

But they might someday. Or some other publisher would. "Thank you. You've given me a lot to think about."

She stood in the middle of the room, with her fingers spread wide as she shook her hands and arms. "Shake it out," she whispered. *Deep breath. Count to ten.* "Shake it out."

A walk would help, but the idea of encountering even her landladies while in this hyper-anxious, easily triggered state only sent her heart rate higher.

She thought instead about the custard and sherry trifle she'd share with her very nice landladies upstairs. Their laughter and kindness. *Deep breath. Count to ten.*

She remembered the heart-bursting first time she'd finished the Great Bay Temple quest in *Zelda: Majora's Mask* and the game reunion of Anju and Kafei. *Deep breath. Count to ten.*

She wrapped her arms around herself and recalled her mother's hugs. *Deep breath. Count to ten.*

She imagined she was in a conservatory filled with honeysuckle, her favorite scent. A sound of wind moving through tall trees, her favorite sound.

Surprisingly, the humor in Diana's eyes suddenly captured her mind, disrupting her calming litany. But not in a bad way. *Deep breath. Count to ten.*

After a few minutes she was able to put on her custom mix of unmeasured, ambient music. Nothing to overwhelm her ears or loud enough for her landlords to hear. It simultaneously filled the silence and made her space quieter.

The afternoon sun was lovely on the small garden. The crocuses were still up and there might be daffodils soon. Computer prodded to life, she slid into her desk chair and placed her hands on the keyboard. Six years ago her custom-built desktop had been the latest powerhouse and perfect for the gaming world. Now it was capable of word processing, basic research, streaming YouTube, and reading the news. Anything else she needed she could get with a library card, and if there was one place in the US that guarded privacy, it was libraries. Completely disconnecting from high tech and the gaming world had made her realize how little she needed it to tell her stories of adventure and intrigue. Stories about luck and hope with a touch of magic and the inexplicable, undeniable power of love.

Her current heroine, Susannah, stranded in Tuscany during grape harvest was deciphering a perplexing message that would reveal a murderous plot against her. Familiar ground. Welcome ground. Other places and people to think about.

She'd decide how to respond to the letter tomorrow.

CHAPTER FOUR

A break in rehearsals allowed Diana to spend the next morning at the Boston Public Library. Secure computers gave her the chance to log in and answer email from family. They were also, of course, great for research and maps, and their digital trail was regularly deleted by the library's privacy settings. Her iPhone had been turned off the morning she'd left home weeks ago.

A glance at local police call records and a couple of hashtag searches showed no official or gossip chatter about a certain oil family socialite guest of a certain hotel having reported anything missing. She hadn't expected there to be. When only one item is not where it should be and other far more valuable items are, the first conclusion would be that the missing item was lost, not stolen. It was the best possible outcome.

Relieved, she turned to email and spent a few minutes reminding her brother that while a wedding was momentous, it was not a worldwide holiday. She also found the official invitation from her future sister-in-law for Diana to serve as one of the seven maids of honor. It would be her eighth walk down the aisle for someone else, and she had the poufy-sleeved dresses to prove it. She did like William's choice of wife and was pleased to be asked, but she dreaded the addition of yet another biliously hued gown to her closet at home.

The last bit of her hour's allotment of computer time she used to read up on Anita Topaz. According to Reynard House, Topaz's publisher, "the young romance superstar from the wrong side of the tracks has vaulted to the top of best seller lists everywhere, and now makes her home in New England where she tends her beloved roses and watches tall ships skim across Massachusetts Bay."

Oh she did, did she? Who had written that drivel?

Diana's success at finding a photo of "Anita" was limited to a press release from a publisher that had since been bought out by the Reynard Media Group monolith. The same photo was on the back of Anita's first book, *Lord of the Lady*, and it showed up in a very recent romance fan site discussion group speculating about why Anita Topaz was so secretive. The photo was clear enough to know that there was no resemblance between this willowy blonde with her face half in shadow and the lanky dark-haired eccentric Diana had met yesterday.

After logging out and clicking the button to erase her search history, Diana headed upstairs to the fiction section. Sure enough, several copies of *Lord of the Lady* were on the shelf. The earliest edition had the picture, while subsequent printings displayed only the short bio. The photograph wasn't as closely cropped as the one online, but there was no way to discern height, for one thing. The pose and lighting were generic—it might have been a stock photo, like the kind put in picture frames for sale. Diana looked more like "Anita Topaz" than Paris Ellison did.

It was that last thought that set her pulse to beating in her throat. She smiled at Anita's picture as the familiar, welcome rush of a new challenge coursed through her.

Lost in churning possibilities, she wandered into the coffeehouse across the street and was staring into the bottom of an espresso when she remembered the time. She scrabbled the burner cell phone out of her purse and clicked one of the few numbers stored in it. William answered just before she thought her call would end up in his voice mail.

"I thought you'd forgotten." He sounded as if he were right next door, but her half-brother was probably up a mountainside with his bike.

"I got caught up answering your ten emails about your big, fat English wedding. All of which you could have asked me when I called."

"I needed a paper trail to forward to our mother. Otherwise she is happy to speak in your name—you know, *Lady* Diana would absolutely agree with her—for everything from the dinner menu to the color scheme. So she casts two votes on every proposal. She and Millie's mum have already gone twelve rounds."

She was grateful to be missing every possible minute. "Sounds epic."

William's high-pitched half-giggle was a dead ringer for his father's goofy laugh. "That's an understatement. Millie's mum is made of the same velvet steel we know so well. It's not as if anyone is going to ask us what we want. We've fled Mote Hall and are toughing it out in Madeira."

"Sounds rough."

"We're wasting away."

"I got Millie's official invite to be a bridesmaid. That was lovely of her."

"She's a lovely person." He sighed gustily.

"Besotted," Diana accused.

"At least I know what it feels like."

Ouch, Diana thought. "That's harsh."

"Sorry, really only teasing you. Men are shits, and you have every reason to be picky about them."

She forgave him, primarily because she knew he really was teasing. "Well, Millie got herself a good one."

"Be careful now. Someone might think you like me." He ignored her feigned laugh. "Which brings me to another delicate matter. It seems that our mother, the Countess, thinks that I need to invite a groomsman to your liking to join the wedding party. So that you have a date."

"Bugger that." Diana realized she'd raised her voice when the man seated next to her, also on his mobile, turned away in annoyance. One reason she spent most of her time at home plotting how soon she would leave was her mother's unsubtle matchmaking. "I refuse to be set up—"

"I was thinking of Evan—"

"If you invite Evan to be a groomsman I will stuff the mattress on your honeymoon bed with gorse." There was a short silence, during which Diana hoped he was replaying the few but effective times she had carried through with threatened reprisals. She was much smaller than he, but she was older, and William didn't have a devious bone in his body. "I am not dating him and have no intention of dating him."

"But he lingers so hopefully. It's the saddest thing I've ever seen."

"He's watched too much *Downton Abbey*. He's got a mouldering estate and thinks I have enough money to save it."

"Eventually you probably will."

"Sure, that sounds like bliss—spending wedded life waiting for *Pita* to die so I can rescue my milquetoast hubby's mansion."

"Dad's last checkup was picture perfect."

"That's wonderful news, thank you for telling me." Diana sent a prayer of gratitude into the ether for continued "all clear" health reports for Anwar, her stepfather.

"So no groomsman upgrade for Evan."

"He's so…unimaginative." She had no ideal mate formed in her brain but she knew what she didn't want: dull, dreary or dumb. "Remember that train track we found in the woods one holiday, all by itself?"

"Yes! We had so much fun with it. Florence was the damsel in distress and you and I the rescuing Mounties."

Diana grinned at the memory. "The Evans of the world don't know how to play."

"I have no unattached whimsical friends, alas, so no bridegroom date for you."

"I'm utterly heartbroken. Smashed." Diana gathered up her empty cup and slipped off the bar height stool so someone else could have it. "Are you up some mountain about to break your neck?"

"This from a girl who got her jollies doing backflips on bits of wood?" His voice thick with excitement and anticipation, he added, "I got it up here, now comes the fun part. It's a twenty percent grade in places."

"Please stay alive until your wedding. I like Millie and want her in the family."

He laughed. "So I can wipe out after the wedding? You'd be losing a brother and gaining another sister?"

"It's a fair trade."

He snorted. "When will you be home?"

"Before too long. I'll let you know," she evaded. She had been planning to head for home but the daring plan taking shape in her head was making her unsure of the next few weeks. "There'll be dress fittings and the like. I won't miss it."

He accepted her promise and she heard the *snick* of his helmet buckle as he disconnected. He thought she was fearless? William liked mountain biking and Florence, though still at school, thought vertical cliffs existed for her to climb. Miraculously, neither of them had suffered more than scrapes. She rolled her shoulder as she pushed out the door onto the street, feeling the click of the pins and metal that kept her clavicle in one piece and her shoulder functioning adequately for daily life.

Normally on Thursdays, when there were no rehearsals scheduled, Diana would head into the North End for a slice of pizza and a walking tour around another landmark of the American Revolution. The job she had come to Boston for was done now, and she always went home after a job. She had no reason to linger.

Unless, that is, she decided to make use of Anita Topaz's letter. It felt like a gift she shouldn't waste. But what did she really know? Not enough to take such a large risk.

She left the coffeehouse and discovered that the soft day had turned to worse. The gray sky had darkened even more, and the wind had come up. It was no fit day to sightsee. Her stomach reminded her that solid foods had been consumed some hours earlier. She could go back to Mona Lisa's for lunch, and see what she might be able to learn from the bartender.

Liking the idea, and the thought of hot tomato soup and the chunk of Irish cheddar they served alongside it, she trekked back to the attic apartment, deftly got into the red wig, slipped in the contact lenses, and opted for no-label jeans and a blouse to complete her Actress costume of the day. She was very glad of her peacoat and gloves. Boston might be further south than London, but it gave the dank, chilled climate a run for its money.

Mona Lisa's was a lot busier than the day before. There was a bartender on duty in addition to Lisa. Lisa looked frazzled and chilled, which didn't bode well for a tête-à-tête about the Paris/Anita setup.

She ordered what Lisa called "her usual" and sipped at the promptly delivered local ale. It reminded her of Jameson's, though it was served far too cold. After a job in South Carolina, Diana understood the American fascination with icy-cold beer. But who wanted brain freeze in the middle of winter? The hot soup, delivered with a clattering rapidity, was most welcome. She wrapped a bit of the cheese in some of the soft French bread and dunked it in the fragrant bowl of red goodness. Her little vegetarian heart sighed happily.

By the time she finished a few customers had left. Though it seemed unlikely, there was a chance if she lingered that Lisa might end up with a little time to talk.

"I'm going to pop into the loo," she said to the man next to her. "Don't let her clear away the rest of my pint."

"She'll have to break my arm." He gave her an offhand grin, then returned his gaze to the basketball game playing on the TV over the bar.

She took her time in the restroom in the hope that more customers would finish their midday visit and leave. She powdered her nose and went over the letter again in her mind. Reynard House Publishers was offering a spree to New York just to get Anita Topaz to a meeting. An hour's meeting. All that expense for so little in return?

A meeting to discuss "RonCon." Which, she'd learned this morning, was an elite invitation-only speaker's event, featuring celebrities and thinkers opining on an array of topics. A review of the previous year's presentations had shown the common thread: how to monetize anything, with a good dose of how to turn a blind eye to the suffering of others while you did so. Capitalism without a soul, which perfectly described the conference's founder and host, Ronald Keynes Reynard.

The same Ronald Keynes Reynard who possessed a nearly three-hundred-year-old obsidian and ram's bone artifact dubbed the Chumash Hammer. Its first provenance was as a gift "martillo y tamborito" from the Chumash tribe to Junipero Serra, and from a time when California was still shown as an island on Spanish maps. Years later, Serra gave the hammer and drum to the chief of the Yokuts. This was all documented in the ledgers of clerk-priests in Serra's service. The drum, made of wood and animal skin, had probably not survived the centuries. Meanwhile, persons unknown had spirited the bone and stone hammer out of the Yokuts's hands. It surfaced again a hundred years later during the Gold Rush through the Barbary Coast's black market. Then it found its way into the clutches of wealthy miners and scions of families who'd moved to new lands to establish new empires.

The photograph in her book was of the Chumash Hammer in its current resting place—a shelf in Ronald Reynard's office, which was on the top floor of the corporate headquarters for Reynard Media Group at East Thirty-Seventh and Park in Midtown Manhattan. She had to assume that all the usual security was in place and possibly quite a bit more. Reynard was a political kingmaker. Having an invitation to meet with him in that very location cut through a lot of red tape and electronic locks.

This was also true: Ronald Reynard liked to use the hammer to gavel in the beginning of his self-named greed-is-good conference. To which Anita Topaz was being invited. Diana's instinct was that the Chumash Hammer would be much less secure at the conference but there would also be a lot more witnesses, some in the form of cameras. A great deal more visibility and risk than she liked.

Well, lingering in the bathroom wasn't going to get her any answers. She'd order another half-pint if it seemed like Lisa would soon be free for a chat. Otherwise, she'd need a Plan B.

CHAPTER FIVE

It was full-on one hundred percent March weather for the walk to Mona Lisa's with her regular brownie delivery. Unlike yesterday, the sun hid behind a layer of high mist while the wind continued to stab into every gap in Paris's clothing. Gusts snatched furiously at the box she was balancing on one shoulder, causing her to clutch it even more tightly. She gratefully stumbled out of the wind to discover that the bar also felt chilled to its core.

Lisa, who had a bright red scarf wrapped around her neck and wore close-fitting fingerless gloves, asked Paris, "How does it feel colder today than it did in December? I don't get it."

"I'm not from around here, remember?"

"Yeah, but you chose it. I was following my heart."

Paris didn't try to hide her eye roll. "Then it has its compensations, right?"

Lisa's ill-humor vanished. "That it does. Warmth at night is not an issue."

"Nobody likes a gloater," a regular at the bar observed. "Have pity on the single people. You're always bragging about you and the missus."

Lisa made a show of staring off into the distance. "Huh, where is it we live? Where are we right now?"

"Crap," he muttered.

Lisa continued as if he hadn't spoken. "Are we in an Irish bar named after an Italian icon owned by a Swedish-American lesbian married to an Inuit woman where a Polish guy named Miguel is complaining about my free speech?" Two other regulars joined her to finish in unison, "We must be in America."

"Bite me," Miguel said. "Please let those be fresh brownies."

Grinning, Paris gestured at the box she'd set on the bar. "You'll have to beg her for them now."

Miguel shrugged. "It won't be the most humiliating thing I do today."

Lisa passed over one of the bags from Paris's box to him. "On the house, sweetie. You know I love you."

Paris was grateful for the bar byplay and laughed along, which had nothing to do with the fact that Diana had emerged from the restrooms and returned to a stool at the far end of the bar.

Lisa handed over the usual cash for the brownies. "Fresh coffee isn't quite finished brewing. I'll bring it over. Lunch?"

"Just coffee today, thanks." Paris made a beeline for the table at the window.

It felt a little bit junior high. Like the whole *Maybe she'll notice me not noticing her* thing. Junior high—what happy memories they weren't. Paris had always been odd girl out in more ways than one. It didn't feel great that after everything else she'd been through she was still capable of drooling over a pretty straight girl.

Lisa herself dropped off the coffee. "Did you insult each other or something?" Paris's puzzled look apparently didn't fool Lisa at all, because she added, "The two of you are aggressively not noticing each other."

"All I did was show her where a postal drop box was. There was no time to become bosom buddies." And it was doubtful that Diana was into bosoms, Paris could have added.

The same thought might have crossed Lisa's mind as well. "She could be more trouble than she's worth."

But it was said with more innocence than necessary. Paris shot her a suspicious look. "That reverse psychology thing won't work."

Lisa shook back her blond surfer girl curls. "Oh honey, you'd be surprised."

She watched Lisa make her way back to the bar and let her gaze casually—she hoped—move on to where Diana had been sitting. Just as she realized Diana was no longer on her barstool, a throat was loudly cleared right in front of her.

"Hi! You *are* a regular here, aren't you?" Diana had what was left of her beer in one hand. A Boston Public Library book bag dangled from the other.

"No more so than you, apparently."

"Not for long." Faint lines of worry edged into the corners of Diana's eyes. "Turns out the production might fold before we get much more than basic rehearsal pay. So I'll be moving on as I'm barely making ends meet as it is. Hate to lose this place for lunch, though."

"I'm sorry to hear that. Yes, this is nice—not too pricey for the basics."

Diana glanced over her shoulder at Lisa. "How does she do it? It's the second of March, she's bundled up in a scarf and still looks like she just got back from the beach. I don't mean an English beach, I mean a South of France beach."

"Her parents mated well, obviously." Paris might have said the same of Diana's parents. A slightly different result—where Lisa glowed like she'd just left off sunbathing, Diana was a shimmer of candlelight with pink cheeks, which made the red hair all the more vibrant. Sun and moon, like flip sides of the same feminine coin.

Paris had to admit she'd always been intrigued by women like Lisa and Diana. Ex-girlfriend Kerry had been that rare creature, a gamer geek who was also a high femme. They all innately understood a world Paris was lost in, like a game where all the symbols made sense to only one kind of player. Paris was never going to earn the Experience Points and Adventuring Gear it took to navigate it—not now, not ever. She didn't want to either, but that didn't mean she wasn't fascinated.

She realized that Diana had asked her a question and was giving her an increasingly puzzled look. "Sorry. Writer's hazard. A thought I was intrigued by."

"Do writers do that? Drift off into thought mid-conversation?"

"This one does."

Diana's expression had turned melancholy. "No rehearsal today, probably none tomorrow. Maybe you could recommend something to do that's affordable to the soon-to-be unemployed? Affordable meaning free?"

Paris gestured at the book bag. "You're doing the best one already."

"I was thinking of something out in the fresh air. Though today it's beastly outside."

"You haven't been here long?"

"Only a month or two. You could call me a traveling actress. I scrape by. Well, not always." She shrugged. "I sold my car a while back. Can't afford a smartphone. For the thrill of the greasepaint it's worth it. This is disappointing though. I was hoping not to have to move on for at least three more months."

Paris wasn't sure when it happened, but Diana was now sitting across from her, explaining the life of an ever-hopeful itinerant actress. Her freckles seemed lighter today, as if the depression and stress of probably losing her only source of income had drained some of the life out of her.

"Most people settle into a community and get regular jobs and when the semi-annual production is announced they go out for it and mostly, they get the gigs. I hate the waiting around. And most of the regular jobs—I'm not fond of them either."

"So what all have you done?"

"I've been Desdemona in Detroit, Mustardseed in Memphis... Ferris Bueller's sister in a really weird adaptation of the movie. That was in Belfast. I've lost track of all the times

I've been cast as 'best friend of the lead plus understudy to all female roles'."

"Doesn't it get tiring, all the moving around?"

Diana's shake of the head was emphatic. "Not in the least. Play's the thing. I've learned to travel light."

There was almost a warning in those words and Paris felt a chill. "Where are you from? I can definitely tell you're not from here."

"Derry." At Paris's continuing look of non-comprehension she added, "Northern Ireland. I've worked hard on my BBC broadcaster accent. So I sound like I'm from nowhere and everywhere in the UK." She cracked a lopsided smile. "You lot are fairly daft about accents, so I seem to get more parts here. Though I can do American broadcaster too." She fluttered her eyelashes and cleared her throat. "*We'll have film on this new development and more at eleven.*"

If Paris had had her eyes closed, she would have thought it was a different person speaking. Diana's voice had lost all traces of lilt and picked up the narrow nasal tones of a generic Hollywood performer. No longer a memorable voice, it was still modulated, a bit husky and with a touch of honey. "That's impressive."

"Just takes practice and the mindset. Acting is what I'm good at. I'm hanging in there until other people think so too." She sipped at her nearly empty beer. "So what are you going to do about your problem?"

Paris was puzzled for a moment, then remembered that Diana had seen the letter. "I haven't decided," she said in a none-of-your-business tone.

"I'm nosy. I know. I'd give my eyeteeth to go on a trip like that right now. Though not by air—I'd take the train."

"Why the train?"

"I miss them. Trains are big all across Europe. And security at airports is so tedious."

"Well, I won't be going by plane, train, *or* automobile."

"They'll take no for an answer?"

She'd told herself she'd decide tomorrow and now it *was* tomorrow. But she didn't need someone to pressure her. Paris bled off a pulse of anxiety by drumming her fingers on the table. "They have to."

The rhythm of Paris's nervous tapping was the only thing that broke the silence that fell. Paris realized they'd arrived at that awkward moment when the other person expected her to pick up the conversational ball and bat it back. Conversation became harder when her anxiety was high.

It was a profound shock when Diana reached across the table to still Paris's drumming fingers. Her hand was warm and gentle and so was her voice. "It'll be okay."

Paris was stunned. Why, instead of panic, did she feel more at ease? Hopeful even? "I don't think so. They really don't want to take no for an answer."

"And you really don't want to go?"

"It's not about what I want. I can't." Diana's eyes held a question, and Paris was afraid of what it might be. She slipped her hand from beneath Diana's. "I want to write books and be left alone."

Diana let out a sympathetic sigh. "The limelight isn't for everybody."

"Speaking of writing, time for me to get back to work." Unable to soften the abruptness of her departure, Paris was still pulling on her coat as she cleared the bar's green door. All the way home she cursed her rudeness, even though she knew there were things about her that would never change no matter how much she wanted them to.

And yet, that was a lie, in this case at least. Bailing out of the bar hadn't been driven by her familiar friend Anxiety. She wasn't running toward the calming familiarity of her keyboard.

She was running away from Diana's unsettling, disconcerting, magic hands.

CHAPTER SIX

"What was that about?"

Diana was startled out of her deep study of the bar's closed door. She turned a sunny expression toward Lisa, who set the vanished Paris's mug of coffee on the table. "I'm not quite sure."

"I might only see her twice a week, but it's enough to know she's not ordinary, that's for sure. But then everyone in this bar is a bit odd. People show their edges to bartenders."

Diana had to ask. "Including me?"

"Oh yeah."

It was intriguing to consider what this observant woman might believe she'd discerned when Diana's masks were so firmly in place. "What makes me odd?"

"For one thing, I wouldn't have pegged you for a butch fetish."

She'd been expecting to be told that her accent was fake or that Lisa had spotted the wig or colored contacts. A butch fetish? What did that even mean? "What makes you think I have one?"

"Femme to femme, honey, I know all the signs. I married one. But…"

Now Lisa's sharp eyes were studying Diana with far more intensity than Diana had wanted. "But?"

"Paris might not be your type—oh hell!" Lisa left the conversation as abruptly as Paris had, heading toward the sound of breaking dishes and curses emanating from the kitchen.

Diana's sigh was a mix of relief and vexation. The chance for a casual talk had come and gone, and she hadn't done well with what talk there had been. She swallowed the last of her beer and left, not wanting to pick up the conversation again. If Lisa thought her interest in Paris was an attraction to female masculinity—was that what Lisa had meant by butch? If so, that was fine. Better than the truth.

As she walked to the T station and then endured the rattling, crowded journey home with her books, she carefully reviewed everything Paris had said and done. The impression Diana had had of her initially, that of a dog kicked one too many times, hadn't changed. But there was more than that. A rapid rise of nervous tension stretched and thinned Paris's composure, like a balloon on the verge of popping. The flight out of the bar after Diana had touched her had been edged in panic. Whatever caused that was deep, deep down, possibly hardwired.

If Paris had some kind of anxiety issue it would explain the reluctance to avoid whatever public pressures would result from her success as a writer. Stage fright was real too, after all. Diana didn't suffer from it, but she had seen it run the gamut from a quick heave before the curtain rose to flat-out paralysis in new and veteran performers alike. Paris's reluctance might be the product of self-knowledge. When she said she couldn't do it, she might mean literally that.

Lisa's description of Paris as "butch" also shed some light on the one and only photo of Anita Topaz. Had it been Paris herself or the publisher that had decided the reading public preferred a fake glamour gal instead of a hoodie-clad lesbian? Sometimes clothes illuminated the person wearing them. Sometimes they were about fitting into a situation. And sometimes they created a convincing cover, as Diana knew only too well. Lisa had seemed to be talking about something else, though, something that wouldn't be easily covered up by long hair and fake eyelashes.

On the gymnastic circuit there had been overt rules: thou shalt be covered in small, lean muscles, have no body fat and look like a girl. Judges liked cute little dolls who spun like tops. Judges did not like big muscles or plain faces. Gymnastics competitors routinely wore hair ribbons and sparkly clips and makeup, even those who loathed all of it. Playing within the rules was sometimes the only way forward.

Her back was unhappy with the jolting subway ride but the wind had succeeded in pushing the storm clouds inland. When she alighted near her temporary home the day had softened. Bright, cheerful sunlight was visible on the harbor. She picked up a peanut butter and alfalfa sprout sandwich at the corner deli—a bizarre and oddly addictive flavor combination—and took it home for supper later.

Eyeing her small living area she realized she had been looking forward to leaving it as soon as she knew her last acquisition had reached its destination. But she'd made up her mind, it seemed. She'd stay long enough to see if there was any chance of leveraging what she knew about Paris and Anita Topaz into a meeting with Ronald Reynard.

Piecing together what she knew, Diana predicted that the next time Paris would go to Mona Lisa's was Monday. She would keep to her own routines until then.

Wig off, contacts out, she swapped out Irish Lass's blouse for a Cambridge T-shirt. It was scarcely two o'clock. The sun would be out for a few hours more, maybe. With a Red Sox hat pulled snugly over her wig-matted hair, she buttoned her peacoat and headed back down the stairs.

A half hour later she was just another Bostonian enjoying the chilly sunshine on Long Pier. The tang of salt water in the air made her think of boating with her stepfather and brother. Summer seemed a long way off, but maybe this year she'd stay home at Mote Hall for the season. Well, it was easy to think she could, though it never worked out that way.

She quelled the unusual pang of homesickness with sizzling salty fries served up in a cone of newspaper and liberally doused with malt vinegar. They were too skinny for proper chips, but close enough.

She found a corner of a bench in the sun and out of the wind, and watched the tour boats and ferries come and go. Finally she opened her new paperback, acquired from the chemist's shop near the underground. She was going to get to know Anita Topaz better.

CHAPTER SEVEN

She hadn't shied away from Diana's touch.

The memory of the gentle touch and her atypical reaction haunted Paris for the rest of the day. Had it been loneliness? When she'd moved here she'd welcomed solitude with all her broken heart and aching spirit. Was she finally easing out of the grief and paralyzing memories?

The usual calm of her desk didn't help her focus and her word count goal for the day was toast. She'd baked herself out of ingredients and had meant to stop at the grocery on the way home, but in her haste to escape Diana and the questions she stirred, she'd forgotten.

The situation had only improved slightly by the following afternoon when two knocks on the door at the top of the stairs broke her out of pointless churning. One knock from her landladies meant they had extra dinner or tea if Paris was interested. She was free to ignore it. Or she could carry up a plate, fill it and go back to her own space. Two knocks meant they needed help with something, or had plans more social than the neighborly, communal sharing of extra food.

Whatever it was they needed, it was a welcome relief to have something useful to do. Not writing was exhausting.

Miss Grace Lambeth and Miss Adya Richards were both looking back on seventy if they were a day. Paris liked them both, and had felt safe with them from the first moments of meeting them. They had asked no prying questions and taken Paris at face value with a genuine acceptance that had been exactly what she'd needed. She had slowly realized they'd spent decades of their lives avoiding questions from the world and so they asked few questions about other people. Paris had thought their reticence ideal. Now she saw that it was the sad legacy of a lifetime spent hiding their relationship.

"Come in, come in, dear." Grace Lambeth was presiding over her beloved teapot, carried with them from Ireland decades ago. Paris had never been much for fancy tableware, but the porcelain's simple decoration of trailing stems and soft green shamrocks had immediately charmed her. She happily slid into the chair Grace waved at. The scrubbed oak table was solid and grounding, the heart of the house. Grace shared food on it alongside whatever protest poster or flyer project Adya was masterminding. At the moment the surface held only the tea service, which meant Adya was resting between causes.

Grace beamed at her from soft blue eyes. "One or two, dear?"

"One, please. Did you need me to lift something for you?"

"No, we're celebrating. There's even some of that delicious trifle left if you would like a treat."

"I couldn't." At the moment, the thought of sweet and boozy trifle made Paris a little nauseated. Hot, fragrant tea would be very comforting.

Adya Richards banged in through the kitchen door, her faded black hair, liberally streaked with white and gray, standing on end as if she'd been out in a nor'easter. Paris had never seen her looking any different. Grace often said that Adya ran through life as if the Devil himself was after her. To which Adya always responded, "Of course he is."

"Did you find it?" Grace filled the third cup of the three on the tray, used the delicate silver tongs to drop in a single cube of sugar and handed it to Paris.

"Last place I looked. I put it all on top of the dryer," Adya answered breathlessly as she took a proffered cup for herself. "Thanks, love."

"Isn't everything the last place you look?" Grace's lined face was free of sarcasm, but there was a hint of mischief in her voice.

"Smarty." Adya shook her head at Paris. "Now that I've found the good silver, don't you know she'll be talking about how it needs polishing."

"You know that it will." Grace deeply inhaled steam from her cup. "Irish blend today, imported." She nodded at Paris. "We wouldn't be able to afford the real thing if it weren't for you, dear."

Paris watched the two elderly ladies sip their tea almost in unison and marveled at the tangible silent communication between them. Clearly, they had something to tell her. The last time they'd had such a sit-down over tea it had been the sad news that her rent would have to go up seventeen dollars and thirty-four cents due to utilities. Back then a minute flicker of Grace's eyelashes had cued Adya to broach the subject. Today it was Adya's playful wink at Grace that had Grace returning her teacup to the saucer while taking a deep breath.

Sensing that Grace was searching for words, Paris warmed her hands around the sturdy china of her cup. The exterior was a basketweave pattern, and tracing the fine lines with her fingertip was calming while she waited.

"Go on," Adya urged.

"Well, it might seem a bit silly, given that we're so far on in years," Grace began. "But rights are rights and—"

"We're getting married!" Adya burst out.

"No way!" Paris clapped her hands in both surprise and happiness. "Are you sure?"

"Am I *sure*?" Adya grinned as she eyed Grace speculatively. "After all these years, I guess I'm stuck with her."

"Have you told folks at church?" The weekly trek to St. Anthony's was rarely missed and Thursday mornings were devoted to a women's group Adya said was full of "cheerful troublemakers."

"We're going to, after, and show them the certificate."

Paris heard hesitation in Grace's voice. "Do you think people will be surprised?"

Adya lined up her teaspoon with the edge of her napkin. Then said, "I think they will."

"Maybe not as much as you think," Paris speculated. "I mean, I knew the moment you opened the door, when I came about the ad for the rental."

"People see what they expect to see. It's comfortable," Grace said.

Paris remembered Diana saying much the same thing. "It's true. When I see two women together I assume they are a couple, and it makes me feel happy. It's a compliment."

Adya nodded. "I didn't use to think that way. I thought I shouldn't assume unless the person said so officially, like I was shaming them by thinking they might be like us. Then I was reading one of Grace's paperbacks—"

"You didn't dog-ear the pages, did you?"

Paris sipped her cooling tea as they quibbled over who treated the books better. Most people would find their happiness contagious, and it usually lifted Paris's dark moods. But happiness was something Paris had little fundamental faith in, not anymore. The same tide that lifted them up had sucked Paris under and rolled her over in the deep. She'd spent the last five years gasping for air.

"Don't you think dear?"

Paris wasn't sure what she'd missed, so she punted. "Is it for me to say?"

Adya spread her hands in a plea. "You're the tiebreaker. Chocolate with raspberry or vanilla with lemon?"

"Chocolate." Adya immediately looked pleased while Grace seemed crestfallen, so Paris hedged by amending, "Both?"

"Now there's a thought," Adya said in a placating tone. "Instead of one big one we could order a smaller one of each."

Grace lifted the teapot to top up her own cup. "Father Christopher—we had to talk to him about it, of course. We decided to talk to him because he mentioned, just in passing, that he's pleased with the direction of blessed Pope Francis's recent statements on the matter, don't you know? Father Christopher is a Jesuit, after all. He went all over the world after seminary, and even on one of those Greenpeace boats." She patted her wispy white hair with a blue-veined hand even though the bun was as tidy as always. "So we talked to him about what we wanted to do. Father Christopher of course said he can't conduct the ceremony, but there are no rules about who can bring food to share after Sunday service, and no reason he can't read a verse aloud if he feels moved to do so, you know, because he can read verse any time he wants. Perhaps Song of Songs 8-7."

"We haven't decided," Adya said quickly.

"I know, love." Grace winked at Paris, which Paris took to mean that Grace had decided. "So we thought we'd have cakes brought in and show people what we'd done. The Sunday following the big day."

"We'll find out who our friends are," Adya muttered.

"Did you tell the Kerns?" Paris had met the twice-a-week bridge partners several times, and she knew Grace and Adya regarded the other couple as their family.

"Bill and Marva are fine with it." Grace favored Paris with a sunny smile. "They weren't the least surprised. Marva said they'd figured out a long time ago only one of the bedrooms was slept in and were waiting on us to say something. They didn't want to pry."

Adya's worried expression had cleared. "They're going to pick us up and whisk us to City Hall and be our witnesses. We think a couple of Tuesdays from now. On the anniversary of the day we met."

"That was at a peace rally, wasn't it?" Paris asked. Both ladies nodded, all smiles at the shared memory. "I'm so pleased for you both."

"We were going to ask you to be a witness too, dear. But we decided it wouldn't be kind of us to put you in that position, given how you might find it stressful. We don't want to cause you a panic attack."

The genuine concern in Grace's voice brought a prickle of tears to Paris's eyes. "Thank you, but really, the Kerns have known you ever so much longer than I have. And—and thank you for wanting to protect me." The very thought of interacting with an authority that would reproduce her identification in a publicly recorded document set off a trill of worry in her ears. They'd been kind not to ask. Yet she was sorry to miss out. It wouldn't have been nearly as stress-inducing as the letter from Reynard House had proved to be.

"I do have one question for you. It's a big one. Are you ready?" She cheerfully ignored the flare of suspicion in Adya's dark eyes. "Will it be Lambeth-Richards or Richards-Lambeth?"

Both ladies clapped their hands to their cheeks and stared at the other, aghast. Paris smiled into her tea, certain the ensuing debate would be lively.

* * *

The persistent flutter of worry was still there as she sat at her keyboard later, full of tea and half a chicken salad sandwich Adya had insisted they share. Because, according to Adya, she was "looking peaked."

For an hour she'd been trying and failing to pick up the threads of her story. How would she answer the letter? Tell them no and stop asking, or find some kind of compromise that kept Paris Ellison off their radar and Anita Topaz on it?

Was it too much to ask to be left alone to write? Her wildly adventurous stories of travel and fame, torrid sex and passionate love flowed out of her like healing, sustaining magic. All the art she'd seen, music she'd heard, stories she'd read, and dreams out of her head were in a crucible that she heated until precious ideas floated to the top.

Ideas that unfolded like maps to new possibilities. Safe in her own mind she could be anyone in the story. She used words to make the bridges between the world she lived in and ones she longed to exist, filled with people who were flawed and brave. Where there was some justice and a lot of love. Was being left alone to create these possibilities too much to ask?

The light from the desk lamp cast her silhouette onto her screen. She filled in the indistinct spaces with her flat top hair and long lean face, and the thin lips that Kerry had inexplicably said were her best feature. Kerry had seen what she expected to see. She'd thought that when the going got tough, a butch like Paris got tougher.

Paris had thought it was true too. Until it wasn't.

After all, she'd learned early on to live with her anxiety. She'd been incredibly fortunate that her mother had recognized that Paris was wired differently than other children. While she'd insisted that Paris do what she could to cope with her symptoms without disrupting others, it was more important for Paris to learn the difference between *can't* and *won't*. The right medication and consistent practice with behavioral conditioning had transformed her from the freaked out kid who lost her cool over every exam to "you know, the odd girl with the weird ideas."

She had thrived in the world of video game architecture, where appreciation for the whimsy and heart in her story arcs had given her security and confidence. She had been accepted and admired for exactly who she was.

As Adya had said, you find out who your friends are.

There might be plenty of people who liked you—until you wrote something honest that they didn't want to hear.

There were colleagues who supported you—until your agony was too hard to watch.

You could have love that made you strong, and still discover that it didn't make you strong enough.

She opened a new document. Closed her eyes and visualized the monsters of what she called Boss Anxiety. Melting brown ache of despair. The shattering scream of lightning terror. The yellow of shame flooding into Kerry's eyes when she had realized Paris really meant it, that she wasn't going to stay and fight. Something else crept into her thoughts—the quiet lavender of relief when Diana had touched her hand.

She wrote her feelings and fears almost without breathing until her fingers finally stopped moving and her brain couldn't find another word.

Her stomach let out a painful growl as she titled the document with the day's date and closed it unread. Somewhere in the last few hours the sun had set. The wind had come up again, rattling the screen door. Headlights from a passing car turned raindrops on the windows into prisms of orange and blue.

The endless river of anxiety was drained for now, by her own choosing. She turned on lights and closed the drapes to push all the dark away. She owed much to the therapist her mother had taken her to in her teens, who had suggested that Paris's love of gaming gave her many tools she could use to confront and win against Boss Anxiety. Paris had learned to accept that even when she won, like in a game, the enemy regenerated and battled again.

Having to battle it again wasn't failure, it was part of the game of life she'd been given. She hadn't needed meds for several years now. If she needed them again it also wasn't a failure. The battles had gotten easier and shorter, most of the time. This one was the worst in a while. It wasn't just the letter. It was also that her mind had considered, for a long moment, how she might be a witness for Grace and Adya. Go to a place where she knew she'd be photographed and write her real name in a document that would become a searchable, findable public record.

She really wanted to be a witness for them and their inspiring decades of love. A year ago she wouldn't have considered the possibility at all, and that meant something had changed. She would have to think about that.

The final step in her engineered, word-spewing catharsis was deleting the document permanently and letting go of the words and what they represented.

A few clicks and it was done. Battle won. For now.

Sleep. Tomorrow would be better.

CHAPTER EIGHT

At first it was research, and then Diana couldn't put Anita Topaz's books down. She'd gone back to the market multiple times until she had all five. She'd read far too late into the night and then again the next night and the next. Monday morning she was in the corner deli and at the bottom of an espresso before she felt awake.

It was hard to decide what kept her turning the pages. The heaving bosoms of the women combined with the hunky, unshaven guys on the covers made them the kind of book she'd never expected to like. They certainly hadn't been in her curriculum growing up. A good, complicated mystery was her usual go-to when it came to books. Miss Marple and Inspector Wexford were her heroes. There were puzzles in Anita Topaz's stories, sure, but they could hardly be called whodunnits.

Nevertheless, she couldn't stop reading. Heroines fell from grace, or had grace stolen from them. In the struggle to reclaim their lives or simply survive, heroes came into the picture. Through mutually suspicious partnership, the couple triumphed over malice and circumstantial adversity. Best friends and trusted allies were colorful and diverse, including a few gay ones, though none resembled Paris Ellison, the real Anita Topaz. There was always a strong sense of justice at the end of these stories, like in a good mystery. There was also heaps and heaps of hot sex.

Hot, sexy love that went on for hours, nights, days even. That part did seem…unrealistic. She could accept, she thought with a grin, that a cast-off rich girl could find true love in a soup kitchen with a man who was funny and moved like a ninja and treated her with respect and turned out to be an Internet tycoon on the lam from mobsters who thought he had the magic code that unlocked the world's banking system forcing them to run for their lives through every country in Europe and parts of Canada. But sexual satisfaction the first and every time?

That part of the novels was foreign territory for her.

She decided on a second espresso and a bagel. Americans made brilliant cream cheese flavors and so far her favorite was honey and walnut. She licked excess off her fingers and wiped a smear from the dust jacket of her book. At least both models on the cover were in equal though different stages of undress. Still, the hulking beefcake male model looming over the half-naked woman left her cold.

Anita Topaz's couples were on fire with passion for each other. Her personal experience with men was not the stuff of stories like this. Diana had rarely lacked for male attention and what hadn't outright annoyed her as intrusive hadn't moved her much past lukewarm.

She massaged the scar tissue in her shoulder. It was a tangible, visible reminder of a dozen years spent in relentless training with the bare minimum of nutrition. Like a lot of her teammates, her hormonal cycles hadn't begun until late in her teens. Delayed menarche had left a hidden mark on her as well. All the passion she was capable of had been directed at practice, judges, and teammates. It had been nearly a year after resuming a more normal life with more food and less physical challenge before she'd even felt the faintest whispers of sexual awareness.

A decade out of competition and her breast measurement was the only one appreciably larger than it had been at age ten. Her occasional connections with men were short-lived and fueled only by a modicum of attraction toward one who made her laugh, no commitment beyond a bit of fun, and the thought that she ought to make sure everything was at least functional now and again.

She studied the near-clinch pairing on the front of the book again. Her lips twisted as she thought of photoshopping her brother and his wife-to-be's heads on to the bodies of the models. William was head-over-heels for Millie and she hoped they would be happy.

She had made herself happy with acting. She loved the experience of getting to know the rhythm of villages and neighborhoods, and the fellowship that grew out of small communities. At first she'd moved all around Great Britain, then branched out to Ireland and Europe. America and Canada had followed. She went home sporadically, changed out her wardrobe and played the part of the dutiful daughter to the hilt.

Her mother didn't understand Diana's wanderlust, or the fixation on having a never-quite-successful acting career. But the Countess didn't know about Diana's real goals. She would never know that the same part of Diana that had pursued the perfect round off back salto with a full twist mount onto a four-inch wide beam loved the challenge and daring it took to plan and execute a perfect theft.

Like gymnastics, she did it because she dared herself to prove that she could.

She also did it because she couldn't stand to see someone using pottery from a conquered people as an ashtray. Or a sacred fetish as jewelry that happened to match their latest coat. Or a piece of native art to gavel in their greed-is-good conference.

Ronald Keynes Reynard was in her sights now. And it was going to be a *most* satisfying job. It would mean taking a few chances. Risk was a familiar friend. Audacity was one of her strengths, and she was going to lead with that.

Mind made up, she walked home with another bagel for dinner later and to raid her supply of American dollars. The espresso had set her nerves to jangling and she was ready to take action. The costume shop favored by local theater professionals would be opening for the day.

She was in luck when it came to the right kind of wig, but didn't like their offerings of what was literally costume jewelry. They had a faux fur jacket that wouldn't fool any of her cousins, but good fake fur cost more than she had brought with her. Her first throw of the dice was hoping that Paris's knowledge of couture was limited. The second throw was that she would have to use her own jewelry, at least for today's performance.

She turned up at rehearsal at eleven to explain that she had to withdraw because she was being called home. She'd had so many sick grandmothers in the last several years. Fortunately, both of hers had already passed on, so she wasn't creating bad mojo by using them as an excuse.

The understudy for the female players was delighted at Diana's news. The director was annoyed. Darling Jeremy was the only one to express regret with any sincerity. Their response didn't really bother her. She was moving on to a new goal, and she needed them to forget her. Within a week they would.

By one o'clock, after an intense hour in front of the makeup mirror and picking through the selection of clothes she'd brought with her, she was within sight of Mona Lisa's. Over the weekend the weather had turned soft again. Drizzle threatened but didn't come down. The skies were gray, but the wind had stopped, thank goodness.

Not knowing which street Paris would approach from meant Diana had to linger more closely than she wanted. Otherwise, she risked not seeing her arrive. It was a busy corner on a narrow one-way street. Lorries rumbled past. Two industrious young men trundled back and forth with stacks of fragrant boxes on handtrucks, slowly loading a van sporting the logo of the pizzeria. She was apparently downwind of the oven, and the aroma of cheese and garlic made her slightly lightheaded.

One of the fellows gave her a cheeky grin when he caught her watching them. "A kiss for a pie, dollface?"

"No, but thank you." She buried her nose in her book. She was overdressed and quite out of place for the neighborhood. If they returned from their deliveries to find her still "waiting for the bus" they would be curious. Curious eyes were never a good thing.

When her watch ticked over to two o'clock she worried that she'd either missed Paris or today wasn't the day Paris would show up. It wasn't going to be discreet, staking out Mona Lisa's every afternoon.

At two thirty she concluded a meandering conversation with a garrulous older woman who adored Anita Topaz's books and had read the one in Diana's hand several times, and promptly had spoiled the ending which made Diana want to poke her with a pointy stick. Poke her hard and more than once.

She was so annoyed she nearly missed Paris's appearance across the intersection, kitty-corner to where Diana waited. Paris was carrying a small box on her shoulder. More brownies, no doubt. She looked exactly the same. Wind-blown, lanky, with a hoodie zipped to her chin.

After about two minutes Paris's silhouette appeared at the table near the window she seemed to prefer.

Diana cast a speculative eye at the clouds. In about ninety seconds the sun would come out.

Never underestimate the power of good lighting.

Showtime.

CHAPTER NINE

Paris set her delivery of brownies on the bar and told herself she was relieved there was no sign of Diana this time. She'd even waited until later in the afternoon to avoid her. It had taken several days, but she'd regained her sense of equilibrium and gotten back on track for her word counts. For now, she was ignoring the letter—yes, it was cowardly. But life was once again safe and routine, and she didn't want to risk that.

Lisa scooped up the box after pausing to inhale the unmistakable dark chocolate goodness. "The day I'm having— some of these aren't going to make it out of the kitchen. You want some lunch?"

"Is there chowder?"

Lisa rolled her eyes as she echoed loudly, "Is there chowder?"

A chorus of voices chimed in, "Is God Irish?"

"Sometimes you run out," Paris muttered as she made her way to the table at the window. There was no particular reason she wanted to linger. She was hungry, that was all.

Nevertheless, her gaze immediately went to the door when it opened. Not Diana. A small woman, perhaps thirty, in a thick fur coat that fell to her knees. The sunlight streaming in behind her caught a dazzle of emerald stones dangling from her ears, winking in and out of sight behind long waves of honey-blond hair that fell over one eye.

She wasn't the usual for Mona Lisa's crowd and conversations paused. Paris tried to stop watching her but she seemed no more able to resist than the guys at the bar.

The newcomer's gaze swept down the long stretch of gleaming oak where Lisa was wiping up a spill of melting ice, over the tables near the televisions and dart board, and then to the front windows to finally settle on Paris. The perfect pink lips curved in a smile of recognition.

Bemused, Paris caught herself before she automatically smiled back. If she had ever met the woman she would have remembered. She was walking toward Paris now, the coat falling open to reveal a short, slinky sapphire dress. Its daring neckline plunged most of the way to the woman's navel, and framed a necklace of gold links with an emerald teardrop pendant. Paris was certain it was no mistake that the pendant rested between the slight curves of her breasts. Leather boots hugged her thighs and stretched down the shapely legs.

"There you are," she said to Paris in a slightly breathless voice. "We meet at last."

Paris knew she should say something. Instead, she was taken aback by the casual way the woman set her designer-logo handbag on the table, as if she expected to join Paris for lunch.

"I'm sorry," Paris finally managed. "Do I know you?"

The blue eyes—several shades darker than the form-fitting, revealing dress—were full of merriment. "Of course you do. I'm Anita Topaz."

CHAPTER TEN

Paris's brain sorted through the words, put them in different order, replayed them—and they still didn't make sense. There was buzzing in her ears. "You can't be."

"Why not?" The blonde slid into the chair opposite Paris, dripping with sex and money. Her coat slipped farther back on her shoulders, revealing firm lines of muscle and fine bone. The only flaw was an odd bump almost at the point of her left shoulder.

"Is this some kind of joke? I'm Anita Topaz." She glanced around the bar, aware that people were still staring, and why wouldn't they? Their attention twanged at Paris's nerves.

Her movements leisurely, the woman extracted a book from her handbag and slid it facedown across the table to Paris. "You don't look anything like her picture."

It only took a glance for Paris to recognize the damned stock photo she'd taken out of a new picture frame. Too demoralized and run to ground to use her own photo, she'd doctored the image with lots of shadow and sent it along with her submission package for the publishing contest that had put Anita Topaz into print. The soft yellow hair, pink, pink lips, and shining blue eyes were matched by the woman sitting across from her.

One corner of the expressive mouth pulled upward and that's when the truth hit Paris.

"Diana!" Suddenly it was obvious—and immediately bewildering.

She bowed her head in acknowledgment. "What do you think?"

Paris managed to gasp, "Why?"

"I really need a job and I have a plan. It's a little crazy but maybe we both get what we want."

Paris realized that she'd been shaking her head throughout their exchange. The buzz in her ears got louder. "You don't know anything about what I want."

She said it more loudly than she meant to, loudly enough to draw Lisa to their table. To Paris she said, "Your lunch will be out in a minute or two." Her gaze was laden with curiosity as she added to Diana, "Can I get you something?"

Still using that slightly breathless voice that was not the least bit Irish, Diana said, "I'd love an iced tea. Especially if some Grey Goose Citron fell into it."

"You got it." Lisa departed after a narrow-eyed speculative study of Diana's face.

Paris began a furious whispered demand but Diana cut her off with a droll, "Don't you think Anita Topaz would drink top-shelf vodka? That'll be my lunch money for today."

"She doesn't drink—"

"Oh but she does! All of her characters do, so it must be a favorite. They also like chocolate and fresh, crisp sheets." With a lazy fingertip illustrating on her own body, she added, "And right there, the part of a woman's chest where the curve of her breast just becomes visible."

Paris tore her gaze from the spot Diana outlined with her fingertip.

"I'm not saying the heroes are predictable that way, I just noticed that it's the first trait *they* notice, when they realize the lovely lady has all the right ingredients to light their flame."

"You've been reading my books?" It wasn't the question Paris meant to ask.

"I'm a method actor." Diana was all sunny smiles as Lisa returned with the cocktail and Paris's bowl of chowder. She engaged Lisa in a frivolous discussion about the vodka, and Lisa returned to the bar without giving any sign of recognizing Diana.

Paris felt less like an idiot on that score at least. Otherwise, she had clearly entered the Twilight Zone.

How was it possible to be sitting at her familiar table, with an ordinary bowl of soup, a prosaic bag of oyster crackers alongside, while across the table was a siren of a woman claiming to be... Well, claiming to be her? With hair product, eyeliner, and lipstick? Long, sexy legs, a prowling walk, and confidence in the power of her charm? Every bit the kind of woman Paris wasn't.

And yet, if anyone were asked to pick the Queen of the Bodice Rippers, who would they choose? Not the skinny, angular, beige-skinned butch whose only foray into the beautification department was strawberry ChapStick. And that only because anyone who didn't use some kind of balm in a Boston winter was asking to be lipless by spring.

She knew the answer to the question, had always known it. People would rather see female success as blond, pale, and pretty, as if a woman's fame and fortune were like beauty itself—unearned gifts from the gods, not the result of grinding work and nurtured talent. People saw what they wanted to see, even when it was a willful lie. She'd fallen into that trap when she'd sent in a photo so polar opposite to who she actually was.

"No," Paris said. She wasn't going to double down on a mistake.

"The soup isn't what you wanted?"

"No, you can't go about pretending to be Anita Topaz."

"Don't you even want to hear my proposal?"

"No." She stirred her chowder, wishing she hadn't ordered it. She wanted to leave but if she bailed, Lisa would want to know why. She didn't want to explain any of this to anybody.

"It would be only for that meeting they want. To go and tell them face-to-face to stop asking. I can do Garbo." Diana struck a tragic reclining pose and intoned sadly, "I want to be alone…"

Well, damn it. The part of Paris's brain that wanted Boss Anxiety to leave her life forever, and would do anything to get some peace, thought that was a feasible idea. But the part of her brain that *was* the anxiety immediately cowered at the possibility of being discovered a liar.

She'd have to run again, the voice of anxiety warned. She'd have to find a new place to hide and she liked where she was. She'd been safe until—until the letter. Safe until Diana showed up with her magic hands and now her ridiculous ideas.

"You wouldn't have to pay me much, only enough to live on until the meeting." There was a whisper of desperation in Diana's voice. "That's a couple weeks rent, some food money. It would give me enough time to line up my next gig. Without having to sponge off my parents who think I ought to be a dental hygienist and marry the richest patient I can find."

Suspecting she was being teased, Paris risked a glance at Diana's face. "What happened to your freckles?" Again, it wasn't the question she meant to ask.

The blue eyes blinked in surprise. "Full coverage foundation. Are you listening?"

"Yes. Still no." The eye color must be contact lenses. Was the blond hair real, or the red hair she'd worn before? Or neither? Diana was like a gamer's avatar with swap-out options. If so, did that make Paris the game? Or was life in general Diana's playground?

"It would get everyone off your back. I could do imperious. Eccentric. Or Tipsy McStaggers. If they think you'll be an embarrassment—"

"N-O. No."

"Can I have your oyster crackers? If you don't want them."

Paris sighed and handed them over.

Diana tore open the packet and popped several of the tiny saltines into her mouth. "Thanks. I skipped lunch and the vodka is going to my head."

"That's not good for you."

With a gesture at herself, Diana said, "This took more than two minutes in front of a mirror."

"I'm sure it did. What did you do to your shoulder?"

Diana reflexively glanced at the telltale bump. "War wound."

Sure. That was believable. "Which war?"

"It was a conflict of many nations."

"Right." Paris made herself eat her soup and a long silence fell between them. When her spoon scraped the bottom of the bowl there was only a thin line of liquid left in Diana's cocktail glass. "Look, I'm sorry you went to all that trouble—"

"It's not the first time I didn't get the part after killing it in the audition. I did get her right, didn't I?"

Paris did not want to admit that Diana did in fact look the part. "Anita Topaz doesn't exist—except in that stupid picture."

"Was the picture your idea?"

"It was the publisher's annual manuscript contest. They wanted a photo with the submission, and I wanted my odds to be the best possible." And she hadn't wanted anyone who followed gaming to recognize her. But she wasn't going to tell Diana that.

"And judges like glamorous blondes," Diana said, half to herself. "This dress has landed me more than one part."

"I'll bet it has." Paris didn't mean to sound so fervent, and Diana's brows immediately lowered.

"They get to look. Nobody gets to touch."

Lucky Nobody. Paris was flooded with relief that she hadn't said that aloud. "I can't do it. So no. Thank you for—for being concerned about me."

"Well, enlightened self-interest played a part. I am about on my last dime and it's official. No more play paychecks. The idea of a luxury weekend and theater and free food, it was really tempting."

"It wouldn't work out."

"You could change your mind. I'll hold out hope." Smiling, Diana slid a piece of paper across the table. "My phone number. Just in case."

"I won't change my mind." She tucked the paper in her pocket. It wasn't as if she could leave it on the table for anyone to find.

"I don't suppose you'd sign my book, would you?"

"I—Nobody has ever asked me to do that before."

"I promise not to put it on eBay."

Diana's American accent had slipped a little. She still didn't sound at all like Irish Lass had—more British than that. The sheer flexibility of Diana's voice and manner would be fascinating under other circumstances. "How do you think Anita would sign it?"

"With a big red marker, and she'd add XX-OO-XX at the bottom."

Paris frowned. "You know, Anita is sometimes called the Queen of the *Smart* Bodice Rippers."

"I know. I saw it on the covers of the first two books. I really like that the women are smart and ambitious and, well, know how to do things. They're competent. And take care of themselves before they meet Mr. Right."

"I think smart women are sexy," Paris admitted.

Diana blinked. "So smart women don't like red ink and X's and O's?"

"Maybe some do." It was oddly thrilling to consider how to sign the book. That she'd published five and never done it before was a cost of her seclusion. Like standing up for her adorable landladies at their wedding, it was another experience sacrificed at the altar of safety.

She set aside the sharp prod of bitterness. "I only have an ordinary pen. It'll have to do." She scribbled a few words, signed "Anita Topaz" awkwardly and pushed the book back across the table to Diana.

Diana opened the book to the cover page and read aloud, "To the most amazing actress I know." The smile she gave Paris was dazzling. "Thank you! That is the best review I've ever received."

"Lisa still hasn't recognized you."

"I am good at my own makeup and costume." She tucked the book in her handbag. "And I don't suppose I could ask you for one small favor?"

"You can ask," Paris said warily.

"I don't suppose you'd buy my drink?" Diana's eyelashes fluttered so hard and obviously that Paris had to laugh.

"Sure. Not a big deal. I was going to offer." Which was the truth.

"Thanks." Diana rose gracefully to her feet and snuggled her fur coat around her shoulders. The boots added at least four inches to her height, but she still seemed tiny. Fragile even, Paris thought. "See you around maybe."

"Maybe."

She blew a kiss to the guys at the bar and then the door closed behind her. A moment later she passed the window and Paris watched her until she was out of sight.

She was relieved. Diana's frivolous, risky proposal was out of her reach.

Lisa filled the seat that Diana had vacated. "Spill it."

"I don't—"

"Yes you do. That was quite possibly the strangest woman to ever walk in here, and that includes you."

"Why am I strange?"

"A, you bake brownies for a bar. B, you don't need the money. C, you don't even drink."

"I told you, I anxiety bake and I don't want to eat it all by myself. I'd end up with a coronary."

Lisa cocked her head. "D, you're a butch that bakes and you're single. I mean, that right there puts you the category of Things that Make Me Go Hmm."

Paris dug in her pocket. "I got this letter," she began. Her head was spinning. "Look."

Lisa unfolded the paper and read it. "Wowie zowie. *Hamilton* tickets? You're going, right?"

"I can't. I don't want to do their conference talk, and besides, they think I'm someone else." As Lisa's eyebrows shot up, she hastily added, "I mean, they don't know I'm me. Who I really am."

"A butch who bakes?"

"Yes, they don't know the lesbian thing. They don't publish queer books. Plus they think I'm a willowy fragile blond bombshell."

"Why would they think that?"

"I may have sent them a photo, years ago. Which I totally regret now," she added hastily.

"A photo like the woman who just left? In the really bad fake fur?"

"It was fake?"

"Yes, most fur is fake these days, but this was *bad* fake fur. But I'd bet my eyeteeth that those mammoth rocks she was wearing were the real deal."

Diana the starving actress had real emeralds? "You really didn't recognize her?"

"I felt like I'd seen her before. Like a bit part in a movie."

"Change the hair to red," Paris suggested.

Lisa gaped. "You're kidding. That was Fiona?"

"Fiona?"

A fine line appeared between Lisa's eyebrows. "The actress. Tomato soup and a half-pint. Fiona."

Paris didn't know if she should tell Lisa that "Fiona" also went by "Diana." If she'd felt bewildered before she was way past that now. "That was her."

Lisa's brow was furrowed. "So she found your letter the other day. This letter?"

Paris nodded.

"And now she wants to pretend to be you for this meeting. *Hamilton* tickets, weekend in the big city, all that."

It was Paris's turn to gape. "How did you figure that out?"

Lisa's shrug said that it was obvious to a child. "It makes sense."

"On what planet? Who wants to bamboozle a conglomerate with boatloads of lawyers on speed dial? Not me. I'm already on shaky ground having sent in a fake photo for that contest. I can't double down. And I *don't* want to go to their freaking meeting."

"You should go." Lisa said it with an air of finality, as if she'd run the entire game play through in her head and had the inescapable winning play strategy. Her certainty was deeply annoying.

Paris pushed back her chair, ready to flee. "We're not going to agree."

"You should go and be you. Don't worry about the photo. Let them see *you*. The real you. That'll be the end of it."

"Thanks for the compliment," Paris snapped.

"Don't be thick. They want *her*." Lisa pointed in the direction Diana had headed. "Every newscaster on their network looks like that. But they've got you. If they're chauvinist assholes—and they probably are—the meeting will last five minutes. There's a chance, I suppose, that they could be decent people. That they'll listen to you explain that you can't do public appearances and leave you alone."

"Have you ever read anything about the CEO, Reynard? He's Jabba the Hut and thinks he's Han Solo. I'd have never chosen them as a publisher. Just my luck they bought the one I had."

"He's not Jabba the Hut. Don't give him that much credit "

"Okay, you got me there." Paris's laugh turned rueful. "I can't. You know why."

"I know that it wouldn't be easy." Her eyes were more sympathetic now. "I never had anyone make a video game where the goal was raping and dismembering me. I can't even imagine it and that's probably good. I get how scary that was."

"And then they told the world where I lived." Paris rested her elbows on her knees, though she was still primed to head for the door.

"Little dick asshats. Do they run Anita Topaz's life?"

"No. But they still scare Paris Ellison. They're still out there."

Lisa was shaking her head. "But that doesn't mean you can't go to this meeting. You say 'This is me, I'm of no use to you the way you want,' and you tell them to get someone else. Then you go see *Hamilton*. Come home and write books. It all works out."

"And if they decide I've been a fraud and dump Anita Topaz?"

Lisa's eyeroll was epic. "Laugh all the way to their chief competitor. Honey, you've got bank and you're bankable as a writer. Surely that counts as some kind of armor."

Paris shook her head. "You make everything sound so simple."

"You're not the first person to tell me that." She waved a hand as if to vanquish all such criticism. "Look. I don't have anxiety disorder and I'm not an introvert on top of that, so, yeah, I know, I look at it differently than you do." She glanced at the far end of the bar where loud words were being exchanged over baseball and politics. Twisting her long hair around her hand she pushed back from the table. "You can do it Fiona's way if you want. Though I don't know where she got those emeralds."

Utterly bewildered and bemused, Paris watched as Lisa approached the argument, timing the release of her hair so it spilled around her shoulders in a dazzling distraction. "Fellas, fellas," she cajoled. "Don't make me shoot you."

CHAPTER ELEVEN

With a wave at Lisa she headed out in the opposite direction from Diana, even though that meant going the long way around to the grocery store. At least the wind had finally let up and the sun was warming when it peeked between the clouds. Laden with chocolate chips, flour, sugar, and all the other necessities of her break-even brownie-making sideline, she made it home feeling as if she'd escaped from sirens trying to pull her into their alluring vortex.

Diana's phone number felt like fire in her pocket. She immediately dropped it into the kitchen junk drawer where, like so many of her favorite utensils over the years, it would never be seen again. With any luck.

She was putting the groceries away when Hobbit scratched at the door. He preferred mornings, but sometimes he showed up for tea as well. "Beggar," she said as he coiled past her ankles to sniff disapprovingly at his bowl. "Just how many houses do you hit in a day?"

Hobbit assumed a stony vigil over the empty dish and fixed her with his yellow eyes.

Paris caved in five seconds. "What? You don't like that I'm so judgmental about it? Truth is truth, buddy."

She was setting the bag of dry food back into the cupboard when the answering machine picked up an incoming call.

An unrelentingly perky voice announced herself as calling from Reynard House. "Mr. Reynard has personally asked me to reach out to you about an exciting new agenda item for the meeting. A teleplay of *Hands Off the Merchandise* is being negotiated! Mr. Reynard is trying to arrange for you to also meet the screenwriter who might be taking on the project. We are all so thrilled to be able to elevate the Anita Topaz brand to such a high level. I am looking through the file for the meeting and I don't see that we have noted your arrival time. I would appreciate it if you would call me back…"

The voice was still talking but Paris couldn't take it in. They were offering a *movie* deal.

Diana's plan floated through her mind. Then Lisa's insistence that Paris should go, and it would all be okay.

"Foul word," she muttered. Then burst out so loudly it echoed, "Foul, foul, foul word!"

The answering machine let out an off-key beep as the call disconnected.

What was she going to do? They were determined to make Anita Topaz more famous. Yes, yes, yes, this was a happy problem. Lots of people would give up body parts for an opportunity like this.

The encounter with Diana underscored the cherry on top for them: sure Anita made them money, but they also thought she was their version of an ideal female. That's who they wanted as their Reynard Media Group Publishing Poster Girl.

Also true—book money paled next to movie money. It raised the stakes all around. If she still said a big N-O to personal contact and publicity, they'd probably move on to someone more agreeable. Anita Topaz was a name but this business had a lot of names.

When women interfered with making money, the world was merciless. She could never forget that. Anonymous Internet trolls had threatened her life, sent the most ugly and disgusting pictures, and loaded emails with viruses and ransomware. Reynard House wouldn't do any of that. It would be bloodless: they would fill her place with another player without a moment's hesitation.

And she'd lose a possible *movie* deal. Just like she'd lost her old life and a girlfriend and signing books and talking to fans at ComicCon and PAX West.

All the bitterness welled up, stunning her to tears. Her mother would call this maundering a foolish waste. Bitterness will rob you of your will to overcome, she would have said. She missed her mother every day, and yet was glad Momma hadn't been around when ugliness had pulled her daughter's life down into the deep.

Wiping her eyes, Paris struggled to take a few calming breaths. Anxiety was popping at her eardrums and had leached color out of her vision. Too many choices, too many unknowns.

Honeysuckle and gentle surf. *Deep breath*. Her adorable landladies getting married. *Deep breath*.

After a few minutes she could take comfort in the soft purple curtains at the kitchen window and the steady crunch of Hobbit enjoying his snack. Another near miss from a full-out anxiety attack—she couldn't go on like this. Ignoring the situation wasn't working. She had to make a decision.

One of her biggest triggers was too many choices. Struggling to anticipate every possible outcome put her mental processes into a spiral loop that eventually crowded out everything else. It was probably why she had felt so comfortable gaming. Choices were limited, outcomes were knowable. There was always an off switch, and it was possible, even advisable, to start over sometimes.

Go to the meeting: yes or no? It was a binary choice, really. Only two options. "If I hadn't sent in that damned photo they might not be bothering me. But I did and they are."

She blew out air so hard Hobbit paused in mid-crunch to scowl at her. "Next life I want to be a lesbian's cat. In Cat World it's possible that thin, yellow-haired creatures aren't the be-all and end-all."

Yeah, you can blame other people's prejudices, she thought, but you leveraged it. You picked thin and blond and so, so white. She knew exactly what her mother would have called that: *complicit*. Now she was hoisted on her own lack of ethics.

"Is that the bed you made all by yourself?" Her mother's deceptively quiet voice played in her mind. "If you get in and pull up the covers, don't blame the bed if you can't sleep."

She reheated coffee in the microwave and took the steaming mug to the sofa. Hobbit immediately joined her, burrowing into her thigh while lightly batting her arm with a paw until she obediently stroked his side. After a few quiet minutes with her mind whirring while Hobbit purred, she felt able to pick at the problem again.

Though not a valid excuse, the photograph had been armor that she'd felt she'd needed at the time. Her terror of being found had been real, and she'd had real evils to fear. But—a new thought entered the situation analysis. She was stronger now than she had been five years ago.

She scritched lightly under Hobbit's chin, enjoying the thrum of his purrs against her fingertips. "It's like I've been on a long, fun but really safe quest and built up supplies and experience. All of a sudden the quest is harder and scarier. But there are good rewards at the end. A movie deal is a dream come true, isn't it? A game winner after I had to start over from scratch."

At the sound of her voice Hobbit had opened one eye, but quickly closed it again.

"How can I complete this quest without losing any of the lives I have left? What are the rules and are there any exploits?" All the questions of Gaming 101. Practice helped. Ignorance hurt. Experience mattered. She definitely had more hit points than five years ago. A movie deal? That was a lot of Experience Points and gold for future questing.

Her fear was that if she played the Anita Topaz Famous Writer avatar too publicly, the pack of ravening jackals who'd ganged up on Paris Ellison could decide to play with Anita Topaz the same way. The day they'd doxxed her home address on Deep Dungeon had taught her that those assholes really did mean to do her harm. They really hoped someone would rape her to death. They really wanted someone to take pictures of her dismembered body. She was nothing more than a woman-shaped toy like the ones they so enjoyed brutalizing in their games. The panic attack had been the worst of her life.

Her mistake had been talking in public about how uncomfortable it made her to see even pretend women treated that way. After her blog post there had been two hours of "Attagirl! Great post! We need to talk about this." Then the mob had arrived, like the endless stream of orcs at Helm's Deep. No Gandalf rescue at the last minute. No Galadriel with magic gifts. Every ally had been overwhelmed and drained until it was only her and so many of them.

"Ow! Stop that or I'll put you out." Hobbit's whack of claws to her hand reminded her to keep petting. "Spoiled rotten, that's what you are. And you probably think I should have stayed. After two months of it, I was all out of hit points and on my last life. Kerry told me to fight. She thought I just simply wouldn't. I knew I couldn't. I couldn't have another panic attack like that." The loss of control, the feeling of strangling and drowning, the inability to hear or talk, coming out of it in an emergency room, terrifying minutes of not being able to speak enough to explain to strangers that it wasn't a drug overdose or anaphylaxis—never again.

The life she'd created by fleeing to the opposite coast had torn out her heart in more ways than one. She'd lost Kerry. She'd learned to play the game of life by going around the battle with Boss Anxiety. Anything that could be a trigger was off limits. Whatever it took to feel safe was Winning.

And she'd been winning, damn it.

Now Reynard House was imposing new rules, like a game designer who decided the play wasn't hard enough.

New rules meant new strategies for winning—wasn't that what a game designer would say?

Thinking about it that way was a comforting framework. If at some point she no longer felt safe, she could freeze the game and leave it, couldn't she? If they continued to change the rules, then Finn and Lisa were right, other publishers would play the game with her. She would not lose her livelihood a second time and that reality meant she had resources she could use.

"Is there some part of their game I can play safely? What do you think, Hobbit?" A flick of the cat's ears was all the answer she got. "I'm five years older and stronger. I have bank and I've proved I can make someone money in the mainstream world. That *is* a new kind of armor. I didn't have that before."

Inexplicably she pictured Diana smiling at her.

Well, that was a pretty enough picture, but Diana, or Fiona, or whatever her name was, she wasn't real. The quiet calm of her touch had been a fluke, and wishing that they'd met under different circumstances didn't change a thing.

"Can I go to their stupid meeting, let them get a good look at the real me, and tell them to their face that I'm not going to be their dancing bear? And say yes, they can make a movie based on one of my books? Anita Topaz gets a big level up—if I don't pass out or drool on myself."

She pushed Hobbit off her leg and carried her coffee into the bedroom. Bouncing on her toes in front of her desk, she reached a state of hard-won calm. Lisa, for all her high-handed interfering advice, was right.

"And if they say no, sorry, no beautiful femme blonde means no deal, I go play the game with someone else who'll play the way I want. I'll listen to Finn about getting an agent finally."

She could deal with those choices, she abruptly realized. They were clear. What she had to believe was that she could physically handle the stress of the meeting.

Diana was in her mind again, sapphire dress and emeralds and fur. Skin as smooth as rose petals. A walk that said "Look but don't touch."

Ignoring the tingles in her stomach and elsewhere, she shook the delectable image from her mind by reminding herself that Diana liked using multiple names and pretended to be people she wasn't on *and* off stage. If Lisa was right, the jewelry was the only thing about Diana that was real.

Well, other parts of Paris speculated, there were definitely a couple of items that had seemed very real. Small and firm and...

Wrenching her mind away from the image of the emerald pendant and where it had delicately rested on Diana's chest, Paris worked on strengthening her resolve. There was no way in hell she could carry off thigh-high boots and a fur coat the way Diana had. But a couple of couture suits, silk ties, designer cuff links—that she could manage. Clothes were a kind of armor, and she could be a sharp-dressed butch with no apologies. Anita Topaz didn't have to worry much about money. Time to make a big withdrawal.

She could take the train, even, and pay cash. Reynard House was making the hotel reservations for "Anita"—they never called her anything else. The electronic payment of royalties to Paris Ellison had been set up with the previous publisher. Now that she thought about it, Paris wondered if the gaggle of marketing interns even knew she had another name. Fine, so she'd be "Anita" from the moment she left home. All in all, the trip wouldn't generate much for one of her former stalkers to find, even if they still had bots out there sniffing cyberspace for her name in play somewhere.

She really didn't *want* to do this, but she *could*. She knew the difference. Her mother would be proud of her.

The memory of her mother's hugs brought up tension-relieving tears and she gave in, flooded with relief to know what she was going to do. Hobbit decided her sniffling around the house for the next quarter-hour was the final straw and asked to be let out. She locked the door and blew her nose.

Heck, she'd get to see *Hamilton*.

CHAPTER TWELVE

Once she'd made up her mind, Paris resumed her daily life. At the keyboard, Susannah discovered the identity of her nemesis and left Tuscany for the Riviera to search for an old flame. The outline for the novel continued to unfold as she'd planned. Best of all, words flowed easily and on schedule. At this pace she'd be ready for a break about the time she left for New York.

Her landladies' occasional interruptions to discuss attire and corsages for the wedding were welcome. They were delighted to hear she was going on a short trip. She'd warned them that Hobbit might come calling while she was gone, but really, there was no way that cat would ever starve.

She also set aside time to go shopping in Back Bay where a women's tailor measured every inch of her. She returned the following week to pick up the results: three suits, a sports jacket, an array of trousers and button-up shirts, plus a bewildering assortment of suggested ties. She tried everything on, taking in the color pairing recommendations as best she could. It was all in service of the quest she'd assigned herself, which she now dubbed "Storming the Office Building."

The tailor, after demonstrating all the fussiness that befit someone in her profession, had finally knelt at Paris's feet to tweak the legs of the power suit pants. "In loafers or dress shoes these will fall perfectly."

Paris eyed her Doc Martens in the mirror. Much as she loved them, they weren't right for the steel-gray power suit. "I'll be sure to pick up a pair." She tightened the knot at her collar slightly, liking how the wide red silk shone against the royal blue of the shirt. *Sharp-Dressed Butch*—achievement unlocked, she thought.

Unbidden she wondered if Diana would approve, then kicked herself for thinking about her at all.

On the way home, laden with a zippered garment carrier and a heavy shopping bag, she chastised herself again for dwelling on Diana. The whole crazy proposal had been a chance intrusion into her life. Diana/Fiona/Anita, she reminded herself, had probably not told her the truth about anything. Yet thoughts of her intruded at odd moments throughout the day and especially in that fleeting-flying moment before falling asleep. The junk drawer where she'd dropped Diana's phone number sometimes caught the light like it never had before.

If her life really were a video game of course she'd open the drawer and find the phone number glowing with magic. But she had no clue as to which kind. More Gaming 101: You never knew about random objects given to you by mysterious characters. And Diana was all that. Mystery and risks and outlandish plans. Improbable, and impossible to forget completely.

The Friday morning she left for New York she was glad to have practiced the tailor's recommended Windsor knot several more times. Her hands refused to stop shaking. The mirror said the steel-gray suit looked just as intimidating as it had in the tailor's shop, but it also revealed her ashen face. A new haircut, sleek on the sides and longer on the top for bravado, wasn't quite long enough in the front to hide the fear in her eyes.

The cab she'd reserved came on time and everything at the Amtrak station went smoothly. But the train was held outside New Haven for reasons unknown and Paris thought she was going to sweat through her shirt. Instead of arriving at the crowded underground of Penn Station at one o'clock, it was well past two. She'd hoped for a quiet thirty minutes in her hotel room to gather her wits. Instead she dashed in the hotel's front door, asked the bellman to hold her suitcase, and dashed back out to the waiting cab.

The next gauntlet was the security screening at the Reynard Media Group home office. Paris gave the meeting details to a guard who looked up something on his computer screen, then waved her through the scanning gate. Her pulse rate rose nevertheless. It was the building itself—cold, steel, echoing. It didn't help that she was now several minutes late.

Helpfully, the elevator was an express that only stopped at the top four floors. It opened directly into the reception area where a petite brunette in a tailored navy blue jacket and skirt immediately greeted her.

"You're here for the meeting?"

"Yes. Anita Topaz," Paris said. It was as cold in the office suite as the lobby downstairs. The air was sterile. Glass and chrome walls were the backdrop to framed posters featuring personalities from Reynard News who were also Reynard House top selling authors. They were either silver-haired mature men in dark suits or yellow-haired younger women in sleeveless blue dresses. The men had the same steely-eyed gaze while all the women smiled in the same cheerful degree. They struck Paris as media cookie cutters, remarkable only in their conformity to a bland corporate type.

If the receptionist found Paris out of the ordinary she gave no sign. She tapped at her paper-thin tablet and gestured for Paris to follow her. "Right this way."

The thick gray carpet underfoot quickly muffled all sounds from the reception area. The hallway was very long and ended at massive double doors. Nearby office doors were closed and blinds drawn over hallway-facing windows. It was the perfect game tableau, Paris realized. There could be a different quest battle behind every door. The floor could turn to lava at any moment.

Such thoughts were not helping her heart rate. Cold sweat dripped down her back. There was no stopping now, but her throat had tightened and she wasn't entirely sure she could speak. *I will not have a panic attack.*

"Go right in," the receptionist said, with a gesture at the double doors.

Paris nodded her thanks, squared her shoulders, and opened the right-hand door into an expansive conference room. *I will not have a panic attack...*

The eastern wall was all glass and faced a stunning view of Midtown skyscrapers and the East River. Being able to see outside immediately made it easier to breathe. Fighting to stay focused, she skirted the long wooden table that gleamed with varnish and looked as if it had never been used. The only occupants were clustered at the far end near a buffet table and bar. A glance at her watch said she was five minutes late and they appeared to have begun some aspect of the meeting without her. Deep rumbles of mirth from several men twined with a woman's sharp laugh.

She had no choice but to go forward. So you're a little late, she told herself. It was fashionable, wasn't it?

The length of the room gave her the chance to take a couple deep breaths. As she approached the group she reviewed her plan. Introduce herself. State her intentions. If it started to go badly, she could leave whenever she wanted and call Finn. This encounter would be draining, but it wouldn't kill her. She would not have another panic attack.

One of the men finally noticed Paris's approach. He was probably on the other side of sixty and his wide-set eyes were dark. She recognized him by his bald head and the massive bulk of his shoulders. Somewhere in his past he had supposedly played football, but the athlete was long gone. What remained was the bull of American media: Ronald Reynard, entertainment czar, CEO of Reynard Media Group, and the corporate overlord of Anita Topaz's publisher. Though the letters had been signed by him, she hadn't really expected him to personally show up.

His expression was not welcoming. The other men were completely focused on the woman, whose back was to Paris. A long French braid hung down her spine, shining like a rope of gold against a pale neck and a sleeveless dress the color of an American Beauty rose.

Paris opened her mouth to apologize for her tardiness, but her gaze fixed on a heavy emerald earring that swayed from a delicate earlobe. From there she took notice of the woman's left shoulder where the flawless toned line of muscle and bone was broken by a bump—and Diana turned her head to see what Ronald Reynard was looking at.

Their gazes met. Diana froze, but only for a moment. Then her expression eased into careless lines as she turned to Reynard. "Excuse me. My driver must have a message for me."

She met Paris while there were still a few steps to go. "Ellis," she said, just loudly enough, "is something wrong?"

There was so much wrong. So very much wrong. Paris couldn't find any words.

Under her breath, Diana said, "Don't hate me. I have them eating out of the palm of my hand."

"I—I—"

"Ronald, I'm so sorry. Can you excuse me for a minute? This won't take long." Diana tucked her hand ever so casually under Paris's arm but her fingers curled around it like iron.

She was being marched toward the end of the room. Every second that ticked by was another one where she didn't tell Ronald Reynard the truth, didn't expose Diana as a fake. She should detach herself, go back, explain.

How could she possibly explain?

They were in the hallway, all doors near them closed, before Paris found her voice.

"You walked in here and told them you were me?" she asked in a furious whisper.

"I didn't tell them anything. Nobody even asked me for an ID. They *assumed* I was you. The receptionist announced me and Ronald Reynard is calling me Anita like I was at school with his daughter."

She was right, Paris thought. Nobody had asked her to prove she was Anita either. Which had nothing to do with anything—Diana was *not* Anita Topaz.

"This is ridiculous," she hissed. It was simply not fair that Diana, in her high-necked cocktail sheath and tantalizing high-heeled patent leather pumps, looked like the Anita Topaz Reynard Media Group wanted. She was not as outrageously sexy as she had been in the thigh-high leather boots and the dress cut down to her navel that she'd worn at Mona Lisa's. Instead, this rendition of Anita shimmered like a flawless gemstone against the gray-and-glass backdrop, not so different from the women whose pictures hung in the lobby. "We're going to get caught."

"Only if you let on," Diana whispered loudly. "I thought you weren't coming."

"I told you no to this—this—madness." How was this turning into her fault? "Was I supposed to call you up and say 'By the way I'm going so don't you show up to the thing I told you already not to show up at'?"

"What's done can't be undone." Diana's accent had been wavering between Hollywood and BBC, but settled back into Hollywood. "Surprise of the day is that Ronald Reynard is escorting me personally to the theater tonight. I'll do something inappropriate. Spit wine in his face. Say something feminist. And that will be that."

"You can't do that," Paris hissed. "I changed my mind because Reynard Entertainment might make a movie out of *Hands Off the Merchandise*. I really want that."

Diana looked momentarily nonplussed. "Well, that's a coup. Um, how should I play it then?"

"You're not playing it—"

"Of course I am. How about I say yes to everything, sign nothing. And tell him to have his people talk to my people, thanks for the play, buh bye. Okay?"

"You don't even know who your people are. I mean *my* people."

"So tell me."

The door opened behind them. Ronald Reynard asked solicitously, "Can I be of assistance?"

"No, no." Diana waved an elegant hand. "Ellis knows what to do. She's my utility infielder, you might say. Driver, assistant, bodyguard." With only the slightest pause she added, "My grandmother is poorly."

Reynard expressed his sympathies, all the while drawing Diana back into the conference room.

Just as Paris thought she had found the ability to speak, Diana sketched a parting salute and the conference room door closed with Paris still standing in the hallway.

She couldn't make herself go back in. Her feet refused to move in that direction. When someone came out of an adjoining office, their curious look sent Paris back to the reception area and into the elevator.

Halfway to the ground floor she blurted out, "Now I'll never see *Hamilton*!"

The other occupant didn't seem startled. "You and me both, mate."

CHAPTER THIRTEEN

Reynard's hand at the small of her back made Diana cringe. The stage she'd set for herself was dissolving under her feet. She'd told herself that her charade wouldn't harm Paris, might even help her. But now, clearly, there was more at stake than she'd known. Reynard was the one with the object she wanted to take, the reason she'd come here. Paris shouldn't be the one who lost.

Clearly, she had misread Paris. Given all the signs—the agitation and the stubborn refusal to even discuss a plan—the last eventuality Diana had expected was for Paris herself to show up. That was her own hubris, performance over-confidence. She'd tried a new move without adequate preparation and the balance beam had smacked her right between the eyes.

For a split second she hadn't even recognized Paris. A gray-silver suit with a royal blue Oxford shirt that set off a perfectly knotted red tie with brushed gold tie bar—Paris was as sublimely turned out as William had been at his graduation from Regent's Park. Her short brown scruff of hair that had looked as if she'd cut it herself was now trimmed and stylish, cocky even. The exposed ears revealed two small gold studs in the right ear which matched a solo stud in the left.

"Your driver is interesting." Reynard sounded as if he wanted to use a different word.

"She certainly is. She's become part of the family. We all love her." Don't babble, Diana warned herself.

"Still," he added in that sonorous tone of speaking the final word that was already grating on her last nerve, "I prefer women like you. Who look and dress like women."

Paris looked like a woman, Diana nearly retorted. Sure it was a man-cut tailored suit and tie, but if a woman was wearing them, they were a woman's clothes, weren't they? And it looked *right* on Paris. She looked confident and smart. Diana pushed away the voice that whispered, "And dead sexy."

His thinking was just like that of coaches and judges in women's competitions who thought a double-twisting layout was better if the gymnast was wearing lip gloss and eye shadow.

What it really means, she thought viciously, is that women should look like he wants them to so he can decide if it's attractive. If he can't fantasize about her, she doesn't look like a woman.

She *really* wanted to take the Chumash Hammer, that relic he treated like a toy, take it right out from under his flabby nose.

But she couldn't hurt Paris to do it.

Bugger all, this was a mess.

That she'd said nothing in response to his comment didn't seem odd to Reynard. He was that kind of man, Diana thought. Clever, but like many of the men in his strata that she'd met, he had a huge blind spot about women. Because some women could be acquired like bottles of wine, he thought they all could be. Their silence was of course agreement.

All in an instant she realized why Reynard annoyed her so much. He reminded her of her father.

Her mother was ruthlessly devoted to maintaining her social status, a trait Diana disliked. But she could humor it for the simple reason that her mother had taken toddler Diana away from a man who would have eventually broken her bones too. And over the years that followed, her mother had presented Diana with a stepfather and two half-siblings who were all very easy to love.

Meetings with her father were always strained. His tendency toward violence when crossed seethed under every gesture, every word. Reynard set off all the same alarm bells. They'd been ringing from the moment they'd met not ten minutes ago, but his immediate disdain for Paris, a woman of no sexual or business use to him, had let her clearly hear them.

"Now where were we?" Reynard handed Diana a fresh glass of champagne. The so-called business meeting was basically a cocktail party, and so far no one had said a serious word about future plans.

She faked a sip at the champagne and addressed one of the other men. "John, I think—do I have your name right? There are so many of you." Six men in all, including Reynard. The other five were here to be pleasant but certainly not to lead. She knew their names from the public organization chart, but Reynard's introductions had been so perfunctory that she hadn't been able to match all the names and faces. John Newsome was the head of the publishing house, that much she'd put together. "John was telling me about the latest corporate changes."

"Reynard House," the dutiful John resumed, "has been newly reorganized to optimize our media group's twenty-first century approach to the new consumer. With global opportunities that marry live arts to news and entertainment, reality programming and—"

"Yes, yes," Reynard interrupted. "RMG has all the tools to take Anita Topaz into the stratosphere of popularity. But we'll need your help to do it. Think of the boost and buzz if you appeared at the next RonCon with a featured talk about writing passionately and growing brand loyalty."

"Do those two things go together?" She looked at Reynard over the top of her still full glass.

"You'll convince people they do. We have a number of pros who can work with you on the mechanics of the presentation and get it finalized in time. Don't worry your beautiful head about that. I'm not sure I understand why you haven't agreed. Perhaps we can sweeten the pot a little?"

His oily regard made her tiny sip of champagne sour in her mouth. "It's not the incentives. I know this might sound unbelievable, but I have a deathly fear of crowds. I hardly ever come into Manhattan. Public speaking is impossible. I get so overwrought that I sometimes faint. So I simply don't do it."

There, she thought. I've tried to express Paris's situation.

"That's no trouble at all at RonCon. The audience can be darkened. You'd never see them."

"I'd know they were there." Diana gave him her best disarming smile. "That's why I said no to even having this meeting at first. Though it's lovely to be here and meet all of you, I feel like it's under false pretense because I can't agree to public speaking."

Reynard looked at her as if she were a child refusing to eat a new food. "I think if we tour the facility you'd become more comfortable."

She wondered if Paris had to deal with people telling her that her fears were inconsequential and easily fixed. "It wouldn't—"

His geniality cracked slightly. "Let's not close the door on possibilities. I'm certain we can find a way to work together."

It was the minute shift in posture by two of the men that cued Diana to their discomfort. So she wasn't mistaken about his meaning. You idiot, she thought. He's not a man you can be alone with. What's worse, the men who work for him know it too.

She made a show of selecting some grapes from the buffet and putting them on a plate. It gave her a chance to put down the champagne she had no intention of drinking. "I'm terribly interested in the idea of a movie. I know I'm not supposed to have favorites, but *Hands Off the Merchandise* is my favorite book so far. It would make a great movie. All those *Devil Wears Prada* sets and glamorous models in the latest fashions."

"We agree," dutiful John said. "We'd love your input on the essential story line that would carry a two-hour movie. It would be impossible to replicate the entire book without making it a miniseries."

"What about a miniseries?" Diana batted her eyelashes.

"Miniseries are dead," Reynard said.

Another man, as memorable as a cotton swab, came to life. "What about as a flagship event on the release of RMG Streaming Entertainment?"

Diana said, "What an intriguing idea."

Reynard scowled.

Cotton Swab wilted.

"Something to talk about over dinner," Reynard pronounced. "We have reservations at The Spotted Pig. Do you know it?"

"I've heard of it. How wonderful." So they were to dine together and go to the theater together? She ought to have anticipated that, but she'd not met Reynard. Clearly, this was his idea of mixing business and pleasure. He was making it clear that money was of no consequence. Yet, like her father, she knew he would add up every dime he was spending and put it on her account. In his mind, she would owe him. Her father had wanted compliance with his choice of schools, social contacts, and living arrangements. Reynard wanted her business capitulation. He also wanted her body because he found it attractive and that meant he was entitled to it.

No doubt he would take her back to her hotel. And then she'd have to kick him in his privates. Which would put Anita Topaz's future—and Paris's—at risk.

You fool, she told herself. You bloody, stupid fool.

CHAPTER FOURTEEN

Paris literally did not know what to do, so she did nothing but wander. She supposed it was a blessing the train had run late and she hadn't tried to check in at the hotel—Diana had obviously already claimed the reservation. It looked as if she'd spent quite some time getting costumed for the meeting.

Starving actress, my eye, Paris thought, recalling the emeralds and the perfectly tailored dress. What was her game?

Meanwhile, the hotel wouldn't give out another key just because Paris said she was also a guest. She supposed she should be angry, but she wasn't. Maybe she was too stunned. Or did it mean she agreed with this crazy plan? Had seeing how easily Diana was accepted as "Anita" changed her mind? Diana had said she had them in the palm of her hand, after all.

But Diana was a fraud. If she'd lied to Lisa, to Reynard, then it was simple logic that she'd lied to Paris as well. Nothing good would come from a pile of lies.

Park Avenue's shadows gathered early. The Empire State Building glittered with gold and silver beauty, but her pleasure in it was dimmed by the honking of cars and constant jostling of people moving in all directions at the same time. Whichever way she turned she was going upstream.

Weary and chilled, she let her nose follow the sharp aromas of curry and cinnamon into a warm side-street diner. The ginger dahl was filling and not too spicy, and she chased it with a decadent rice custard topped with chopped lime and toasted coconut. For a few minutes she pretended she was back in San Francisco enjoying a similar meal, comfortable in her job with just enough money to get by, future no more certain than the gaming marketplace itself.

Food helped. Her brain slowed. She realized now it was a bad thing that she had no way to communicate with Diana—but how could she have known she'd need that phone number out of the junk drawer? And it wasn't as if there were pay phones anymore. A quick glance around confirmed she was the only person in the diner who wasn't also tapping at a phone. They would have to figure out a communication strategy if this plan was going to succeed.

She snorted into her last spoonful of dessert. Was she actually considering this lunacy? She'd gone over to the Dark Side.

Heartened by the meal and soothed by a lovely hour of quiet bliss at the Fifth Avenue public library, she walked the dozen or so blocks to the theater district, thinking she would possibly run into Diana when the play let out. One look at the crowds changed her mind, and instead she made her footsore way back to the hotel to claim her suitcase and take a seat near the elevators.

Uneasiness crept up on her as she waited. What was taking so long? Were the staff aware of her waiting? What if she were challenged? Finger rolls kept her from fidgeting in the chair, and she distracted herself by thinking about her character Susannah and her daring plan—yet to be written—to steal information that would clear her family name.

Just when she thought she'd have to start pacing she heard Diana's voice. In fact, she suspected the loud laugh had been meant to carry because there was relief in Diana's face when she spotted Paris. Reynard was with her, his hand possessively clutching her arm.

"Ellis, you're an angel, waiting for me." Her eyes widened slightly at the sight of Paris's suitcase.

"Uh, your missing bag arrived just now. Ma'am." Paris had no idea what a driver-assistant-bodyguard would call her employer.

"Awesome!" Diana gave Reynard a sunny smile. "Items go missing all the time, don't they?"

"Crime is an epidemic in this country." Reynard finally let go of Diana's arm, but only because Diana had leaned over as if checking the suitcase more closely.

"They said it was misdelivered," Paris offered. Her shirt suddenly felt itchy, and she realized it was her skin crawling. An anxiety spike bled the bright yellow and blue walls into black and white. Fortunately her vision steadied, but only after a long, deep breath she hoped neither of them noticed.

"Just one of those things. Happily resolved." Diana, who had moved closer to Paris, favored Reynard with another smile of beaming pleasure. "It has been a spectacular evening. I'm incredibly grateful." She put out her hand, palm down.

To Paris's amazement, Reynard made a show of kissing Diana's hand with a half bow. "My Queen, the pleasure has been all mine."

Paris swallowed down a queasy pulse in her stomach.

"As fabulous as this day has been, the crowds were very large and I'm exhausted. Beauty sleep must be had."

Reynard hadn't let go of Diana's hand. "You won't forget about brunch tomorrow?"

"Of course not. I'm looking forward to it and meeting your charming daughter. I've heard so much about her." She relaxed any grip she may have had on him and Reynard had to let go of her.

Turning to Paris, Diana said, "Are the accommodations to your liking?"

She didn't know quite what to say. "Yes, certainly." She realized that Reynard was still within earshot, and he was watching them closely. "Ma'am," she added belatedly as she rang for the elevator.

They were thankfully alone as it bore them upward.

"I gather that went well," Paris observed.

"Too well." There was chagrin in Diana's voice. "I'd forgotten about men of a certain age. His charming daughter is older than I am."

The oddness about him holding onto Diana's hand so long clicked into place. "He wants to sleep with you."

"He sees something he wants, he expects to get it then and there. That you showed up helped snap that assumption." She fervently added, "I was so glad to see you."

"And you did the rest with body language," Paris mused. Everything from the set of her shoulders to the grip of her fingers. Had she ever given the women in her books such subtlety? "Where did you learn to do that? I wouldn't have a clue."

Diana looked at her oddly, but the doors opened and she led the way to the end of the floor. "You didn't get a separate room, did you? This suite has two bedrooms. We could play polo in it."

"I didn't want my name in the hotel records. In case…"

Diana had flipped the lights on to reveal a spacious living room, all in ivory and gold brocade. In addition to two sofas and several side chairs there was a fully stocked bar and a burnished mahogany table that would seat six. The curtains had been pulled back to show off the view of an adjacent roof garden lit up with strings of white lights. Their glow faded into the sparkling skyline of Midtown. Directly in front of the window was a fainting couch covered in gold velvet.

"Wowza." Now that they were away from Reynard, Paris's anxiety abated. So much so that she could picture Diana lounging seductively on the couch. Stop that, she told herself, or you're no better than the slimy guy. "This could be a film set."

"I need a shower." Diana's face paled and fine lines appeared around her mouth. "I've been on for hours. He took me out after the play for drinks with no food so I'm buzzed and not in a good way. My back is *killing* me. Can we wait to talk until I've cleaned up? I know you want to talk."

That was putting it mildly. Even as she told herself that Diana's stiff movements could be an act, and that Diana/Fiona/Anita had lied about everything, Paris set aside her objections and questions for the moment. "Yes, okay."

Paris stood staring at the bedroom door on the right, now closed behind Diana, then rolled her suitcase into the bedroom on the left. Don't unpack, she told herself. It makes this normal.

None of this was normal.

If the ruse was found out, well, Reynard didn't seem the forgiving type. He seemed like a lecherous bully, and they shouldn't be playing games with that kind of man. They should leave. Now.

At least that's what common sense dictated.

She ordered room service.

CHAPTER FIFTEEN

There was little that a hot shower couldn't make better, Diana decided. The Tylenol-3 would take a little while to kick in, but the steaming hot water immediately took her back pain from vivid red to a bearable yellow. She wanted more than anything to tumble into the luxurious bed with the soft sheets and sleep for twelve hours.

That wasn't going to happen. Even through a layer of silky shampoo suds and luxurious soap, she was certain she could feel waves of Paris's anger and disapproval. Fine kettle of fish this was, indeed.

She scrubbed harder. Reynard made her feel dirty and everywhere he'd fondled her arm was soiled. Part of her would happily abandon her private mission. Every encounter with the man was going to be about as pleasant as a stroll through a sewer.

Part of her was even more determined to do something, anything to thumb her nose in his face. Even better if he never knew it, which was her style. She didn't think her father had ever missed the Sami stone bowl he'd occasionally used to put out a cigar. It was how, at every compulsory meeting with him, she had been able to smile and ignore his threats. Some day she'd go to Sweden and visit it in its new home where it was treated with respect.

But taking a swipe at Reynard, however deserved, put Paris at risk. The Chumash Hammer, so old and so delicate, wasn't worth mucking up Paris's life. Paris would have to agree to going forward with the plan to take it, and that was bloody unlikely. Diana's priorities could hardly matter to Paris, and why would Paris do anything to jeopardize a movie deal?

If she didn't tell Paris her real objective, could she convince Paris to at least let her go on pretending to be Anita for the rest of the weekend? Convince Paris to go home and leave it alone? Could she get another meeting with Reynard, this time in his office, where the Chumash Hammer might be on a shelf? Or in a display case? It wasn't as if a lock would stop her if she had enough time. Was any of that possible without also being groped—or worse—by the man?

She scrubbed harder.

What could she offer Paris that would assure her that the ruse couldn't harm her? Nothing plausible. Paris was no fool. And she didn't want to fool Paris anymore.

She hadn't come to any decisions even after she wrapped herself in one of the thick hotel bathrobes and toweled her hair until it stood on end.

It was a shock, as she looked at herself in the brightly lit mirror, to realize that it had been years since another human being had seen her naked of makeup and not in a carefully chosen costume. Even with her family she was who they wanted her to be. Light and fun, athletic, pretty and clever. Biddable, until she took off for parts unknown for weeks on end.

So used to seeing her eyes with colored contacts she peered closer and wondered if the basic brown had gotten darker over the last couple of years. Were her freckles more vivid as well?

The longer she looked in the mirror the more she replayed that moment when she'd seen Paris in the conference room. She'd been horrified. And then deeply, stunningly pleased. A hot flush had headed south from her heart. Just remembering it woke up the sensation again.

No man in an Armani suit had ever made her feel as if a spotlight had illuminated sheltered, deep places, places she'd decided didn't exist for her. Places this woman could reach. She searched her eyes again for a clue for what it meant, but had to turn away from the disquieting feeling that she didn't know the woman in the mirror.

She couldn't go on hiding in the bathroom. She had set a job in motion. Nothing else should matter. The safest course of action would be to convince Paris she could go home. Go home and let Diana take care of Reynard.

Convince her to leave, she told herself again.

Except she didn't want to.

She belted the robe more tightly and felt absolutely naked.

CHAPTER SIXTEEN

Paris lost track of time as she looked down at the soothing, mesmerizing patterns of cars crisscrossing Fifth Avenue. Her clue that Diana had rejoined her was a patch of white in the window reflection, which turned out to be a hotel robe.

"The light in there is too darned good. New wrinkles," Diana announced.

Turning from the window, Paris began, "Is that what you think we have to talk—"

Diana had brown eyes. Short, wavy brown hair.

Her freckles were more visible than ever. In bare feet she couldn't have been taller than five feet or so. In the robe it was clear that the rest of her, all the muscles and simple curves, was quite real.

For a long moment Paris had no breath at all. Every time she laid eyes on Diana she was a different woman, and it was dizzying. Why wasn't she worried? But it didn't worry her—it was fascinating.

Fascinations can be fatal, she warned herself.

Diana was shaking her head. "No, it was a shock is all. There's horrible lighting where I'm living now."

Paris knew a distraction when she heard one. "Tell me the truth, Fiona."

Diana's eyes widened. "Lisa told you my stage name? Fiona Mahoney."

Stage name? Damn. That was plausible. "Why did you tell me 'Diana'?"

"I was startled. *You* have two names."

Diana had a positive gift for making Paris feel as if she were being unreasonable. "So what was your plan here? You lie to Reynard for the weekend, and then what?"

"I told you. This was too good to pass up." Diana's back was to the window now, and she looked even smaller with robe sleeves dangling well past her hands. "And I figured I could convince them that I'm not their girl when it comes to publicity."

"You mean *Anita* isn't their girl—and how are you convincing them of that? Looking like a million bucks, being charming and flirty?"

"I looked okay?"

"Like you don't know that every time you look in the mirror?"

"I'm not supposed to know. Modesty and all that."

At this rate Paris was certain she was going to give herself an eye roll headache. "Exactly how is Reynard supposed to find your rendition of Anita unpalatable?

"I read up on him first. I thought I would do the falling-down-drunk thing, but I can't afford to be vulnerable to that man. No woman should be." Diana seemed to search for words. "I miscalculated. I am thinking now if I start saying 'patriarchy this' and 'misogyny that' he might lose interest without it being disastrous. For you."

"I'm glad you're finally thinking about me."

Diana's gaze never left Paris's face, but she said nothing.

"So your name really is Diana?"

"Yes. Diana. Diana Beckinsale."

"You're not Irish. Not from Derry. That whole accent and story was fake. Where are you really from?"

"Kent. Well, near there." At Paris's continuing look of non-comprehension she added, "South of London, about halfway to Dover."

Paris felt herself relaxing, as if somehow everything was okay. But it wasn't. Diana had a knack for making her behavior sound perfectly reasonable. And yet a powerful, unscrupulous businessman thought Diana was Anita Topaz, and he thought Paris—who *was* Anita Topaz—was Anita's hired help. How did there get to be so many lies in such a short time?

Diana stepped further into the light, her disarming spray of freckles stark against pale skin. Her soft brown eyes were remarkable not in their color but in their depths. She was nothing like the siren Anita or the lass Fiona. Something else. More dangerous, Paris thought.

"I didn't think he'd be so... So... Jabba—"

"—the Hut," Paris finished.

"Like he was going to lick my face any minute. I get why you don't want to deal."

"That's not why, actually. It's not like he's ever going to want to lick *my* face."

Diana flushed. "Probably not. I'd guess you're exactly the kind of woman that makes him feel inadequate, and that's all your fault."

Paris had to agree. "He looked at me like I was unnatural. Trust me, though. It's not the first time in my life I've gotten that look."

"I'm sorry," Diana blurted out. She pushed back the drapes to expose even more of the view. Her back to Paris, she continued, "I didn't mean to do anything to make you worried. I thought you'd find out after the fact that they'd decided to leave you alone. If they mentioned the pleasure of meeting you, you'd probably figure it was me and you wouldn't be able to find me..." Her voice got very quiet. "It wouldn't do any harm. I didn't think that part through, I guess. I just wanted..."

She turned from the view with a gesture. "I just wanted all of this for a couple of nights. Not to worry about money and have a hot, hot shower. God, it was a religious experience. And see *Hamilton*. It was *brilliant*."

"I wouldn't know," Paris reminded her crossly. She had reason to be angry, she thought, and it seemed very important to be angry about, well, *something*.

"I didn't think you wanted to."

"You really have no idea what I want," Paris snapped.

"That's quite clear to me now. I am sorry." She sighed, then brightened. "Where did you get this smashing suit?"

"I think it's more to the point where a starving actress got her clothes. And jewelry." There, she was proud of herself for finally asking something that mattered.

Diana hesitated.

Remembering Lisa's comment about the emeralds, Paris insisted, "The truth. You're not here to live free for a few days."

"I went home for the clothes. And to visit family. I always have the emeralds with me."

"You had that dress at home?" It had looked as if it were sewn on her, and Paris was now well aware how much hand-tailoring cost.

"Yes. And a few others that were suitable upmarket corporate chic. The emeralds were my father's mother's."

"So you're not a starving actress and your parents don't really want you to be a dental hygienist."

Diana shrugged as if every part of this conversation was normal for her. "My father's views are of no consequence. My mother would be both pleased and horrified if I did something conventional."

Why horrified? Paris didn't know where to start. It was a different part of her that asked, "You like the suit?"

Diana cocked her head, her gaze traveling over Paris's body. "Very dashing. You were the best dressed person in pants in that room. You put the men to shame."

"I'm not a man."

With a fervent edge Paris didn't know how to interpret, Diana breathed out, "I know that."

A knock at the door startled them both.

"I ordered food," Paris explained as she went to answer it. "You seemed… I'm hungry."

"Me too." Diana pulled her robe more tightly around her as she stepped out of view from the door. "For the record, Anita Topaz eats like a bird. Reynard eats like a toddler. Gobbles down what he likes and picks at the rest like someone put veg in it."

Paris pulled the door open.

Ronald Reynard stood there, a bottle of champagne in one hand.

CHAPTER SEVENTEEN

Diana heard Paris's startled intake of breath and instinctively backed further out of sight.

"Is Ms. Topaz available?"

Bugger all, it was Reynard. As lightly as possible she bolted for her bedroom, closed the door quietly and dashed into the bathroom. Towel, she needed a towel. They were enormous—maybe he'd think it was all the long blond hair he thought she had. She'd have to squint and keep some distance because there was simply no time to put in contacts. Paris shouldn't have to deal with him. She'd gotten them into this mess.

The lecherous wanker.

She wrapped the towel around the back of her head, twisted it in the front and tucked the ends. The weight of it set her back to jangling in distress. She quickly patted her cheekbones with cold cream. Back at the bedroom door she focused on using her Hollywood accent before calling out, "Is there someone at the door?"

There was no audible answer.

Showtime. She began rubbing the cold cream into one cheek and reentered the living room.

Reynard had made it a few feet past the door already. His chest was puffed out, and he loomed over Paris in a way meant to force her to step back. He grinned when Diana came into his line of sight.

Paris was saying, "I'm quite certain she's retired for the evening."

Reynard gestured at her, which made Paris turn to look.

"Ronald?" She crossed about half of the distance to the door, still rubbing in cold cream. "Oh dear, you've caught me out in my beauty secrets."

Very smoothly he explained, "I recalled you saying you hadn't visited The Big Apple before. I wanted to drop this off to welcome you. And make sure the accommodations were to your liking."

Paris had moved away from Reynard, but Diana couldn't risk a look at her.

"This suite is simply beautiful. Ellis and I are extremely comfortable."

"I'm so glad to hear it." He made no attempt to withdraw.

Diana kept massaging cold cream into her cheeks. "Really, your administrative staff did a great job."

"Only the best for the best."

Paris suddenly came to life, moving in between Reynard and Diana. She held out her hand for the champagne. "May I?"

"Oh yes." Diana half turned away from Reynard. "Please put it in the refrigerator, Ellis. Thank you Ronald. It was so thoughtful."

A clatter from the hallway followed by a quiet knock on the door drew all their attention.

Paris cleared her throat. "That'll be room service. I ordered the soup you like."

"Thank you." Diana couldn't think of anything else to say.

The uniformed waiter gave them all a cheerful greeting and wheeled the long cart across the room, where he efficiently moved covered plates onto the table, added napkins and cutlery for two, then finished by decanting sparkling bottled water into two frosted glasses.

Reynard blustered. "If I'd realized you were hungry we could have gone to Sardi's for steaks after the theater. The evening in New York is just getting started."

"I'm a vegetarian," she reminded him. She'd told him at dinner when he'd offered her a steak then as well. Apparently, she thought sourly, steaks and champagne were his aphrodisiacs of choice. She held up her cold cream smeared hands. "As you can see, it was time for repairs. And I am truly exhausted."

A tight pulse in his neck put the lie to his gentlemanly tones. "Then it's time for me to say good night."

She sketched a wave. "Until tomorrow."

Paris had signed the bill for the waiter and opened the door so he could be on his way. She continued to stand next to the open door, looking at Reynard expectantly.

Good heavens, Diana thought, did the man not understand that he literally was being shown the door?

It seemed to Diana that for just a moment Reynard was going to approach her, attempt to touch her in some way. Alas, a dollop of cold cream chose that precise moment to drip from her hand onto the floor. He kept his distance and tipped an invisible hat. "Until tomorrow."

He breezed past Paris and she let the door quietly click behind him.

Diana's arms felt like lead weights. She dragged the heavy towel off her head and used it to wipe the cold cream off her face. A delicious aroma was filling the room and she zoomed toward the table. "Thank you for ordering food. I'm *famished*."

Paris said from behind her, "I don't believe this is about a free weekend. I'd like the truth this time."

"I was only trying—"

"I could have gotten rid of him."

"I wasn't sure. He's going to be the persistent type." She lifted the covers from the dishes. "That smell is making me faint. Tomato soup for two? And grilled cheese?" Diana eased herself onto one of the chairs, and her back immediately felt better. Too much standing, and in heels. Seizing a sandwich half, she dunked a corner into the steaming bowl of soup she'd pulled toward her. She was chewing before Paris had even sat down. "Brilliant. I'm going to live, I think."

Paris picked up half of her sandwich. "You can keep changing the subject, but I'm not going to stop asking for the truth. You're not a starving actress."

"What do you think I am, then?" She immediately regretted the question, but she felt drunk on soup and cheese.

"I don't know. You say you're unemployed but you wear couture and real emeralds." She set the sandwich down again, untasted. "If this were one of my stories you'd be a jewel thief."

Diana coughed in mid-swallow and grabbed up a glass of water.

Paris gaped. "No, dear lord, tell me you're not."

She coughed again and managed to say more or less steadily, "I'm not a jewel thief." Not the way Paris meant, anyway. And to her horror, she heard the half-lie in her own voice.

"What have you gotten me mixed up in?" Paris looked wary and disappointed, mournful almost. Like she was beyond anger. "Whatever it is, I'm a pawn. I know that."

There was raw pain in Paris's voice and Diana again saw in her mind's eye the image of the wary, wounded dog she'd first compared Paris to. A wave of guilt washed over her. She was piling onto whatever it was that had beaten this smart, creative woman down so hard. She hardly knew Paris and she still wanted to tell her the truth. Yet, in all the annals of thievery, no thief ever said it was a good idea to tell anyone.

And that was what she was, a thief. Just not jewels. Well, the Fijian wooden tiki had had small pearls embedded for eyes, but they weren't technically jewels.

Focus, she warned herself. You can't tell her the truth.

But she didn't want more lies between them. It had been such a short time and there were already so many lies. She couldn't add to the list, not when a low, burning turmoil in the pit of her stomach, growing by the minute, told her that Paris might be the source of a surprising revelation.

She tried one last plea. "Can't you just go home? Leave me to clean up the mess I've made? Just…go?"

"I won't even consider it unless you tell me the truth."

"It would be for the best." I'd probably never see her again, Diana thought, and was stunned by how much the idea pained her.

"Maybe the best for you." Paris spread her hands. "How can I trust you? You won't tell me the truth."

The words tumbled out of her. She simply couldn't hold them back. "He has something I want."

"What?"

"I can't tell you. You shouldn't know, I mean, it would make you an…"

"An accomplice? Great. That's great." Paris ran one hand through her hair, making the tantalizing locks that curled over her forehead stand on end. "So you're planning to rob him?"

"No! Yes. It's complicated." Diana quelled the urge to reach across the table and smooth Paris's hair back into order. There was a screaming in her ears. She was blowing it big time. *Idiot, it is impossible to tell the truth and lie at the same time.* "He has something that's not his. I mean it's his on paper. But still isn't his."

"So…" Paris's pallor had increased and her eyes were like liquid rock. "A family heirloom? Something to save the family farm? Your father's honor?"

"No, it's—"

"Don't tell me the plot of one of my own books!"

"I'm not!"

"So what's the truth? What is this thing you've got to have back?"

Diana whispered, "It doesn't belong to me either. I want to send it home."

"Your parents need it?"

"No, I mean—to its own home. Or the most appropriate place I can think of. Probably a museum in California." She closed her eyes and plunged over the cliff's edge. "Without anyone realizing it's gone, at least for a while. Long enough for the museum to establish provenance and stewardship."

There was a silence long enough to make her risk opening one eye. Paris was staring at her and Diana could almost see the whir of brain gears and wheels turning.

"You mean… Like a tomb raider, but in reverse?"

She blinked in surprise. "I guess. Yes, I suppose, yes."

Of all the things Diana had expected Paris to say, it wasn't, "That sounds like the coolest game idea ever."

CHAPTER EIGHTEEN

Paris stared out the window, her brain in a whirl. "So you give people a plausible front, they see what they want to see, and then you pounce."

Diana looked outraged. "It's not a game. Not something I play at for a few hours that doesn't have any real risk."

"Yes, yes, I know that," Paris said crossly. Her head was starting to hurt in earnest. "Can we eat before the soup gets any colder?"

"Nothing is stopping you." Diana had become snappish, which Paris didn't understand.

"All I'm saying," she said after a sip at the tepid but still tasty soup, "is that the idea of raiding for artifacts in order to put them back where they came from is a really great game idea."

"It's not a game," Diana repeated. She mopped the bottom of her bowl with the last of her sandwich. "It's scary and illegal and I could go to jail. In the real world. Not a cyber-jail. Not one where I can push a magic brick or whistle the right tune and escape."

"I'm trying to understand." She was also trying to file Diana's activities into a mental realm where she didn't expect cops pounding on the door any minute.

"Well I don't think you do." Diana was openly pouting now.

"I'm compartmentalizing. It helps me think." The grilled cheese, now lukewarm, was still pretty good. She dipped it in her soup the way Diana had, but took great care not to drip any on her new shirt. A happy part of her brain was thinking about how a game like that would work, and what kind of quests would deal with actual lost artifacts. How to make matching artifact to the right historical timeline part of the Experience Points. How to invite First Nation cultures into the storytelling, music and graphics development. Avatars, gear, even character arcs. Five years ago she'd have been scribbling madly on paper and pinning the sheets on her cubicle wall. "I'm trying not to panic because you've gotten me involved with this…this… criminal enterprise."

Diana ran both hands over her head, scrubbing at her scalp until her soft after-shower hair stood up in spikes. "I didn't ask you to show up."

"This. Is. Not. My. Fault." Paris took a huge bite for emphasis and focused on the adjacent roof garden. She couldn't afford to fall further under Diana's spell. This Diana, even in nothing but a hotel robe, could still be a fake. It did nothing for her composure to think about how close to naked Diana was. Or to consider how adorable the tiny smear of cold cream just under her left eye made her.

"Fine," Diana muttered. "You're not cut out for a life of crime."

"You know, most people aren't. But you're a zebra not horses kind of person, aren't you?"

"What are you talking about?"

"If I hear hoofbeats I think it's probably horses not zebras. You'd be the exception."

"I'm not a horse." Diana gave her a stony look. "Or a zebra. Or anything equine for that matter."

Paris gritted her teeth. "It's. A. Meta. Phor."

"My life isn't a metaphor. Or any of your other fancy words." Diana shifted in her chair with a grimace.

Paris laughed against her will. "Don't play dumb. That's not going to work."

Diana's ill-humor seemed to diminish. "You'd be surprised."

"Exactly how long have you been doing this?" Even as she asked the question, Paris considered that maybe she didn't want to know the answer. Surely the smart plan was to pack up all traces of herself and go home. Instead she wondered if she'd look back on this moment and think, "And that was when I decided prison was okay with me."

Diana busied herself dabbing at a red splotch of soup that had trickled down the front of her robe. "Long enough."

"There is no way forward if you won't tell me—" Her breath caught in her throat as a pulse of hot anxiety burned through the nerves from the back of her skull to the base of her spine. It surprised her, though it shouldn't have. If anything, it was overdue. "If you won't tell me the truth."

"Sure there is." Diana spread her hands and Paris did her best not to stare at the smooth palms and manicured, elegant fingertips. "We play out the weekend and we both head out of here at the soonest possible opportunity. I already told them Anita is deathly afraid of public speaking."

Very quietly, trying to hide the shake in her voice, Paris said, "You want to gamble with everything I have. I will not cooperate if you don't tell me the truth."

"The truth right now is that I've got food in my stomach so it's time for more—"

"Stop it," Paris couldn't help her rising voice. "Enough with the distractions—do you think I'm an idiot?"

"Lord, no."

"Then stop making me play Twenty Questions only you never answer any."

After a pause long enough to make Paris think Diana was going to go on stonewalling her, Diana muttered, "Ten years."

More lies. "You were twelve when you embarked on a life of crime?"

Diana brightened. "I'm twenty-seven, but thank you." She glanced at Paris's face before dipping the edge of her napkin into a water glass to continue worrying at the soup stain. "I started young. With my father and for completely immature reasons."

Paris let out an exasperated huff of air. "You're going to blame this on your parents?"

"No, just my father. And I'm not *blaming* him. He inspired me to do it."

"He's a thief too?"

"Depending on your perspective."

The woman wasn't capable of yes or no answers. Maybe that's why Paris found her so frustrating—conversation with her was full of conditional logic. "What was your perspective when you launched into a life of crime?"

"That he was a brute to my mother. I'd just crashed and burned in the sport I'd devoted every spare hour to from the age of six, and he demanded that I do something meaningful with my life because up until then I'd done nothing but sponge his money."

"So he really did want you to be a dental hygienist?"

"No—he wanted a solicitor for a daughter. Or a politician. Someone he could make more use of than a gymnast."

Paris blinked. "You were a gymnast?"

"Yes." Diana tapped her shoulder where the telltale bump was. "War wound. I told you."

"You said something about many nations."

"The European Games. In Sweden that year. I broke my clavicle in three places and that was that."

"You never said it was gymnastics."

"Of course I didn't get specific. I met you in a bar." Diana waved her fingers as if it all made sense.

Paris could feel a vein throbbing in her neck. "And you were planning to impersonate me, so sure, secrets."

"Yes secrets." Diana's tone was growing increasingly waspish. "I had finished a job and was getting ready to head for home and your letter dropped into my lap. Like my father, Reynard has many objects that don't belong to him and I'm after only one of them."

The gold fainting couch and red curtains were going gray. She flexed her fingers, but that wouldn't help for long. "That makes it all better. After all, it's a reduced sentence if you only take the Hope Diamond and leave the Star of India behind."

"It's nothing like that. My father had a bowl I thought was an ashtray. He treated it like one."

"And it wasn't?"

"It was a shallow carving from the Sami people that's anywhere from three hundred to eight hundred years old. I was listening to him tell me again how worthless I was and watching him stub out his cigar. One of our off-practice outings in Sweden had been to a museum. And the carving looked familiar, like something similar in style that I'd seen there. So I did some research and that artifact had gone missing during World War Two. Turned up in an auction and my father ended up with it. As if it didn't belong to someone else."

Seesawing back and forth between frustration that was infuriating and a grudging admiration, Paris was completely at a loss. The audacity of it, for one thing. It wasn't something she would have ever *thought* to do, let alone actually undertake. "So you just took it?"

"When he was away. As far as I know, he's never missed it. All I had to do then was figure out who to send it to. I didn't want anyone to give it back to him. I found a professor of Nordic Studies, dressed myself up as a messenger and dropped it off at his office at Oxford. I'm guessing he was more invested in finding out where it had originated rather than who the most recent so-called owner was. Because about eighteen months later it showed up as a museum asset in Sweden. I'll visit it someday."

"And you kept doing it?"

She turned her head, but not so far that Paris couldn't see a deeply satisfied smile. "I kept doing it."

Paris had a horrifying realization. "So I helped you mail stolen property, didn't I?"

"You showed me where a box was. You didn't know I was avoiding cameras at the post office—no point in tempting fate that way. It was a brooch of red rock and turquoise, and it was in a photograph from the 1870s. I liberated it from a woman who was wearing it on her scarves. Not a drop of indigenous blood in her, it was just something unusual and cultural and didn't that show how hip she was? She wasn't even trying to take care of it..." She turned her gaze back to Paris finally. The brown depths were shining with what Paris thought was genuine emotion. "Now a native-run cultural archive in Utah has it. It arrived in the mail, out of the blue. It wanted to go home so I sent it there."

A hard ache of longing tightened Paris's throat. Longing for home, the familiar sounds and smells, the "right" air to breathe. She wished that someone could wrap her up safe and sound and send her home.

"I know it's silly. They're only objects. But they've been moved all over the world, handled by people who don't know or don't care to know what they are. After the bowl I spent time using my eyes in places I was visiting anyway. I started scanning through elite auction listings. If you know where to look, there are a lot of little objects far from home."

"Aren't there laws requiring things like that be returned to their original owners?"

"They rarely apply to individuals. I thought seriously about going into antiquities repatriation law, but it didn't take long for me to realize that kind of thinking, the logic of it, is not in my skill set."

Paris snorted.

After a long narrow look Diana continued, "I don't have the patience. I didn't want to spend ten years getting back one painting, like that Austrian woman reclaiming the Klimt stolen by the Nazis."

"So it's been ten years and...?"

"Twenty-two minor items have been returned home. All from settings like my father's."

Twenty-two times. Paris looked down at what was left of the soup. "So taking them doesn't make you any money—what do you live on?"

"My wits."

Paris sighed.

"That was a joke."

The overhead light was suddenly too bright and Paris squinted across the table. She was running out of time for this conversation. Now that Diana was opening up, however, she didn't want to break it off. "Seriously."

"I'm sorry," she muttered. "My grandmother left me a trust fund. Decent of her after raising such an awful, awful son."

"Your father, who inspired you to embark on a life of crime?"

"It's not a *life* of crime. It's months of acting and *minutes* of crime."

"You're right about not having the mindset of a lawyer."

"I need to take some Nurofen," Diana said abruptly. Her Hollywood accent had been replaced with the one that sounded like actors at the Royal Shakespeare Company. At Paris's blank look she added, "Advil, Motrin, whatever you call it. My back is ramping up again."

"You hurt your back too? In gymnastics?"

"Everybody hurts their back in gymnastics. There isn't one former gymnast who isn't walking crooked."

Paris was left to flail in a whirlpool of thoughts and feelings too chaotic to sort out. Not the least of which was the fact that she was anxious on multiple fronts now. They would get caught. Reynard Media Group would tell the world where to find Paris Ellison. Diana would end up in prison. The strangest of all was a sense of grieving: she couldn't see a future where she and Diana ever meant anything more to each other. Not even friends, let alone…

She pushed away the feeling before it could take on a name. But the sharp pulse of yearning for something out of reach grew stronger when Diana took her seat again across the table from her.

"These jobs are like…like the balance beam," she said quietly. "At some point you have to back flip. Where your feet are going to land—you can't even see it when you jump." She lined up the silverware and then pushed it away. "The fourth time, I was after a so-called letter opener. It was in Ottawa at a real estate company some venture capital heir ran as a hobby. I made deliveries of flowers a couple of times to get the feel for it, and when they advertised for a new receptionist I sent in a picture and a résumé." She grinned. "I think the picture did the trick."

Remembering how sensual Diana had looked in the first Anita outfit at Mona Lisa's, Paris agreed. "I can just imagine."

"I really was thinking I'd get the job, find what I was looking for and be gone before they seriously checked my identification. But there it was. The handle was sticking out from under a pile of papers, like he'd forgotten it was even there. He left the interview just long enough for me to put it down my blouse. I hope he thought it got lost in the papers and thrown away— he'd only have himself to blame."

"So nobody noticed you'd snatched it?" It had taken Paris everything she had just to show up to a meeting where she had nothing planned other than telling the truth. "And you walked out with it?"

"If nobody thinks something was stolen, nobody looks for a thief, right? I'm sure he searched everywhere for it when it didn't turn up after a couple of days." A ghost of a smile crossed her face. "I gave the silliest interview ever. And the whole time I could feel that I'd cut myself with the thing down my blouse. It was a sixteenth century Romani throwing knife and still had an edge. Now it's in the Czech Romani Museum."

"What happens if he ever realizes where it is?"

Diana's eyes were shining with triumph. "He'll have a hell of a time extracting it. I'm careful about what I choose. Once an item has been returned to the descendants or caretakers of its closest cultural origin it's going to stay there."

Paris had to close her eyes for a moment. She was approaching information overload.

"That's all there is to it, most of the time. I float in the background until I see an opportunity. Patience, planning, and Bob's your uncle."

Given how the situation with Reynard was going, Paris thought, she was surprised Diana hadn't been caught. "What exactly does Reynard have?"

"A very old ceremonial gift, a hammer that was used to strike a wooden drum. It was made out of bone and obsidian by a tribe that still exists." Diana's voice went quiet and low. "So what do you want to do?"

"I don't know. I have to think." She got up to look at the view again, shaking her hands and visualizing anxiety and stress falling from her fingertips. Her head throbbed. She needed to sift through all the data and break it into smaller pieces where only a yes/no answer was needed, but she had to find some quiet and calm first.

"I'll leave you to it," Diana said. "I need to sleep. We'll settle it in the morning."

Paris turned to face her, but whatever words she had thought to say froze in her throat. In her mind she was closing the distance between them to capture Diana's face between her hands so she could kiss the upturned mouth.

What is wrong with me? Kissing women she didn't know in some hormonal conflagration had never been her thing, let alone courting the real possibility of getting punched in response. Diana might be but little, but she was fierce.

With a tremor of panic that Diana might read her thoughts, she said, "I'll go to bed too."

She bolted for her bedroom and stood behind the closed door, eyes screwed shut until she heard the other bedroom door close.

She paced for a while and went through the motions of getting ready for bed, even though she felt far too wound up to sleep. This is what she got for trying to level up her life—a case of the weak knees for a chameleon madwoman. Fortunately, her body recognized stress-driven exhaustion. Had it only been this morning that she'd boarded the train? Nothing had gone as planned from that moment on.

With the curtains drawn the room was completely dark. The vent blowing warm air became a soothing white noise. The sheets were cool and crisp and the pillow felt wonderful against her cheek. She was asleep in a moment.

CHAPTER NINETEEN

A gentle touch to her shoulder woke Paris from a murky fragmented dream of Susannah running from toilet-plunger wielding rabbits through vineyards in Tuscany. The gate to safety was always at the end of the next row of vines, but Susannah didn't have any magic unicorn dust and was all out of hit points.

The touch came again and she sat up with a gasp. Then clutched her sheets to her naked chest.

Diana looked like a small, cross elf on a bad hair day. Her faded maroon T-shirt bore the white letters *To Sleep Perchance to Dream*. "We have about forty-five minutes to get to brunch. I had no idea I'd sleep this late."

Paris blinked at the bedside clock. It was nearly eleven. "I never sleep late," she said even though it was patently obvious that she had done just that.

"Look." Diana's voice was hoarse with tension. "We can either not show up and I'll call the restaurant and let them pass on the word, and then we split town. Or we can go to brunch and see this through. I'll forget all about the job, it doesn't matter. See through convincing them how wonderful a movie deal would be while they stop asking for personal appearances. And then we're free to leave. Just because Reynard is paying for the room tonight doesn't mean we have to stay."

Paris was intensely aware of Diana's thin T-shirt and how much it didn't obscure. All she could manage was, "Um."

Diana yanked back the curtains and slapped a hand over her eyes. Sunlight streamed in, making what was under the thin T-shirt even more noticeable. Paris stole a long moment to admire the graceful lines of Diana's body then looked away before Diana caught her. "You're not a morning person?"

"I'm not a blinded by the light person." Diana disappeared into the living room and returned with a can of Red Bull. "Caffeine. Come on, caffeine."

"I would give all my fame for a pot of coffee," Paris misquoted, adding wryly, "and safety."

"It is way too early in my day to deal with Shakespeare." Diana took another long swallow from the can. "Coffee takes too long. I'll get you one of these." The moment Diana disappeared from sight, Paris leaped from the bed and yanked open the closet door. She tied the hotel robe closed just in time.

Diana tossed her the energy drink. "We have a performance in forty-two minutes and counting."

"I haven't had one of these in forever. I used to live on them." Paris gratefully popped open the can and drank about half in two long gulps. It tasted like all-nighters, long meetings and burnt popcorn. "Is that what it is? A performance? And we haven't decided if we're going."

"Okay, decide." Diana went to the window and Paris studied her back. "What do you want?"

She wanted to be able to trust that Diana was…Diana. She wanted Diana to look at her again. She wanted to find out what made them both laugh. All of which were too complicated and too scary.

She knew better what she didn't want. She didn't want to ever explain to anyone at Reynard House that the woman they'd met wasn't Anita Topaz after all. They weren't the kind of people to laugh it off. "You promise you've given up the idea of taking the hammer you're after?"

Diana didn't turn. "I've given up on getting it. I don't want anything to interfere with Anita Topaz's future. Your future."

"But you want to go ahead with the impersonation part."

"Movie deal, remember?"

Paris grimaced. "I remember." She'd been ready for her own Storming the Office Building quest. Steeled herself to cope with her own affairs. Part of her was weak and stupid, thinking that Diana would be the better warrior to send into this particular battle. "This is madness."

"It could work. Work out really well."

"Okay." She felt slightly faint. "If you promise no stealing anything."

"I promise." Diana dropped her empty can into the trash. "Shower time."

All through her shower Paris regretted her decision. She was taking way, way too much on faith. Toweling her hair dry she told herself it would only take one phone call to end the whole charade. She could pack up and go home. Get an agent and bury herself in the stories of her own choosing. That was literally the best decision she could make.

It meant saying goodbye to Diana. Who was chaos and confusion and nothing but complications, none of which mattered whenever she was close to her. What was it about Diana that kept her from focusing on the real issues, in the real world, involving real people? Did she even know Diana's real name for a certainty? No, she didn't. Why wasn't she anxious about that?

Instead, she worried that her new designer slacks and button-up under a cashmere pullover weren't right for a power brunch. Great, she was nervous about her clothes. But not about Diana playing the role of Anita Topaz for the likes of Ronald Reynard.

Diana called out, "About ready?"

She stepped nervously into view. "Am I okay for Sunday brunch?"

Diana was waiting for her at the door. Finally, for the first time since waking their eyes fully met and locked. It didn't matter that Diana was again sporting the blond French braid and that her eyes were now blue. Something in those eyes made Paris hungry and more than a little dizzy.

"Yes," Diana said finally. "You are okay for Sunday brunch."

Paris gestured at Diana's sleeveless, belted shirtwaist dress patterned with Van Gogh sunflowers. Her blue high-heeled pumps had small gold stars across the toes. "You look okay for a Sunday brunch too."

"Thank you." Diana led the way toward the elevator bank. "We can do this. It'll be fine."

"Yes ma'am." Paris gestured for Diana to precede her into the empty car.

"Knock off the ma'am thing. Call me Anita. I told him that you were practically a member of the family."

"Anita, I think we're both crazy."

"Possibly." Her lips, lavishly red, twitched into a smile. "I'm used to being crazy all by myself, so this is a nice change."

Paris laughed to cover the fascinated chill of watching Diana become someone else as the elevator doors opened. The set of her shoulders, the tilt of her head, even the way she looked at Paris with a friendly distance—she was not Diana anymore.

Diana's "Anita" smile for the mustachioed bellman was broad and immediate, deceptively unguarded. "How can we get to Salazar's as quickly as possible?"

"It's two blocks," the bellman advised her. "Perhaps three minutes."

"So faster to walk?" Paris confirmed.

"It truly is and it's a beautiful morning out there. Springtime in New York and it's warm, even. Turn right out the door, then left at the first block." He hustled to open the door for them.

She glanced down at Diana's shoes. The little stars caught the light, making it hard not to watch. "Can you walk in those?"

Diana slid sleek, bright red sunglasses onto her nose as she breezed past Paris. "I know how to walk."

"I'm talking about the shoes." The bright sunlight made Paris wish she'd thought to bring sunglasses as well.

Diana gave her an over-the-shoulder look that Paris couldn't decipher. "So am I. I'll show you when we're not in a hurry."

Diana plunged through the clusters of people crowding the sidewalk, leaving Paris to admire the alluring sway of Diana's hips and the powerful flex of her calf muscles. Other people noticed Diana as she passed, some with a look of wondering if she were someone famous. She walked that way—head up, shoulders back and seemingly unaware of anyone else's notice.

They turned at the first corner where the sidewalk was far less crowded and it was easy to walk side-by-side. "And this *isn't* what you meant by showing me your walk?"

"Maybe a little."

"You learned that in acting school?"

"No, I learned it walking a four-inch wide beam of wood—and watching Maggie Smith movies. She could be quite the vamp when necessary. She's more my stature than Audrey Hepburn. I make do."

Yes, Paris thought, she made do. She was suddenly afraid of what might show in her face. "Are we sure I'm invited to this shindig?" As if that was the most perilous part of the outing.

"Who cares? You will not, under any circumstances, leave me alone with him."

"I won't."

"Promise me."

"I promise." Paris wanted to hold her hand. This was a crazy, bizarre game, but they were in it together now, weren't they? "Do you know anything about his daughter? Isn't she going to be there?"

"Supposed to be, but I wouldn't be surprised if she's a no-show. Just his kind of move." Diana's annoyance was obvious. "I looked her up before I got here. She's thirty-four and an only child. Second-in-command of the entire media group."

"So the heir apparent to this highly lucrative empire?"

"She already runs the cable network group. Her mother, who was a model, died years ago. Heather got Daddy's genes big-time. Tall, big shoulders."

"Can't be easy being his daughter. And no doubt a succession of temporary so-called mothers."

"I don't know about that." In spite of their quick pace, Diana wasn't even breathing hard. "It's hard to know what family life was like. She went to boarding school, that I read. As for him, social media photos show a new woman on his arm every month, and he likes them young. None of them seem to ever stay around for long."

"That makes me want gloves when we shake hands. I mean—do the math."

"I have," Diana said grimly. "It's creepy."

They turned the corner, coming within sight of the restaurant marquee. "Sounds like you know his type way too well."

Diana sighed. "He reminds me of my father. And I've met his type more than once."

More proof that Paris knew nothing about Diana's background. The trust fund meant money, and the clothes and social aplomb meant status. She'd been fooling herself, thinking she was beginning to know this woman.

CHAPTER TWENTY

Diana appreciated the cool breeze. It took a step and a half of hers to every step of Paris's, and in heels it was closer to two. She didn't want to arrive in a sweaty mess.

As they covered the last few yards to the restaurant, the breeze lifted into view a green and red flag in front of Salazar's. It was centered by a contented white sheep with a glass of wine in one hoof and a pale lavender stemmed blossom in the other. The sidewalk directly outside was crowded with clusters of people waiting for tables.

She caught Paris's arm before they wound their way to the door.

"Let's catch our breath. We can afford fifteen seconds." She'd had enough stage practice to have perfected a few mental triggers that brought calm before a performance. Paris brought something else to the energy of the setting, like acting a part with a brand-new understudy. Unpredictable, skill level unknown.

Paris had closed her eyes, and within a few seconds her face relaxed. Lines of worry around the firm mouth and long-lashed eyes eased. Unable to stop herself, Diana followed the line of

Paris's jaw to her throat where the skin looked so very soft. Belatedly she realized that Paris had caught Diana's rapt gaze. Heat rose between them as Paris gave her a look of unflinching vulnerability that took Diana's breath away.

Paris swallowed hard, then her lips curved up slightly. "Ready?"

She used Anita's slightly breathless voice and generic Hollywood accent. "Ready as I'll ever be."

Paris blinked. "That's unnerving. I'm never sure who you are."

It was too late to ask her what she meant, but Diana supposed she already knew. When a job was afoot it didn't bother her to be a changeling. It was one of her best skills and she reveled in it. But she wanted to tell Paris not to worry—not to worry about what? That she wasn't a lie? When she'd told Paris only some of the truth? There were still a lot of lies.

She had never felt less prepared to make an entrance. She almost forgot to maintain her Hollywood voice as she gave the tall, brown-skinned hostess her name.

The restaurant was long and narrow, with a tight path between white-draped tables. Paris touched her elbow with her fingertips. Instead of steadying Diana, the light contact fractured her focus. All her maturity, her professionalism—gone in less than a heartbeat. Paris's nearness grew more devastating with every second that passed.

What had happened to the woman who could tell her body, "Tumbling Run Two" and then simply do it? Run, fly, spin, flip-cartwheel-layout-flip, foot-foot, and dismount. She should shake off the contact but she couldn't make herself do it.

She wanted more.

Paris murmured, "Something smells good. I'm starving."

"We're not here for the food." She spoke more sharply than she intended.

Quietly, in her ear, Paris said, "I know that."

Goose bumps prickled across the nape of her neck. Diana attempted to calm herself by studying the decor. Skillful murals of the Mediterranean countryside brightened the walls. She liked that the chairs were eclectic, some metallic gold, others wood, some with tapestry seats and others with tied-on cushions as if their hosts had collected chairs from multiple houses for a large family celebration. The effect was simultaneously classy and homey.

Paris was right, there was a wonderful smell of oranges and roasted peppers in the air. Her focus would steady once she had some food. She enviously eyed an espresso on a table they passed. Her stomach growled—and then she saw Ronald Reynard.

He was scanning his phone with quick grimaces and stabbing at the device as if it were to blame for his displeasure. She had made a promise to Paris, but the moment Diana saw his face she wanted to harm him. Not physically, though the thought of slipping laxative powder into his tea had an appeal.

One of her favorite aspects of a job was being both the director and the stage manager who knew everybody's lines. She liked being in charge of how the scenes would play out. Right now she was in charge of diddly-poo and she *hated* the feeling. Paris wasn't in charge either, and Diana was never going to let Reynard or his ilk be in charge. So what exactly was running the show now? Sheer luck?

She wasn't ready for this scene. Paris's touch at her elbow was all that kept her from fleeing. Too late—Reynard had seen them.

The phone disappeared into his breast pocket. Though it was a struggle to raise his bulk quickly, Reynard rose to greet Diana with utmost courtesy. His manner was infuriatingly proprietary. There was no sign of his daughter.

"A pleasure, Ronald. You remember Ellis of course. Is Heather not joining us?"

His nod to Paris was perfunctory. "She's running late. An old friend is in an important tennis match and Heather is very loyal."

"Terrific. I'm so looking forward to meeting her. What a charming spot you've discovered." She glanced at the nearby empty tables, all marked reserved. "Is there a party arriving?"

"I prefer not to have anyone close enough to eavesdrop." With a flash of almost genuine charm he added, "Or notice that I've ordered two of the rib eyes. Which I recommend."

Paris forestalled Diana's third reminder that she was vegetarian by saying, "Is that what smells so wonderful?"

"Everything here is magnificent. I have a fondness for Basque food," he admitted. "From my maternal grandmother's side of the family." He launched into a pat speech about the old family farm halfway between Bilbao and Biarritz, overlooking the Bay of Biscay. World War Two resistance fighters had changed the family name from Azeria to Reynard in solidarity with their French neighbors.

It sounded to Diana like myth-making at its finest, a practice of the nouveau riche and of dusty monied families alike. Her father doted upon specious bloodlines to polish his already upper crust credentials. Reynard used the humble origins of his grandfather to make his brash, lavish riches all the more remarkable. Neither of them was capable of ever being satisfied with who they already were by birth and by their own effort. Neither would ever look around them and think, "This is enough."

She was momentarily swamped by a flood of affection and homesickness. Her visit home to grab a wardrobe appropriate to Anita Topaz had been too brief. Her mother and stepfather had their flaws, but lack of love and compassion weren't among them.

"I come to this place for its intersection of the French obsession for fresh ingredients and the Spanish love of spice," Reynard was concluding. "I've already inquired and they have St. George's mushrooms today. They're not to be missed."

A waiter was already hovering, eager to explain the chef's special dishes and offer sangria made with Graciano wine, lime, and blood oranges. It sounded delicious, but she was annoyed at Reynard's presumptive order of a pitcher "for the table."

"Heather will be along and we'll order a meal then," he added.

So they were going to sit there at noon and drink with no food? She caught the server's eye. "I'm told you have amazing mushrooms at the moment."

"We do!" The stooped and swarthy waiter was either from the old country or an actor doing a very good job of pretending to be. "*Zizak* in the nude. Roasted with only a touch of olive oil and fresh herbs and served with traditional sheepherder's bread. They are so beautiful, they need nothing more."

"I'm a vegetarian and that sounds delicious. For the table. While we wait for our remaining guest," she added. She saw a flare of amusement in Paris's face.

"I like a woman who knows what she likes," Reynard announced.

"You always say that, Father, but you and I both know it's not true."

Startled, Diana automatically rose from her seat to greet the newcomer. She'd seen Heather Reynard's photos online, and they had accurately captured the physical traits she'd inherited from her father: very tall, broad-shouldered, round-faced. Unlike her father, she gave an impression of fast-moving sleekness. Her stature made her a person you would always know was in the room. And possibly not turn your back on, Diana mused. Burnished reddish-gold hair cut asymmetrically framed a face made expressive by dark brows and eyes. She envied Heather's light jacket of soft blue chambray—the restaurant was a bit chilly.

All in all, Heather Reynard was confidently casual and exactly what Diana had expected. The big surprise was the light, musical voice and a smile that had a natural, easy charisma. Her mother's genes had blended some swan into the bull.

"Anita Topaz," Diana said, extending her hand.

"A pleasure." The handshake was firm and brief. But the oddest expression crossed her face when she turned to Paris, who had also risen to extend her hand.

"I'm Ellis. The amanuensis."

Their handshake continued as Heather asked, "Have we met?"

"I'd remember," Paris said.

"Were you at Stanford?"

Paris mock growled, "Berkeley."

Heather laughed. "Well, we're off to a rocky start."

Diana resumed her seat, unable to say what it was she found disquieting about a completely appropriate exchange. She was relieved at the return of the waiter bearing the pitcher of sangria and a tray of cut-glass tumblers rimmed with sugar.

"Forgive me," Heather said, finally releasing Paris's hand, "for turning into a daughter for a moment. Father, it's scarcely past noon."

"It's mostly fruit juice," Reynard protested, gesturing at the waiter to pour him a glass.

Diana gave in to a flash of contrariness. "I'd love to taste it."

Heather's smile of acceptance had enough edge for Diana to know she'd displeased her. No, she wouldn't turn her back on this woman. She was happily leveraging all the benefits of being the daughter of this pig of a man and would not succeed in making Diana feel small. It was no time to feel upstaged and petulant, like when the big teams with medal prospects marched into the competition arena, lithe and strong and wearing much cooler gear.

She firmly told herself that her chaos of feelings—all of them—had no bearing whatsoever on the business at hand. A reaction to a fleeting touch or wondering why Paris was smiling so much all of a sudden had nothing to do with bringing up movie deals. She was Anita Topaz for a few more hours only, and then only for Paris's sake. All her other plans were dead. And why? Because she felt sorry for Paris.

The lie rang in her ears.

Pity? Her body felt like she'd been in the sun too long— dizzy, slightly fevered, skin on fire. It wasn't pity.

Paris and Heather had launched into a lively conversation about New York. Well, she would envy Heather Reynard one thing: she could talk to Paris without measuring the lie in every word. Diana didn't see how she could ever have that with Paris. She hadn't given Paris a single reason not to eagerly say goodbye forever.

Reynard was also watching Heather and Paris as he chatted with Diana about how doctors really didn't know what was good for anyone. He didn't care for being told to cut down on drinking and to get some exercise, but she didn't think the narrowed gaze was about his health. His eyes never left the other two women. On the one hand it was a relief not to have him fawning all over her. On the other she didn't know what he saw that bothered him.

She followed his line of sight again, imagining herself a Lear-esque monarch watching the heir to the throne with paranoid speculations of disaffection and disloyalty. His mind preoccupied with territory, prestige and his own pleasures, he sat in his counting house, thinking about his property, where Anita Topaz and all the other young, pretty women in his life were bought and discarded.

"I've never been to the Hamptons," Paris was saying. "I grew up in California and worked there for several years. San Francisco has a different heartbeat than New York."

"What an interesting way to describe it." Heather rested back in her chair, shoulders relaxed, arms casually resting on the table. "I've lived in the Hamptons now for several years. It has similarities to Napa Valley, but, as you say, the heartbeat is very different. What did you do in California?"

A trill of alarm sounded in Diana's head. They hadn't discussed any kind of backstory for "Ellis."

"I followed my passion for gaming into design for a while." Paris's shrug wasn't completely natural.

"What's your poison? I'm working on beating the latest *Dark Souls*."

"I'm a bit behind the times. *Zelda*—"

"Who doesn't love *Zelda*?" With an arch look at her father, Heather said, "It's nice to meet someone who appreciates gaming as a pastime."

"It's not that I don't appreciate it," Reynard began. "It has no ultimate reward."

"Except for falling into and becoming part of a story full of self-challenge," Paris said.

"Exactly," Heather agreed. "And how did you meet the amazing Anita Topaz?"

Diana's heart stopped. It was belatedly occurring to her that all she knew about Paris's life was that she wrote novels under a pen name. She hadn't known about California and gaming design. That Paris had had a life before Anita Topaz. *Which of course she had, you stupid fool.*

With a lifted eyebrow glance at Diana, Paris said, "We met in a bar. And that's all I'm saying."

Both Reynards looked slightly taken aback until Paris added, "And whatever it is you're thinking, trust me, you're wrong."

Relief and irony sent Diana into a fit of giggles.

Eyebrow raised, Heather said, "This is a story I think I have to hear."

"It won't be from me. It's Anita's story to tell." In spite of Paris's ease with the words, Diana noticed that her fingers were flexing and tapping lightly on the table the way they had at Mona Lisa's, just before Paris had bolted out the door.

"And millions will pay to read it some day I'm sure." Reynard added smoothly. "Well, we'd like it to be millions."

Diana seized on the opening Reynard had provided. "Wouldn't a movie reach that kind of audience? Or a miniseries?"

Heather's smile tightened. "It would. Reynard Television has a reliable working production network and a vast affiliate base, as you know."

"Vast," Reynard echoed.

"*Hands Off the Merchandise* is a natural for that. I'm very excited that you're interested in making it into a movie. It's a great story," Diana said honestly. Then added hastily, "If I say so myself."

Heather's expression was now carefully impassive, but Diana noted the short glance at her father. If she wasn't mistaken, this was the first that Heather was hearing of such a possibility. Which meant the offer might have been bait and nothing more. Bloody hell.

Heather admitted, "I haven't read it, I'm sorry to say."

Reynard finished his first glass of the sangria. "Too busy with video games and that school."

The faint wince in Heather's eyes told Diana that her father's offhand criticism was not new. The gold-plated life had a cost, of that Diana had no doubt. "My leisure time is quickly booked."

"Understandable," Diana assured her. She cast about for a way to build a rapport with her. "I'm glad you were able to enjoy a tennis match this morning—a beautiful day for it."

Heather's eyes narrowed as if she suspected Diana of sarcasm. "It was an old friend at a Pro-Am charity event. She was paired with Navratilova—not something I wanted to miss."

"I certainly wouldn't have missed it," Paris said.

A long look passed between the two women. Reynard was scowling.

Oh, Diana thought.

Oh.

The waiter delivered the *zizak* mushrooms with a flourish, and not a moment too soon. The chef personally came out to wish them a pleasant meal with an attentiveness that Reynard hardly noticed. The platter was passed around and the conversation turned to safe, easy topics of favorite foods. Diana agreed that the roasted mushrooms were unusually savory and rich in flavor, but she barely tasted them. Her mind was in a whirl.

Heather was a lesbian, like Paris.

So, apparently, was she.

More than a decade of living behind a game face saved her. She stayed in character and said all the right things while absorbing the fact that Heather was gay and Reynard didn't like it. Hence his hostility toward Paris, who, in her man-cut clothes, was telling the world that she was a different kind of woman. A kind of woman that Heather clearly found interesting.

The observing voice that guided her through gymnastic routines and acting performances, that unceasingly coached her on everything from the voice and accent she used, to the set of her shoulders and the extension of her fingers, was urgently telling her that she was staring at Paris. Studying too closely her eyes, her mouth, her hands. If she didn't stop the hunger would show in her face.

"My father isn't quite right when he calls it a school," Heather said in response to Paris's question. "It's a literacy program available to any house of worship. We've found that inability to read English is a significant barrier to any kind of success in life, and if the church or synagogue or mosque will provide the space, we'll provide the teacher and materials."

"Why churches?" Paris seemed genuinely interested.

"Churches, especially in poor communities, know who needs help. They're also trusted by those who attend, making a teacher's acceptance by the students easier. Most of the people we're reaching are girls and women desperate to learn English as a second or even third language. But too many are native English speakers who still don't know how to read beyond *See Spot Run*." Heather seemed almost shy. "I provide the money, mostly. It's an amazing team of people who make it happen, and across many cultures. If there's one thing New York has a lot of, it's diversity."

Paris asked Heather another question while Diana politely listened to Reynard explain everything he knew about Spanish wine. What else could she do? She was adrift with no script. It was like a nightmare of realizing that she hadn't memorized her lines and didn't even know what play she was performing as the curtain went up.

It was easiest to accept the waiter's recommendation of the chef's vegetarian breakfast, and once ordered Diana preempted Reynard's return to the topic of wine he had loved by rising. "Excuse me for a moment."

She took as long in the restroom stall as she dared, glad of the quiet. Finally emerging to wash her hands she was startled by her face in the mirror.

It looked exactly the way it had when she'd left the hotel.

The thought of touching Paris's skin with her fingertips, with her lips, turned everything south of her belly button into molten jelly, and yet she didn't look even one bleeding bit different? Rather than being relieved, she found it unfair. Surely something so monumental ought to show.

Maybe, when she got out of the wig, took out the contacts, scrubbed off the concealer, maybe then she would see it. A stranger's life in her own eyes.

CHAPTER TWENTY-ONE

Paris prayed that Diana came back soon. She was enjoying the conversation with Heather Reynard, much to her surprise, but that didn't mean it wasn't stressful to act naturally while watching every word. She had to be careful not to commit to anything that Diana wouldn't then know as well. The caution, layered on top of the already tense setting of deception, was ratcheting up her internal alarm bells.

I'm the one who is going to screw up. This is not what I'm good at.

When Reynard's expression brightened she was flooded with relief. Diana must be returning.

Heather's gaze also slid to Diana, but her expression remained passively pleasant. What was she thinking? This was the sort of situation where Paris knew she had blind spots. There was one surprise she had sorted out, though: her gaydar was actually pinging for once.

Breakfast was delivered, which turned the topic back to food. Her nerves stopped jangling quite as hard.

"This shepherd's bread is fantastic," she offered into the conversation. The aromas of the potatoes and peppers underneath her baked eggs was making her faint, but the dish was still too hot from the oven to eat. "It reminds me of Irish oat cakes, but with yeast instead of soda."

"It sounds as if you bake," Heather said. "Or do you watch a lot of food TV?"

"Mostly the former. Brownies are my specialty, but I like most everything that has butter and sugar and goes in the oven."

Heather gave Diana an amused look. "She bakes too? Lucky you."

Paris lost what Diana said, but it made Reynard laugh as well. She finally got it—Heather thought she and "Anita" were possibly sleeping together. Or, she was trying to rule it out. Were they giving off that vibe? Diana wouldn't ping anyone's gaydar, Paris thought. But then again, Lisa at the bar wouldn't either. It was that she talked openly of her wife and sometimes donned rainbow-decorated apparel that made it obvious.

"If we have any business to discuss it has to be before I eat all this food. My brain will go to mush," Diana said. "It's all delicious. And Ellis is right about the bread. Purely addictive. Thank you for selecting this restaurant for our meeting."

"I've been thinking over what you said about public speaking," Reynard said. "How are you with crowds, in general?"

Diana didn't look at Paris. "I, uh, it depends how loud and how long. It can be exhausting, as you saw last night."

"A cocktail party, in your honor. It could even be a fundraiser for your favorite cause."

Paris saw Diana hesitate. "Do you mean—"

"At RonCon of course. We could perhaps announce a book/movie tie-in project."

Heather asked her father to pass the bread and said, "I don't mean to be a wet blanket, but aren't the speakers all lined up at this point? Squeezing in another event won't be easy."

"For Anita I think it could be done," Reynard answered smoothly.

"Frankly," Diana said, "while I am happy to have a fundraiser, I am far more interested in learning the next steps to making that book-to-movie project happen. Though my agent should be involved before I commit myself."

"Of course," Heather said quickly. "That's just good business."

Diana's smile held charm, yet Paris saw steel in it. "It'll take some time to work out details, but I'm confident an agreement could be reached."

Reynard pronounced, "Anita Topaz has never been more popular. I believe in striking while the iron's red-hot."

It was news to Paris that Anita was "red-hot." She knew her numbers were strong, but she wasn't burning up the bestseller lists with her own version of *50 Shades of Lots of Sex Play*. Heather also seemed reluctant to do anything quickly. Which of them really ran the business? Or the part of the business that would make this particular decision?

"I know that, Father, but RonCon is only eight weeks away. You know these things take time."

"A standard contract with a signing bonus could be executed in a week." He sliced off another large piece of his rib eye, pushed it into his mouth and chewed only a couple of times before swallowing and replacing it with another bite.

Even Hobbit paced himself, Paris thought. Her meal was cool enough to thoroughly enjoy and every bite was sharp with spice and sweet with tomato. Diana seemed to like her food as well, but she was picking around chunks of artichoke. Perhaps she didn't like them—something to remember.

Mental brakes slammed on. There was no need to remember Diana's likes and dislikes. They were parting ways. There was no reason for them not to, after all. All her anxiety faded for a moment, overshadowed by a wave of regret. How could she feel so drawn to someone who was essentially a stranger? Who lied so glibly?

Lost in unfamiliar emotional territory, and trying desperately not to stare at Diana for too long, she missed the import of Reynard's strangled gasp.

Diana dropped her fork. Then Heather said loudly, "Dad! Are you okay?"

He didn't respond. His eyes were glassy and unfocused. Another gasp.

"Somebody call 911!" Heather was on her feet, trying to pull Reynard's chair away from the table. A nearby couple leapt up to help. The man helped Heather pull her father down onto the floor while the woman peppered Heather with questions in a clipped Middle Eastern accent.

"Does he have a history of heart disease? Is he taking medication? How recently has he seen his physician?" The woman was kneeling next to Reynard now, feeling his throat.

"He's had several heart attacks. Bypass several years ago." Heather's voice was shaking. "He always recovers. Can you help?"

"I'm a doctor. This is quite serious." To her companion she said, "Cardiac arrest. Find their AED."

With a nod he left off loosening Reynard's tie to engage in excited conversation with the waiter in a language Paris didn't recognize. The woman began CPR, counting under her breath as she pumped Reynard's chest.

Diana said, "I'll watch for the ambulance," and sped away.

Paris knelt next to Heather. She wasn't sure Heather even knew she was there. There was nothing she could contribute beyond offering a steadying hand. Then the man was back with a red case that he carefully set down next to the woman. Without a spare word he matched her counting and took over performing CPR while the woman opened the case and pulled out cables and packets.

Paris gently pulled Heather back to give the pair room to work. Within seconds they had opened Reynard's shirt and stuck pads to his massive chest. A few seconds more and a mechanical voice from the AED announced, "Shock advised."

"Everybody clear," the doctor ordered firmly.

Heather jumped when Reynard's body jolted. The man resumed CPR. The woman closed her eyes as she pressed her fingers into Reynard's neck again. "I have a pulse."

Paris slipped her arm around Heather as she slumped in relief. "I think I hear a siren."

Heather nodded while her lips moved in prayer. She was shaking so hard that Paris had to brace herself more securely to give Heather stability.

Diana's voice came from some distance away, clear and commanding, "Medics coming through!" Then, "Put your bleedin' phone down and get out of the bloody way!"

It seemed like only a few minutes had passed before the EMTs were lifting Reynard onto a stretcher. He wasn't conscious. Heather and the two Good Samaritans followed in the stretcher's wake, everything else forgotten.

The waiters and maitre d' were soothing the guests into resuming their meals.

Diana was pale and there was no trace of Anita Topaz's Hollywood accent. "It'll be a bit before I can look at food."

"That was—dreadful. Shocking." Paris felt light-headed, disconnected. She was trying hard not to relive the day her mother had collapsed. She caught the eye of the maitre d'. "I'll take the check," she told him.

"No worries about that," he said. "Mr. Reynard is a treasured customer. There is nothing to settle. Please give Ms. Reynard our best wishes for her father's speedy recovery. You must return another time."

To Paris's surprise the day outside was just as sunny and cool as when they'd arrived. There was still a queue for a table. The normalcy of it all reminded her again of the day her mother had died when she'd wondered how she could be so full of pain and darkness and the sky still be blue. Like the day her contact information had posted onto the dark web and her voice mail counter had started spinning like a roulette wheel. While she was listening to a harsh male voice salaciously detailing all the ways he would torture her, co-workers were ordering out lunch.

Fresh air dispelled most of the light-headed feeling but her stomach was still churning.

"My stepfather had a heart attack," Diana said suddenly. "It wasn't like that at all. He was awake and in pain. But he tried to crack a joke to stop my mother having hysterics. Well, hysterics British style, which means she raised her voice."

"Is he okay now?"

"Yes. Regular checkups, does what the doctor says. Sold half his business to cut the stress."

"That's hard."

"Not really. Half of a lot is still a lot. He's in aluminium," she added.

Grateful for something to smile about, Paris teased, "Why do Brits say aluminum that way?"

"Why do you lot say it wrong?"

"Touché." Paris added soberly, "I hope Reynard's okay. For Heather's sake."

"He's a creep but I don't *want* him dead." Diana shuddered. "I wouldn't mind if he spent time in a long tunnel with a bright light at the end having a heart-to-heart with Jesus before he comes back."

"I'd be happy with that." Paris steered them around a street musician setting up a portable speaker. "Heather wasn't what I expected."

"Me neither."

It was an effort to push away the image of Reynard's body splayed on the restaurant floor. Trying for a nonchalant tone, Paris asked, "Does her official bio say she's gay anywhere?"

"Not that I read. It was a surprise to me. Reynard's not too happy about it."

So Diana had seen it as well. "Did he say something?"

"No, he didn't have to. It was written all over his face." Diana stopped at the crowded corner for the signal and looked up at Paris. "Do you have trouble interpreting facial expressions?"

Paris studied the red light, not sure how much detail Diana really wanted.

"I'm sorry, that was very personal. It's just—you take in the world differently than I do. I'd like to understand."

The light turned green and the crowds of pedestrians divided and flowed around them, but Paris felt alone with Diana. Their gazes locked. Paris felt stripped bare and tears stung in her eyes. "Why?"

Diana's cheeks flushed slightly. "I—just to understand."

Paris had to look away. "You mean like to help with your acting?"

"No, no. God no. I'm sorry!" And she flung her arms around Paris.

The shock of contact overwhelmed Paris's defenses. She held Diana as tight and close as a lifeline. Diana's ear was against Paris's shoulder. This feels so right, Paris thought. Impossibly right.

"I didn't mean to hurt you."

"You took me by surprise is all. I don't have a great track record with people wanting to understand. I explain and most people tell me how to cure myself. Plus the whole incident with Reynard—I'm adrenaline crashing."

Diana let go of her and dabbed at her eyes. "Me too. I'm jumpy. It makes me feel fragile."

The light changed again and Paris seized Diana's hand and dragged her into the crosswalk. "Come on."

"Slow up, good lord. I'm running on tiptoe here!"

Paris laughed. "It'll be worth it." She shouldered open a shop door and pulled Diana in after her, arriving moments before a long line of school kids in matching eye-popping orange T-shirts.

"Ice cream?" Diana peered through the glass at the array of containers filled with creamy, wonderful goodness in every possible color. "You're a good woman. With good ideas."

"I try."

"We hardly had breakfast."

"I know, but don't your people put sugar and cream in tea after a shock?"

"Right, this is the very same thing as a cuppa. Completely medicinal." To the teen behind counter she said, "A scoop of Cup-of-Joe please."

They were soon separated by the press of kids all trying to look in all the containers all at once, but Paris managed to get her order in as well and then pay before the cacophony grew too painful. The tiny shop had no seating, so they escaped to the street again.

"I think I'm going to live," Diana said after tasting hers. "What did you get? I couldn't hear a thing."

"Brownie Almond Fudgearoo. Wanna taste? There's no cooties on this part yet."

Diana lip-nibbled the side Paris pointed at. "That's brilliant. Try this."

Paris tried to be equally delicate with Diana's cone. "I love coffee. That's really good too. Now imagine if our flavors had babies."

"I would gobble that up all day."

The tight fluttery sensation of spent adrenaline eased after another soothing mouthful of ice cream. Paris said, "I can read people's expressions when I'm not stressed. Anxiety disorder isn't like being on the autism spectrum. They're two different conditions, but some people deal with both. What happens to me is like on a phone when an app goes haywire and sucks up all the memory."

Diana's expression was thoughtful even as she chased an ice cream drip headed for her hand. "Except you're not a phone."

"I would love to have an expanded memory card." She made herself not watch as Diana licked ice cream off her red, red lips. "Yes, it's not like a simple reboot or program tweak will fix it. Though I have a lot of tactics for reducing the impact. Certain situations set off the anxiety cycle and I avoid those. When it's triggered—" She paused to lick up a drip that threatened her sleeve. "When it's triggered I have trouble running all the other normal brain activities, like reading people's faces or hearing tone nuance. Or controlling my breathing or voice level. When it's bad my eyes are slow to adjust to light and colors get washed out. I get dizzy and can't breathe."

Diana's eyebrows raised. "And you'll eventually faint?"

"That's happened twice. I'm never doing that again if I can help it."

"I get that. I passed out once. It was not like in the movies, I mean, there was nothing elegant or slow motion about it. I went down like a house of cards. Woke up in hospital. It's horrible, that feeling of your body clock knowing time has passed and your brain having nothing to fill in the gap." Diana pulled back her skirt just in time to avoid a drip, which landed on her shoe. "Bugger all, that'll be the devil to get off."

"We seem to be walking toward the hotel," Paris said. "If you want to change your shoes."

"I have to say, I'm at a loss," Diana said carefully. "I don't know how to help you with the movie deal now. Reynard's in hospital." She didn't need to say that he could be dead. "Everything is up in the air now. I don't know what to do next."

"It's Sunday in New York. There must be tons of things to do."

"I mean about Anita Topaz."

"I think that's moot now, don't you?" Paris judged her ice cream as having reached that perfect soft stage such that a large bite wouldn't freeze her teeth. The chunks of brownie were dense and chocolatey—worth the risk of brain freeze. When she was able she continued, "Whatever has happened, Reynard and the company will take some time to recover. I realize that Heather Reynard might be the new big boss. She didn't sound in favor of making changes to the conference agenda, did she?"

"She wasn't in favor at all. I'm not sure she even knew about a movie offer. I'm sorry about that. It might have only been Reynard's bait."

Paris sighed. "So all this... For nothing."

"We got ice cream."

Paris gave Diana a crooked smile. "You got to see *Hamilton*."

She hung her head. "That I did. I wish I could say I was sorry about that. I really hadn't seen it and wanted to." With a quick glance at Paris she added, "That much was true."

They walked in silence for a few minutes, ducking around tourists craning their heads back to see the tops of the skyscrapers. Paris took note of the fact that dripping ice cream cones meant people gave them a wider berth. That would be fun armor in an urban game—Cone of Large Drippage increases zone of protection. She pushed away the pang of lost opportunities. Being with Diana made the past softer somehow.

Their cones were finished by the time they reached their hotel bellman, who opened the door with a cheery, "Welcome back."

The lobby was quiet and cool compared to the street behind them. Diana was licking her fingers, which was so distracting that Paris almost missed her question. "Were you planning on going back to Boston today?"

"Yes. I didn't think there'd be any reason to linger."

"Someone will miss you if you don't turn up as planned?"

Was Diana asking what Paris thought she was? Anything seemed possible without the shadow of Reynard looming over her. "No. I could stay another night. If you have something in mind."

Diana's head was turned away as she pressed the elevator call button. "As you said, it's Sunday in New York. I'm sure there's a museum or two open. I've heard tales of a very large park. I like this place." She cracked a lopsided smile. "And willingly could waste some time in it."

Only the place? But Paris couldn't bring herself to ask such a perilous question. Her stomach was in a slow flip-flop and all the warnings her head had been sending her went silent. Instead she asked, "Just how many times have you been in *As You Like It*?"

Diana laughed. "I've lost count."

The elevator car was crowded and stopping at nearly every floor, giving Paris a chance to breathe. I get a few more hours with her, she thought. For the moment, it was all that mattered.

CHAPTER TWENTY-TWO

I get to spend a few more hours with her, Diana thought. Not pretending to be someone else, not buried in lies and subterfuge. We can both be…natural.

It was, perhaps, the one thing she was worst at. As a skill it had never seemed important, not the way it did right now.

"I can't wait to get out of this wig," she said as she keyed opened their door. "The scalp glue is itching."

"Isn't it all uncomfortable? The contacts and the shoes and everything?"

"I love these shoes." Diana sighed as she took them off. "But I'm only good for a few hours before my back reminds me of all my previous activities at its expense." She carried them to the sink in the minibar and found the little bottle of dishwashing liquid the housekeepers stashed under the sink. She stirred a few drops into a mug quarter-filled with water and whisked the solution with a coffee stir stick until there was foam.

"You look like you're in a Hogwart's potions class," Paris said.

Diana lifted an eyebrow at the teasing smile. "I wish."

Paris's smile widened. "You were frowning so seriously about it."

"It's a costumer's trick. Works on leather, even fur."

Paris turned away to look at the view. Diana dabbed soap foam over the blotch on her shoe while stealing glances at the long, lean line of Paris's body. Sunlight limned her smooth brown skin and almost black hair with gold. With her shoulders at ease and hands in her pockets she looked as comfortable as Diana had ever seen her.

Comfortable, strong, vulnerable—alluring. Diana forced herself to look at the stupid shoe. Drooling was unbecoming. "Would you like to see Central Park?"

"It is a beautiful day. I have the right Adventuring Gear." Paris turned from the window just as Diana looked up. "Jeans, walking shoes."

"You told Heather you were in game design." She pressed a dry paper towel into the toe of her shoe, hoping the faint outline of the ice cream was gone, but her gaze was on Paris. "What kind?"

"Multiplayer quest and RPGs—role playing games. I wrote and co-wrote story lines and characters. Game dialogue, tutorial scenarios, song lyrics for bards. It was a small company—large now."

"And you left to become a writer? Anita Topaz?" When Paris didn't answer she looked up, worried that she'd once again asked a question that Paris found painful.

Paris had sat down on the fainting couch in front of the window. One hand was idly running over the gold velvet in a way that sent a hot shiver through Diana's body. "Not quite. I left. Then I invented Anita Topaz and went on telling stories. Adventures and love, a touch of magic sometimes."

Diana heard the flash of grief in Paris's voice. She'd already hit a raw nerve once today, and the day had been tumultuous enough. She gave her shoe a final dab and said, "I'm ready for Adventuring Gear too." She couldn't look at Paris at the moment. "Meet you right back here in ten minutes."

The bedroom had been cleaned and the bed made, but clothes were still strewn over the chair from earlier. It seemed like days ago, not only a few hours. She managed to work off the wig without looking in the mirror. She couldn't find the courage for it. The twisted braid was a little loose now, but what did it matter? Her role as Anita Topaz was over. Now she was Diana. A Diana with no agenda except to spend time with another woman, a woman she found fascinating and attractive.

Was this a date?

No.

Yes.

No—a date required mutual interest. She'd been so gobsmacked by her own feelings and their sheer intensity that she hadn't a clue about what Paris might feel. While she was well aware that a wide range of men usually found her attractive, especially when she meant to use their befuddlement to her advantage, she didn't know if women were the same. Women like Paris, that is. A lesbian. A butch, Lisa had said.

Paris *had* agreed to stay another night. She'd been under the influence of shock and ice cream, though.

A quick rinse in the shower removed the heavy foundation and eyeliner she'd used to create Anita Topaz. Feeling much fresher she pulled on black jeans and a royal blue silk blouse, adding a simple gold chain and twisted knot earrings. Her beloved peacoat would be perfect if the day turned chilly.

The makeup mirror reflected a face that looked a little pale. She thought of Paris's hands stroking the velvet on the couch. A tremor of desire showed in the tightening of the fine lines around her mouth. She wanted to cover them with foundation, change her face, make it a mask.

She settled for a little mascara and a light touch of blush. And felt naked. She added Maniac Red lipstick for courage.

From the depths of her largest suitcase she found an over-the-shoulder leather bag perfect for the accumulation of treats to take home. Her sister-in-law-to-be liked a super sweet, sticky pecan and toffee concoction she might be able to find. She dumped the contents of this morning's purse into it and added a traveler's tube of Nurofen tablets and an energy bar.

Feeling almost giddy and not wanting to jinx it by wondering why, she found Paris leaning against the bar, an open can of soda in hand. She looked just like Paris-from-the-bar, too. Simple jeans, sturdy boots, and a dark green hoodie over a T-shirt with an elfin gaming character Diana didn't recognize.

"Ready?"

Paris shook her head as if to clear her vision. "You're…you."

"I'm me." Diana spread her arms with a shy shrug. "About to go out in the world using my real name. It feels kind of weird."

Paris slung a lightweight backpack over one shoulder and said nothing, but the slight lift to her eyebrows was enough.

"And you think I could use more practice at it?" She slid a bottle of water from the minibar into her bag. "Want one?"

"Good idea." Paris tucked it in her backpack's side pouch. "More practice at what?"

"Using my real name and not feeling weird about it."

Paris held the door for her. "I didn't say a thing."

Diana bounced on her toes in front of the elevator, loving the luxury of wearing trainers. "You didn't have to. Behave, Ms. Paris Ellison."

Paris flushed. "I shall attempt to do so. You don't make it easy."

Diana waited for the elevator doors to close before she asked, "How do I make it difficult for you to behave?"

Paris let out a strangled half laugh and simply shook her head.

"What?" Diana's teasing air faded at the look in Paris's eyes. The elevator car seemed to shrink and fill with heat, waves of it that Diana felt in her face and her ears, her palms, between her legs. It was frightening, almost painful, and impossibly full of wonder. She gasped and closed her eyes when Paris's fingertips grazed her cheek then gently cupped her jaw.

Paris kissed her, her lips warm and soft against Diana's. It was so welcome that her fears melted, leaving amazement and desire behind.

"Oh," she whispered when Paris stepped back. She opened her eyes in time to see Paris forming the words, "I'm sorry," but

Diana didn't want to hear that it was a lapse in judgment or that the ice cream had gone right to her head. She laughed, giddy and breathless. "You're wearing my lipstick."

"Oh." Paris wiped at her mouth.

She found a tissue in her bag. "It's not your shade."

The elevator pinged. As the doors opened Diana wasn't entirely sure she heard Paris right. But she thought Paris said, "I'd like it to be."

CHAPTER TWENTY-THREE

Idiot, idiot, id-i-ot.

Paris decided she'd lost her mind. The shell she'd built around herself for safety was cracked to pieces and now she was being stupid, reckless. As if she didn't know perfectly well that when you're playing a new game where you don't know the rules, kissing mysterious women in elevators was a bad idea. Where would it end?

Diana had diverted to chat with the concierge, and was asking for tips on getting around the city. Her face was still glowing from the shower, and she'd quickly reapplied her lipstick—it was as if the kiss had never happened. Which was for the best, Paris thought. Just pretend it never happened.

"Most people use Lyft or Uber these days." The young man's voice was as pale as he was.

"We don't have smartphones," Diana said. She was using the accent Paris had decided was her real one. It sounded very English private school, but was lower in pitch than either the Fiona or Anita voices.

His nearly white eyebrows shot up as if their lack of tech was shocking. Yeah, Paris thought, that's the strangest thing about the two of us.

"Then of course a cab will do. The subway is very efficient and will avoid the traffic, but Sunday service isn't as frequent." He pulled a map out of his desk drawer. "Personally, I'd take a cab to the park. My favorite place to start is Strawberry Fields. Tell the driver to go this route." He drew circles in several places, refolded it and handed it to Diana.

"Ready?" Diana's eyes were bright and eager as she turned to Paris.

"Yes," was all Paris could say. The truth and a lie all at once. She was getting good at it because she didn't feel a single pang of anxiety.

The next few hours were bliss. Paris decided the sun was brighter because the shadows over Anita Topaz's future were gone. There were hints of spring in all directions, from the brave shoots coming up through the sidewalk cracks to the colorful pots of flowers in front of stores and peeking over balconies. It felt as if winter had lasted forever and was finally losing its grasp.

They alighted alongside Central Park and followed the signs to Strawberry Fields. A pond with frogs and lily pads attracted tourists and their phone cameras. A bridal party posed in their finery with the green of the park behind them. Every time someone shouted, "Congratulations!" the bride and groom waved. A picnic with two men and three kids, all five of them different colors of the human rainbow, had a boom box playing, "All You Need is Love."

Diana read all the historical markers, stopped to watch an artist sketching, and peered at the little signs that gave the botanical names of the trees and flowers. Paris watched her breathing all of it in and wondered if she'd been born with double curiosity points.

"A donut with peanut butter in it?" Diana pointed at the vendor cart. "That sounds disgusting."

"It's dipped in chocolate," Paris pointed out. It sounded good to her.

Diana was digging in her purse for her wallet. "I have to try it."

"But you think it's disgusting."

"What if I'm wrong?"

Paris watched her conclude the transaction, chatting with the vendor about business and the weather. Once she had the treat in her hand she gave it a steady look, took a deep breath and bit into it.

"Well?"

Diana chewed for a while, her face impassive. After swallowing she said, "I wasn't wrong."

"You are so weird," Paris said. "It looks delicious."

Diana grinned and handed it over, then drank deeply from her water bottle. "Never make me peanut butter brownies, okay?"

"Okay." Then she wondered what world would have to exist where she could make Diana brownies. She wanted to live in that world. But it was nowhere near the one they actually occupied. The donut was fresh, the chewy-salty-sweet peanut butter and chocolate combo exactly what Paris thought it would be. Yummy.

They rambled through the Ramble, doubling back on footpaths with a general plan to reach the other side of the park to find real food and very cold drinks.

"Look! How fun!"

She followed Diana's pointing finger and saw a dance lesson in progress. The bright trumpets of Latin music reached her. The instructor was showing off footwork while a dozen students in pairs copied the moves.

"I think it's the mambo." Diana tossed her bag on the ground close by. "Let's try."

"I'll step on you."

"I won't break. Your other hand goes on my shoulder—" She peered at the dancers. "I'll lead. I step forward, you step back."

She managed to avoid tromping on Diana, but just barely. "I don't think Doc Martens are made for this kind of dancing."

"We're doing fine—and step, two, three. Everyone over there—and step, two, three—is sixty or older—and step, two, three."

Paris had noticed. Kerry crossed her mind, because the idea that they'd grow old and happy together had been where Paris had hoped they were going. A future like that seemed impossible with Diana. They were very different people living in different worlds with different rules. She wrote that sort of story in her novels, and it always worked out—but that was fiction.

Diana was impulsive about life. Dancing in a park, trying a new food even if she suspected it would disappoint. The most impulsive thing Paris had done recently was kiss Diana in the elevator and it had exhausted her supply of risk-taking. Even if it had been so worth it.

She could protest all she wanted about not knowing why she'd done it, except the fire in her hands where they touched Diana was very clear with the answer. She was attracted to her, in a big way, and what was she going to do about it that didn't make her like Reynard? And didn't leave her broken with regrets?

"And step, two, three. There!" Diana gazed up at her. "You're good at this, you know."

"My mother loved to dance to Big Band. We cleaned the house on Saturdays and listened to Glenn Miller."

"Did she dance professionally?"

"No, she was a medical technician. A wonderful mom."

"It sounds like it." No longer following the music, Diana swayed closer to Paris. "What's the best lesson she ever taught you?"

Paris thought about it. "Even if the world is falling apart around you, how to get up and get on with it."

"Keep calm and carry on."

"Like that. After she died I found a little notebook in her night table where she wrote down what I took to be her regrets. They all began with 'I wish I had' and ended with 'and I ask God's forgiveness.'"

Diana's head was nearly on Paris's shoulder. "What kind of regrets, if you don't mind telling me."

Paris breathed in the scent of Diana's shampoo. "The notebook was about fifteen years old. The very first entry was about not marrying my father. That she never tried to find him. He took off after she told him she was pregnant, after all, but she wrote that she'd never known if she'd done the right thing, struggling on her own instead of forcing him to pay child support which meant letting him into my life." Her mother had rarely talked about him and Paris had never felt the urge to track him down either. "One of the latest entries was that she wished she'd looked into her roots earlier. She'd gotten her DNA done. She had no idea she had Central and South American ancestry."

"Ah." Paris could feel Diana smiling. "That's why you mambo so well. And your mum loved Shakespeare, which is another point in her favor."

"She was a voracious reader. Stacks every week from the library. I've always been grateful she didn't name me Tybalt."

"Or Ophelia."

"I am so not an Ophelia."

Diana laughed. "I went to school with an Ophelia and the Good Lord help you if you ever called her that. She went by Gemma."

"I never wanted to go by another name, until Anita Topaz."

"Where did you come up with that?"

"Anita was my mom's middle name. Topaz was her favorite gemstone. That picture wasn't of me, but at least the name was part of me." She added quietly, "I miss her. This morning—Reynard—it reminded me of the day she died. A series of strokes, out of the blue."

Diana nodded and moved closer again, this time snuggling her head on Paris's shoulder. "I'm sorry she's gone."

Paris managed to say, "Thanks," as she battled the usual flush of tears that accompanied thoughts of her mother. They were swaying together and a breeze ruffled through Paris's hair. "What about your mother? What's the best lesson she taught you?"

"I'm not being a copycat," Diana said. "But it's the same thing. Keep calm and carry on. Don't whinge and remember people are counting on you. She's a very decisive woman, my mother. She doesn't tend to revisit her decisions. If she's made a mistake she will simply go about fixing it. No hand wringing. No excuses." Diana's fingers moved rhythmically over Paris's shoulder. "She regretted marrying my father. Will admit that she overlooked his previous two marriages and the stories the ex-wives told because he was a big social step up. His eight-hundred-year-old family line mattered a lot to her. But she didn't hesitate to leave him when he demonstrated that the stories were true. The second time he hit her she wrapped up her broken arm, took his bank book, packed up me and my Paddington Bear, and went to the cop shop to swear out a complaint."

"That was brave."

"I think so. She had some money and a lot of status, which made it easier, but not easy. The older he gets the less effort he makes to hide what an awful man he is. I keep thinking I'll hear some day he's in jail. He ought to be."

"So you took the—what was it? A bowl?"

Diana was so close now that Paris could feel her smiling. "Yes I did. It was very like him, to collect things and then abuse them."

She felt the slight shudder that ran through Diana's body and hugged her, savoring the soft touch of Diana's ear against her jaw.

"It worked out. She remarried, never regretted that. And in the totally weird way of English family names and titles, if you were ever married to an earl, you're a countess for life. Purely a courtesy, but she revels in it."

Paris laughed. The music had stopped but she wasn't going to let go. "Diana?"

"Hmm?"

It was the sunshine and too much sugar, she tried to tell herself. The truth was that Diana fit in her arms, and holding her close, at least for now, filled all the places that she thought she'd never open again. "Can I kiss you?"

"That's funny," she said. She pushed Paris back slightly. "I was just going to ask you that question."

Startled, she asked, "Why?"

"Symmetry." Paris didn't know what to make of the light in Diana's eyes. "I didn't do my part earlier. I think—I think it would be even nicer if I did."

Only two days ago she'd screwed up her courage and embarked on this trip to take control of her future. Not even a month ago she hadn't known Diana existed. Five years ago her soul had been stretched so thin she'd felt see-through. Boss Anxiety was whispering in her ear that her battle with it never went away, could not be defeated, and this woman was unpredictable, lied easily, jaywalked through life, would never be the calm stability that kept Paris safe.

And she was aglow with life and strength, and Paris wanted so much, so very much, to believe the other voice in her head, reminding her that she been hounded by evil yet survived by clinging to her own stories of valor and love, hope and beauty.

Why couldn't her stories come true for her?

All these thoughts whirled through her brain until, standing on tiptoe, Diana kissed her.

It was the touch of hesitation and awkwardness that swept away Paris's doubts and ignited her desire. For all that Diana could look like a woman fully aware of the power of her sensual charms, it was not the kiss of a practiced seductress. It began slightly off center and Diana corrected with a little laugh after their noses bumped. Then there was the soft, vulnerable contact of their lips in full acceptance of intimacy.

Diana cupped a hand behind Paris's neck and Paris surrendered to the dizzying spiral of passion. Her arms went around Diana as their lips parted to allow a deeper exploration.

Her skin came alive, as if she'd left perpetual winter and stepped naked into the blaze of a summer sun. Prickles at the top of her head became an effervescent cascade of tingling that swept down her body. She wanted to feel Diana's skin on hers and had to consciously still her hands before they wandered to the soft curves and swells where she wasn't yet invited.

Diana broke off the contact with a gasp that was halfway between surprise and a laugh. Her gaze was somewhere near

Paris's collar. "That was—that was quite nice. Though I can't claim a lot of experience at this."

"You've never…" Paris wasn't surprised.

"Not seriously. Not…" She finally looked up again, eyes full of light. She pressed her lips lightly to Paris's again. "It didn't feel like this."

Paris ran her hands up Diana's arms. "How does this feel?"

"Like a backflip on a balance beam."

Did she mean frightening? "You can't see where you're going to land?"

Diana was smiling as she shook her head. "Gymnasts don't jump unless they know where they're going to land." Her hand slid slowly down Paris's chest. "If I can find the courage to jump, I know exactly where I intend to land."

The sudden confidence and intent in Diana's eyes took Paris's breath away. She was full of questions again. Not the jumbled frustration she had felt with Diana so often, but the normal questions of confused arousal and attraction. Was this only for tonight? If Diana hadn't really been with a woman before what would she like? Was this about sex or something more? She thought for a moment about Kerry and how naturally inevitable their relationship had seemed, like jigsaw pieces that fit easily and made the expected, pleasing picture.

She and Diana fit, at least it seemed like it, but it wasn't an easy or predictable fit. She had no idea what picture they made together.

She kissed Diana again, this time with a smile. "I think," Paris said softly, "if we don't get something to eat neither of us will survive the rest of the day."

She didn't say, "Let alone the night," but she could see the thought reflected in Diana's eyes, a gleam both shy and bold.

They held hands as they left the park and finally settled on an eatery with a hipster-funk vibe Paris recognized from places tech workers hung out in San Francisco, complete with a long list of craft beers. What had attracted them was the equally long list of vegetarian tapas. Diana led the way to a table on the sidewalk where they could still see the park.

Diana perused the cocktail menu. "I want something frothy with an umbrella in it."

"It sounds delicious. I'm in deep need of an iced tea."

"Do you drink?"

"No. It makes me more anxious. It also doesn't mix well with my meds, if I decide to take something."

Diana regarded her seriously over the top of the menu. "Do you often?"

"Not for a couple of years now. I have lots of tricks I try first." She added with a smile, "Spells and magicks. Eye of newt and toe of frog…"

"Wool of bat and tongue of dog," Diana finished. "Never done *Macbeth*. What kinds of spells do you use?"

"There's the 'Reset Button.' I tell myself if I start over my physical routines to bleed off the stimulus, the anxiety that's built up will have to reset too. Like in a game."

"That makes sense—an interesting way to look at it."

"You mentioned stage fright last night. Do you get it?"

Diana shook her head. "No, and I think that's because of the athletics. Doing a floor exercise, for example. That's a performance in addition to being a showcase of skills. A bell goes off in the venue, and I take a deep breath and go. Since about age nine when I started the junior circuit. There is no time to be afraid. You don't survive in a lot of sports if you can't perform in an instant."

"How high up did you go?"

"I was an Olympic alternate once. Just missed out."

Paris realized it was the first time she'd seen anything like bitterness in Diana's expression. "Nobody got injured or sick?"

"It was not to be." She shrugged, but the loss still seemed poignant to her. "Will you think me an awful person if I confessed to wishing someone would get the flu? Or pull a groin muscle? Nothing permanent," she added hastily. "Only enough to knock them out of the competition."

"I think that's just human nature. You didn't poison anyone." She tried not to make it sound like a question.

Diana burst into laughter. "That's definitely not in my skill set! No, I watched from the sidelines for the entire tournament. The next Olympics was after my injury, so I was all the way out."

I love watching her laugh, Paris thought. "How did it happen?"

"I misjudged. A mental error. I've watched the video so many times and it all came down to the position of my wrist when I started to mount the beam." Diana demonstrated with her arms held out in front of her. "They were supposed to be like this." She made a minute adjustment to her left hand, rotating it slightly clockwise. "They were like this. Yes, it was enough to throw my balance. My hands slipped and my shoulder kept right on going. It was a difficult mount."

"Such a tiny thing."

"So that's how I crashed and burned. What about you?"

Paris raised her eyebrows.

"You crashed and burned in something. You said you left your job and *then* became Anita Topaz on the page. That you moved all the way across this really huge country of yours also says something happened. Relationship breakup?"

It was Paris's turn to give a not very convincing shrug. "That too."

They paused to give the waiter their order of drinks and added street tacos and plantain fritters.

Paris moved her fingertips lightly on the table surface as she summoned up the brief history of the total destruction of her life. "I blogged about video games. Reviews, and stuff like that. One day I decided I was tired of the endless stream of games that used women in violent and degrading ways. How often single shooter games ran through rooms of women who were obviously prostitutes. How killing women in the games was something both the good and bad guys did equally without remorse. How women's suffering was used as art design in a way that men's suffering never was."

"And there was blowback?"

"To put it mildly. I was called a saboteur, a spoilsport out to ruin what was only a game—and those were the mildest attacks.

I got death threats, ones that local police called 'credible.' I got hate mail—email and the real thing. A virus took down my company's servers for a couple of hours. And then they put my address on the web in really bad places—not just my address, but a picture of the outside of my apartment building and tips on how to get past the lobby. Over something that was *only* a game."

Diana covered Paris's hand with her own. "That must have been terrifying."

"It was." Diana's touch was equal parts soothing and arousing. "My girlfriend at the time was also in danger. I mean, when they found out I was gay the bigots joined the misogynists and then the racists showed up. A woman, a homo, and skin not white? Who did I think I was? It was ugly on steroids. They threatened me, my girlfriend, and any of my family they said they'd find. My mom had passed away the year before. Those—" She changed her word choice. "Those idiots made me glad she wasn't around to see it. When I miss her every day."

"None of that is fair or right." There was a mist of tears in Diana's eyes.

"No, and nobody could do anything about it. They were real and they meant what they said."

"Your girlfriend dumped you?"

"Not really. Not the way you mean. She thought I should stay and fight. Fight an enemy I couldn't see. That had thousands of real live fanatics egging each other on. I had no defenders— at least no one brave enough to wade publicly into that kind of testosterone cesspool. Eventually some psycho was going to try to hurt me. I had a panic attack—worst of my life. It wasn't going to get easier or better and I promised myself I would never have one again. I decided to leave, go underground, get myself off the grid completely. She didn't have to do that, and didn't want to. So… It was over. Just two people who suddenly weren't in the same space anymore."

"The appetite may sicken and so die."

Happy for a change of subject, Paris said, "*Twelfth Night* is my favorite."

"Mine too," Diana agreed. "How long ago was all that?"

"Five years, a bit more. I found a new place to live that I liked. I started writing fiction. I entered a contest on a whim and got lucky enough that it felt like the universe evening up the scales a little bit."

She might have added that sitting in a New York café on what seemed very like a real date looking at one of the most fascinating women she'd ever met and contemplating the sound of her breathless whispers—all of that also seemed like the universe finally giving more than it took.

Even if it was just for one night. It would be worth it.

At least that was what she told herself and for the moment, she accepted the lie.

CHAPTER TWENTY-FOUR

Diana was used to noticing how people moved. Weighing their gestures, interpreting their vocal tones. Theater—and her style of thieving—happened by interplay. Cause and response. Nuance and improvisation.

All the many ways she'd spent most of her life working in reaction to other people hadn't prepared her for sitting in a taxi next to a woman she wanted to touch. She had never focused on a gymnastics judge's expression the way she watched Paris's face as she spoke to the driver. She had never followed anyone's line of sight to know what had drawn a smile.

It was all new.

She slid her hand into Paris's as the cab carried them back to the hotel. It had never seemed like an overture to intimacy before now. She hadn't thought about hands—certainly not another woman's hands—as sexual. She had taken notice of how Paris tensed her fingers to lessen her tension. Now she was studying those fingers and feeling just a bit faint.

It wasn't until they were alone in the hotel room, staring at each other with nervous smiles, that Diana felt completely helpless. It had been easier with the few men she'd known. They had had their agenda and got what they wanted. She'd felt removed from their experience and been disquieted by her lack of response. She'd blamed it on her nearly dormant hormones, but maybe she'd been waiting for women. Or at least this woman.

There was nothing dormant about the pulse between her legs and the heat of her ears against her scalp.

"We don't have to do anything," Paris said. "We flirted. No pressure."

Did Paris not want to now? Diana was at a loss to interpret her expression. "Why do you say that?"

"You look scared."

"I am, a little."

"I wouldn't hurt you."

"I know that. I wouldn't hurt you either."

Silence again. Paris had moved toward the window, all the way across the room. The late afternoon sun had dipped behind an adjacent building, leaving the room warm and softly lit.

She laughed and said, "Want to mambo again?"

Paris grinned. "Maybe I should lead this time."

Her coat and bag slid out of her hands onto the floor. *Pretend the bell just went off*, she told herself. With that thought she launched across the room, vaulted the sofa with a one-two landing, spun into Paris's arms and knocked them both onto the fainting couch.

Paris let out a surprised *oof*, but she was laughing. "I have been thinking all along that this thing was conveniently placed."

Diana gazed down into Paris's face, liking how her eyes lightened when she was amused. "This may be my favorite dismount of all time."

Paris's hand was behind her neck then, pulling her down. Their mouths met in a rush of shared air and breathless heat. Paris's hands on her back were strong but suddenly even the thin silk of her blouse felt like too much of a barrier. She managed to get the blouse unbuttoned and the front clasp of her bra undone. Paris sat up, yanked her clothes over her head and all at once their breasts touched. Skin melted to skin.

Paris's tongue and lips at her throat sent a flush over Diana's chest. She'd thought her nipples not particularly sensitive to anything but cold but now they seemed on fire. The brush of Paris's fingertip against one drew a throaty moan from deep inside her that she didn't recognize.

She arched her back in an offer that Paris seemed to understand. Fighting back tears, she clutched Paris's shoulders while the flutter of her tongue and the edge of her teeth reduced her to shivers. How could anything feel so good? How could she survive if she were naked, and Paris touched her in all the places that ached for release?

Her imagination was feverish with visions of Paris's mouth and fingers exploring her. Shoes thumped onto the thick carpet. They struggled with zippers and yanked garments around knees until they were both naked and stretched out alongside each other.

Paris's pelvis was against her thigh. *Oh-oh-oh* echoed in her head.

I know my body, she thought. The memory of her first release move on the bars—her hands hadn't wanted to let go but she made them. She commanded her body, knew every muscle and bone. But she hadn't known her skin could feel *this*.

Paris whispered something. It took Diana a moment to realize it was her name. The tingling of nerves and the fire on her skin were overtaken by a sense of awe. How could she crave something that she'd never desired before? She'd been in locker rooms all her life, in gyms, at tournaments, at school. Had never thought twice about being naked in front of other women. She'd admired, much as she did statues and paintings, the beauty of women's muscles and bones.

How had the sight of Paris's taut nipple transformed her aesthetic appreciation into a stomach-clenching desire to taste her skin? To fall into Paris's body with hunger in spite of fear?

She gave into the desire, bent her head to take one nipple into her mouth, teasing it with her tongue. She heard Paris exhale a moan and she wanted to hear that sound again and again.

"Wait," Paris whispered.

"I'm sorry—was I too rough?"

"No, but let's do this first." Paris pulled them both to their feet, leaving their scattered clothes. "Beds are more comfortable."

"Yes they are." Naked and laughing, Diana moved into Paris's arms. "And step-two-three."

"No, no, no." Paris's stern tone would have been more successful if her lips hadn't been curved in a smile. "Like this. Kiss-step-two-three."

Hands fumbling and teasing, they stumbled their way into Paris's bedroom. A yank of the covers sent turn-down chocolates and pillows flying. Not knowing where the confidence came from, Diana curled onto the crisp, cool sheets and crooked a finger at Paris. "I have a different dance in mind."

Paris's smile faded as she joined Diana on the bed. Brushing her lips against Diana's, she said, "Only if I can lead."

"For now," Diana said as she pulled Paris on top of her.

She thought for several minutes that her skin would peel open or her brain would go off like fireworks. Kisses and soft breath on her shoulders, her stomach, followed by the nip of teeth on the underside of her breast, at her ribs. All causing lights in her head to snap on with a sharp flash that forced her to close her eyes so she could focus on the path of Paris's tongue from her belly button and downward.

She'd read the articles in *Marie Claire* and *Cosmo*. They used phrases like "feels great" and "favorite thing." But now she was recalling passages in Anita Topaz's books when heroines expressed joy and amazement, surrender and strength, and a surprising sense of feeling beautiful and whole when their lovers breathed in their sexual scent. Breathed it in and then opened them with lips and tongue, what Paris was doing to her now.

The intimacy of it made her gasp for breath. She was dissolving and tightening at the same time. She didn't know what to do except welcome so many sensations, all at once. She reached down, hoping to touch Paris somehow, and found the soft brush of Paris's hair. Paris's hand met hers then, and they joined palm-to-palm, fingers clenched until their contact was the only anchor Diana had.

Paris's voice sounded almost broken with need. "I want to go inside you."

"Yes," Diana managed, though she wasn't sure she'd actually spoken.

Paris seemed to have heard her though, because she felt Paris's fingers where her tongue had been. Her legs went limp and a flush of deep pleasure spread over her body. A small portion of her mind marveled that the soles of her feet could feel on fire from the inside. And so did her thighs and her breasts and all the places where Paris was touching her.

Paris was like a magician, working some spell of freedom on her body where the promise of ecstasy came with searing truth. There was no mask to hide behind. Loving this was who she was. An unsuspected and brilliant truth.

Her eyes were full of tears. Not fear, even though she was breaking to pieces. It was that everything she could feel was being touched by Paris from the inside of her, and she was going to cry. If she didn't faint or dissolve or scream first.

Paris was holding her with one arm, murmuring soothing words while her fingers kept working magic deep inside her. Warm lips at her earlobe sent another shock wave over her damp skin.

"You're making me crazy," Paris whispered. "That you love this."

She tried to answer and whatever sound she made brought another whisper.

"Relax. We're in no hurry. We can do this all night."

I won't survive. The idea that she could relax when something so profound was happening seemed ridiculous. But she tried to take a long, deep breath and to her amazement her arms and shoulders melted into the bed. The only part of her that seemed alive was her heart, beating a pulse so strong and steady she could feel it against Paris's fingers as they moved slowly and precisely inside her.

Paris made a sound of deep pleasure. "That's better, isn't it?"

She tried to say yes but Paris kissed her and the taste and scent of herself on Paris's lips stole her breath again. She'd never struggled so hard for words and so she said yes with her tongue and bit gently at Paris's lower lip.

Brown eyes gazed into brown eyes. Diana hoped she never forgot the bell sounding in her heart. Everything fell away but the glow in Paris's eyes. Paris was seeing right into her, and that moment of profound nakedness sent her body into shaking tremors that made Paris cry out.

"Beautiful, beautiful, stay with me," she was saying and Diana realized there was more. She was climbing a ladder and falling at the same time. The only safety was in Paris's eyes and Diana stayed there until her head fell back onto the pillow and she felt utterly undone.

CHAPTER TWENTY-FIVE

She was having a dream she didn't want to leave, but when Paris realized the dream was mostly a replay of the night with Diana, she risked opening her eyes. They had never closed the curtains and bright daylight and blue skies declared that it was early to mid-morning. Closer to breakfast than lunch, Paris decided.

Turning her head slightly she took in the sight of Diana, sheet pulled up over her breasts, hair in a glorious mess and face relaxed in deep sleep. It was a lovely sight.

Don't get used to it, she warned herself.

She carefully edged out of the bed and found the hotel robe for a quick visit to the bathroom adjacent to the suite's living room. Splashing water on her face finished waking her up. She, too, looked relaxed. Why wouldn't she be? Last night... She had nothing to compare it to. Sex had been good with Kerry and the few others before her. Last night had been different in ways her brain hadn't yet sorted out.

The sight of their abandoned clothes sent flutters through her stomach. The memory of Diana's mouth on her body made her dizzy enough that she had to make herself focus on the matter of breakfast. She didn't want to call room service—that could break the spell that had bound them so closely together.

She'd seen a coffeemaker and a selection of single brew cups in the kitchen area. There were some hermetically sealed cheese and crackers in the minibar and a banana in the fruit basket. Breakfast in bed coming up. After a brief panic that there was only decaf, she found a fully leaded dark French roast and brewed two cups. The cupboard held swanky dishes with the hotel's monogram and there was even a tray—perfect.

Diana had shifted position. She was snoring, ever so slightly.

Don't think it's adorable, she told herself, though it was already too late.

She set the tray on the bedside table nearest Diana and fanned coffee steam in her direction. Diana made a soft sound but didn't open her eyes. Paris decided that perhaps a slightly more personal wake up was in order. She edged back into the bed and slid across to nestle against Diana's warm back. After a few moments she felt Diana take a deeper breath.

Brushing her nose against the soft neck, she whispered, "Good morning."

Diana made a murmur of pleasure but then her entire body stiffened.

"What is it?" Fearing Diana was startled or offended by the intimacy, Paris put a few inches between their bodies.

"My back," she croaked. "Give me a minute."

"Can I get Advil or something for you?"

"Do I smell coffee?"

"You do."

"You are a good woman. I'm the Tinman and that's my oil can." Diana took a deep breath and slowly rolled from her side onto her back. "That thing we did?"

"Yes?"

"We shouldn't do that again."

Her stomach flipped over. "Oh."

"I mean the thing when I was—and you were—" Diana made a diagram with her hands. "That thing."

Relieved, Paris grinned at the memory. "I did admire how limber you were. But I can live without it." Lightly, even though it felt like a dangerous question during daylight hours, she asked, "What about the other things?"

Diana turned her head to give Paris a wide grin. "I can do with more of them, sure. And pills."

Paris leaped out of the bed. "Where are they?"

"The white leather bag on the dressing table. With a red zipper."

There was no white bag on the dressing table in Diana's bedroom. "I don't see it."

"Maybe I dropped it into my suitcase," Diana called back.

"Found it!" She lifted it from on top of a pile of silky black undergarments, any one of which would look marvelous on the floor next to the bed.

Diana was sitting up against the pillows looking wan, which quelled Paris's libido for the moment. She handed over the bag and stepped into the bathroom to get a glass of water. By the time she returned, Diana had upended the bag and a jumble of items had fallen across the bed—two bottles of pills, a wrapped set of slender tools Paris took for manicure equipment, and a pouch out of which a small electronic device had tumbled. She couldn't help but pick up the most interesting item—the chestpiece of a stethoscope.

"Playing a doctor lately?" Too late she considered the fact that she might not want to know.

"No that's for…" Diana's pale face was abruptly flushed.

"Seriously?"

"Old-fashioned tools still work in a digital world."

"So sometimes you actually crack open a safe?" The image was laughable. But then this was Diana who excelled at looking like what people wanted her to be and not what she was. Except last night—that hadn't been an act. Or did Paris desperately want that to be so?

"Do you want me to answer that question?"

Paris pushed down a swell of anxiety. This is what life with Diana would be like and she was crazy to be daydreaming about making her breakfast every day. "I still want only the truth."

"A desk drawer with an ordinary lock doesn't take long to open if you know what you're doing. Half the time a credit card will do it." Diana picked up the tools Paris had thought were for manicures. "These are much faster."

Lockpicks, not cuticle utensils. She set the stethoscope back on the bed. "And this?"

"It uses any headphones."

"For safe cracking?" She flexed her fingers against her robe and took a moment to focus on the glass and steel panels of a building several blocks away. She couldn't remember a time when making sure curtains were pulled all the way closed hadn't been part of her nightly routine.

"It has a number of uses." Diana opened one of the bottles and shook two pills into her hand.

Paris handed her the glass and watched as she tossed the pills into her mouth and chased them with a large gulp of water. "I'm sorry about your back."

Diana's face went pink again. "It seemed like a good idea at the time."

"It really did."

Diana speared a piece of cheese. "Thank you for this."

"It was my pleasure."

Diana's gaze was on Paris's hands. She gave herself a little shake and said, "So when you do that—stretch out your fingers like that, it's to help with feeling anxious?"

Suddenly shy, Paris busied herself with peeling and slicing the banana. "Physical response to physical signals. I visualize excess energy shaking off my fingers like raindrops."

"This conversation is making you anxious?"

"Yes."

"And knowing why I open locked doors and that I try hard not to take undue risks doesn't change that?"

"Knowledge isn't that kind of power. Knowing what tends to trigger an episode doesn't get rid of the trigger. It only helps me mitigate or avoid it."

She accepted a slice of banana offered from the tip of Paris's knife. "Like being allergic to bees. You avoid the bees, but you're still going to puff up like a marshmallow in a microwave if you get stung."

"The early stages aren't as obvious as anaphylaxis," Paris said drily. "Like I'm sure people don't know you're in pain from your back most of the time unless you tell them."

The sheets over Diana's breasts slipped slightly. "I stand up as tall as possible when it starts up. If I can I'll sit down."

Paris lightly touched the irregular bump on Diana's shoulder. Her skin was intoxicating to her fingertips—she couldn't get enough.

Diana turned her head to watch Paris's hand. After a deep breath she kissed the back and said, "Breakfast first."

Whatever else the morning brought, that was enough of a promise for now. With a parting caress, she was content to move to the foot of the bed where she could look at Diana and the tray was between them. She wanted breakfast too, and more coffee. She also wanted a shower, preferably with Diana.

What she didn't want was to go home. Sitting cross-legged on the bed, she smiled as Diana gobbled up every bite of food that Paris didn't get to first.

"What's so funny?"

"I like that you like food."

"I do like food. And I know that feeding the machine means the machine gets to work." She popped the last piece of banana into her mouth.

Trying to occupy her eyes with something other than Diana's every move, Paris studied the objects from the white leather bag Diana had swept to one side while they ate. Paris picked up the electronic device that had slipped out of a protective pouch. It wasn't very big—about the size of a portable power pack. There was an on-off switch, a minute numeric keypad and a single row LED display. Less functionality than a handheld video game.

"That is my little friend *Sissone*," Diana offered. "Scissors."

"I'm going to go out on a limb here and say that this is not for cutting paper."

"No." She sighed. "I don't want to—I mean, I don't mind telling you what that is. I'm not sure you want to know."

"I do. I'm telling myself it's an academic curiosity."

Diana cocked her head, then pointedly looked down at her naked-under-the-sheets body and then at Paris in her robe. "Sure. Academic."

"That's not what I meant, and you know it."

"I certainly learned a lot last night."

"So this is academic for you?"

"It was definitely something we both seemed to have needed."

There was no point in arguing about the obvious. "Are you trying to pick a fight?"

"Yes. Because this is anything but academic."

"I know. I'm trying to lie to myself in what is a very odd situation."

"Because anxiety?"

"Because human." Because she felt like her heart was on a bull's-eye and Diana was a huntress with a full quiver of arrows.

They stared at each other for a long minute. Though she was as usual feeling completely in the dark about what Diana was actually thinking, Paris's heart was pounding.

"I don't know how to do this," Diana finally said. "So I'll show you what I do know how to do."

She picked up the lockpicks and *Sissone* and threw back the covers. Paris followed her into the other bedroom. Diana fished the hotel bathrobe out of the closet and shrugged into it. Pulling the door farther open she exposed the front of the small safe set onto the middle shelf.

"Go ahead and lock it," she said.

Paris punched in a code and shut the small door. The mechanism whirred and the display announced it was locked.

The LED display on *Sissone* was lit. Diana pressed it above the keypad on the safe and less than a second later the mechanism whirred again. The display read, "Unlocked."

"Holy crap," Paris said.

"It sends a series of common signals that tell the chip inside that the matching unlock code has been entered."

"So anyone in the hotel can open the safe in a second?"

"Anyone who can afford one of these. Which was expensive. I mean sports car expensive. Maybe not an Italian one, but nearly. It also works just as fast on many types of hotel doors."

"So in movies where they have their high-tech gadget spinning through all the possible codes—"

"They're doing it the long, hard way. But it's not as if I'm a tech wizard. I had the money."

Paris said exactly what she was thinking. "I'm glad you're using your powers for good."

Diana laughed. "Well, sometimes it's to satisfy not so noble feelings. If *schadenfreude* was a deadly sin I'd be in trouble."

"Kind of like using the dark magic of your enemies against them."

"That's karma."

"Karma takes too long." Paris slipped an arm around Diana and pulled her close. "I know that in one of my books the characters would head right back to bed at this point."

"I noticed it didn't take much for them to do that."

"I really would like a shower."

"Preferably not alone, I hope."

"Definitely not alone."

Diana spun out of her arms, losing her robe in the process. "But no hanky-panky until there's hot water."

There was a great deal of soap and shampoo put to proper use before suds proved useful for a foamy massage. Diana's fingers were strong and firm as they worked their way up Paris's spine, then she rinsed it off and opened another bottle. "Moisturizer for in the shower. Great stuff."

"If it makes my skin feel like yours, I'm all for it." Paris braced herself against the shower wall, her nipples like rocks in spite of the steam and warm water. Diana's palms smoothed the lotion across Paris's shoulders and down her arms, over her ribs and across her belly. It didn't seem like any part of her was out of Diana's reach.

The feeling of Diana's small breasts against her back was welcome, but the moment lasted only long enough to realize that Diana was sliding down to her knees. A kiss punctuated with a nibble at the base of her spine sent shivers shooting through her arms and she turned around to see Diana gazing at her with an undeniable hunger. She spread her legs and hoped they wouldn't fold up—and they nearly did when Diana buried her face between them.

Her moan of pleasure echoed from the damp walls—then Diana coughed.

And spluttered, and burst out laughing. "I got water up my nose. I'm sorry—" She clutched Paris's knees with a loud wheeze.

Paris's frustration dissolved into laughter as she helped Diana stand up. "Sex in the shower is fraught with peril."

"Oh dear lord!" She snorted and made herself laugh again. "Such an elegant woman I am."

"I have to say—there's a reason I prefer beds."

"Well, let's go with that idea." She reached for a towel as Paris turned off the water.

A few minutes later, enjoying the as yet unrumpled sheets of Diana's bed, Paris asked, "Where were we?"

"I think what really matters is where I was." Diana knelt between Paris's legs and used both hands to caress the inside of her thighs. "This is where I want to be."

Diana didn't stop this time, devouring Paris with a lusty urgency that drew a long groan of pleasure from a place so deep Paris had forgotten it was inside her. Diana's damp hair was cool against her thighs but there was an untamed fire burning across her skin. She gave herself to it until she was completely consumed.

When her ragged breathing finally calmed she realized their fingers were intertwined. She tugged on Diana's hand and Diana scrambled into her arms, cheeks flushed, hair tousled and looking pleased with herself.

"Is it always like that?"

"It's the goal." Paris pulled her close with what strength she had left.

She was content to doze, but even so, she knew it wouldn't last. Sooner or later housekeeping would tap on the door and eventually the hotel would call asking if they intended to check out. Her brain wished life had a freeze frame, just for a moment like this.

CHAPTER TWENTY-SIX

Diana startled awake at a knock on the door of the suite. The delicious dozing state slipped away as she heard the door open.

"Housekeeping," a woman's voice called.

Paris mumbled, "Uh-oh," and pulled the covers over her, which left Diana naked.

Diana quickly called out, "Could you come back, please?"

"Of course, ma'am." The door shut and all was quiet except for Diana's pounding heart.

Paris stuck her head out from under the covers. "All clear?"

"Yes, and thanks for leaving me *déshabillé*." She grabbed a handful of sheet and at least covered her lap, even though the housekeeper was gone. Paris grabbed them back and they rolled into a happy tug-of-war that ended with Paris behind her and her hand between Diana's legs. She buried her face in the nearest pillow and reveled in the feel of Paris's body alongside hers. Then the spiral of pleasure took over and she said yes to all of Paris's whispered questions. Yes, and more.

* * *

We can't fall asleep again, she thought some time later, though they were in danger of doing exactly that. It was good that Paris's eyes were closed, however. Otherwise she'd see how hungrily Diana was looking at her hands and they would both be lost again. But she couldn't stop looking at them. They were instruments of extreme pleasure and intense intimacy—and they were too close to her for rational thought.

She needed to be rational. She wasn't here to have an affair and neither was Paris. She was no longer here to take back the Chumash Hammer. It was time to go home, enjoy her brother's wedding and be Diana with her family again. After that… She pushed the thought away.

Outside the window there was blue sky streaked with pale clouds and the promise of sunshine where tall buildings didn't block out the light. She didn't want to leave this hotel room, not even the bed. Not if it meant distance between her body and Paris's.

"I think we have to get up." Diana kept her gaze on the window.

Paris sighed and the bed shifted as she got to her feet. "More coffee?"

"Okay." Don't look, Diana told herself, but she couldn't help but watch as Paris left the bedroom. "I should start packing, I suppose. I have more stuff than you do."

She caught a glimpse of Paris in the kitchen area, standing still with her arms held out slightly from her sides. She flexed her fingers and shook her arms before beginning the process of making more coffee.

Goodness, her backside was sexy and firm and…

Focus, you twit! Accept reality, Diana told herself. Being around you makes her anxious. You're a trigger and not good for her. Who you are and what you do isn't compatible with what she needs. You have chemistry in bed, and that's all it is. You've both had your fun. You've had a time of self-discovery. Now it's time to move on.

She kept repeating this litany as they raided the increasingly depleted minibar. Cashews and dried cranberries filled a few of the empty spots in her stomach.

"You look worried." Paris finished a packet of crackers that came with peanut butter and jelly spread.

"I've been thinking." Desperately, recklessly thinking, she could have added.

Paris narrowed her gaze, but she was smiling. "Should I be worried?"

"Not sure. I, well, I'm wondering if we might get somewhere by dropping off a note for Reynard. Get well or something. Since we were there."

Paris made a peanut butter-muffled sound that might have been, "Hell no" or "You're barmy."

"And write in it something like 'get better soon, can't wait to talk about the movie with you.' Wouldn't that say don't call me unless it's about that?"

Paris swallowed. "You'd have to get in all that gear again. Be Anita Topaz again."

We wouldn't part ways for another couple of hours, Diana thought. She was willing to do nearly anything for a few more hours. "I don't mind, not at all. It seems like basic courtesy. Given what happened. Yesterday. In the restaurant." Even to her own ears it sounded weak. There was no reason for Paris to agree.

"Okay."

Diana blinked. "You're sure?"

Paris was staring at a point above Diana's head. "Courtesy, and I get that reminding him about the movie is a good thing."

Don't analyze this, Diana thought. "We can get checked out of here and leave our bags with the bellman."

"Have a real lunch," Paris added.

"Yes please. Okay. Well then."

"Sure."

"All right. I'll pack."

"Me too."

"Stop that."

"Stop what?"

Diana decided that Paris was too good at raising just one eyebrow. "Standing there all naked and edible."

Paris pointedly looked Diana up and down. "Said the kettle to the pot."

"We don't have time. And don't say 'the lady doth protest too much.'"

"And yet, you just did."

Diana stuck her hands out in the universal crossed-fingers-warding-off-vampires gesture. "Keep your distance." She scampered for her own bedroom absolutely certain she could hear Paris's eyes rolling.

CHAPTER TWENTY-SEVEN

"I remember there was a drugstore on the corner near the RMG building," Paris said. "We could get a note card there. Something blank and you could write flowery whatevers."

"You should write it," Diana suggested. "Keep the handwriting consistent with whatever they have." She shot a glance at the cab driver, who seemed oblivious to them.

Paris nodded absently. "Sure. Let's get the card and then decide what to write over lunch."

Diana's stomach growled and she saw Paris smile. "Every time you say lunch my stomach goes into flips of joy."

The same response happened every time she looked at Paris, to the point of absurdity. Paris had chosen to wear the tailored suit again, and it was delicious and devastating. It's all chemistry, she told herself. As they browsed for a greeting card she was reminded of when she was a little girl and the nanny would blow soap bubbles after tea to coax her charges to run about the garden. William had delighted in popping them while Florence had been too small to do more than fall on ones that made it to the ground.

Diana had played a different game, maybe because she was older. She'd let one float onto the palm of her hand and see how long it would stay there. Could she walk all the way across the garden with it? Could she carry it inside? What would keep it safe?

The tiny drugstore was a long way from the garden at Mote Hall but she was trying to do the same thing, wasn't she? They were in a magic bubble and she was trying to preserve it for as long as possible.

But all bubbles eventually pop, she reminded herself.

"How about these?" Paris handed over a three-pack of classic white cards with a red and purple geometric pattern on the front that, when held further away, became a flower.

"Perfect I think. Exactly what Anita would choose."

"There's a deli next door." Paris sounded somewhat desperate. "Lunch rush might be about over."

"Sounds great."

They fussed together with a self-check machine, feeding in bills and throwing in odd change until it was enough. A scant minute later they were sliding into a booth. The service was blissfully fast which made Diana's stomach happy. But it meant that the meal would end too quickly when she wanted it to last the rest of the day and all night.

"What's your favorite type of lunch?" Paris took another large bite of her egg salad sandwich and made a noise that sounded very similar to ones she'd made this morning. "This is killer good."

She gestured at her chopped salad with spicy pecans and bits of what claimed to be Irish blue cheese, though there wasn't enough for her to tell if that was true. "I like this a lot. Promise you won't judge?"

"I already know that grilled cheese and tomato soup make you drunk."

She had to smile at that. "If I'm raiding the kitchen for just myself, I eat olives, pickles, and hummus. All together."

"Adventurous. But then I knew that." They shared a goofy smile.

Paris abruptly asked, "Is your mother really a countess?"

Diana wondered what prompted the question. "She gets to put it on stationery and calling cards. Bricks and benches all over Maidstone, Mote and Leeds proclaim it. But it's a courtesy title, like mine."

Paris's eyebrows shot up. "Like yours?"

"I'm the daughter of an earl. I don't really like using it, but technically I'm *Lady* Diana Beckinsale."

"It suits you."

Diana tried not to stare as Paris licked mustard off a fingertip. "How so?"

"You act like a lady."

Paris's cheeks abruptly flushed, and Diana was sure her cheeks were red too. This morning she had been voracious and loud. "In public," she said. They grinned at each other like loonies.

Finally, Paris continued, "Plus it has an elegant ring to it. Mellifluous."

"*Doctor* or *admiral* would sound good too, but I'd have to actually earn those." She frowned at her salad. "It's the only thing of his I've kept, mostly because it makes Mum happy to call me that, especially when I'm in trouble. My grandmother left him out of her will to the extent that she could."

"You ended up with emeralds from her, right?"

"And a flat in London that an agent leases out for me." Paris had said she wanted the truth. "I have lots of bonuses from birth, none of my doing. I enjoy it, but I'm also trying to leverage it in a way other people can't."

"Because that's who you are."

She speared a grape tomato to add it to her bite of rocket and pecan. "Can I ask you a weird question?"

"Sure."

"If you were out walking in the wood and you came upon a train track, not connected to any others, just one all by itself, what would you do?"

Paris cocked her head. "A lone train track?" She narrowed her eyes as if expecting a trap of some kind. "I'd cast a spell to detect enchantments and curses."

"I mean in real life."

"So do I. It's very suspicious, a train track by itself. I mean, if you came upon a flying carpet in the woods, you'd ask a few questions before you got on." She gave Diana a sidelong glance. "Wouldn't you?"

"Sure, of course." She didn't even convince herself with her answer—she'd get right on that flying carpet and ask questions later. "Anything else?"

"Walk up and down the rails to see if I could balance, maybe with a book on my head. I have a backpack, right? So there'd be a book." Paris's expression was the picture of innocence. "But first I'd put my ear to the rail to make sure there weren't any trains coming. Just to be safe."

Diana burst out laughing though part of her wanted to cry.

They were on their third refills of water when Diana ran out of ways to keep lunch from ending. The card was written, addressed to Reynard care of Heather.

It was Paris who finally said, "I guess we should see about Storming the Office Building."

"Storming?"

"We're on a quest to deliver this." For the first time since they'd ordered, Paris's fingers were lightly tapping on the tabletop.

"I think we can talk our way in without actual storming needed."

Paris didn't dispute the assertion, and that was exactly what Diana did. She put all her charm front and center, telling the beefy guard that it was a follow-up to the appointment she'd had on Friday.

"I see you right here in the log." He tapped at the screen and added with a smile, "And I remember you."

She heard Paris stifle a snort.

"I can't think why today's appointment isn't listed. We're to meet with people in the media group's offices this time, not the publisher's. About a movie."

"They'll sort it out upstairs. Have a good meeting." He turned to help the next person in the queue.

They said nothing in the crowded elevator though Diana was acutely aware that Paris was taking long, deep breaths. She pressed the button for the top floor and suppressed a wave of guilt. For a few more hours with her she was putting Paris through this completely unnecessary visit, without a thought to how it would make Paris feel.

Full of regret, she opened her mouth to suggest they forget about it, but the doors opened and the flow of bodies carried them out of the car. Like the floor where the publishing house was situated, the decor was cold steel and silver light with touches of RMG corporate blue. Instead of large photos of their media celebrities, there was only Reynard himself smiling over the reception area like a benevolent monarch. The facing wall was also Reynard, an enlargement of a black-and-white photo taken decades ago in a college football uniform spattered with mud.

There was no forgetting where they were.

Paris's fingers were flexing against her slacks.

Diana took her own deep breath and approached the exceedingly thin young woman at the desk. "I was hoping to get a moment with Heather Reynard."

"Do you have an appointment?"

"No, but we were at lunch with her and Mr. Reynard yesterday at Salazar's when he was taken ill. I'd like to pass on a card to wish him well. Have you heard any updates?"

The receptionist, who had seemed ready to deliver a well-rehearsed speech about the necessity of appointments, said instead, "He's holding his own, we've been told." She swiped across the thin tablet she'd picked up from the desk. "Lunch yesterday? You're Anita Topaz?"

Modern connectivity to the rescue. "Yes, and my assistant Ellis."

"One moment."

The receptionist had just pushed back from her desk when Heather herself appeared from an adjacent hallway, saying into her phone, "It'll be several weeks. Route everything on that through me until you hear otherwise."

She stopped walking when she saw Diana and Paris, dropping the phone into her suit jacket pocket. "Anita, Ellis—I've been meaning to ask someone for your contact info all day. You were so helpful yesterday. I don't know how to adequately say thank you."

Diana smiled her thanks at the receptionist before shaking hands with Heather.

"We wanted to leave this with you." Diana held out the card, which Heather tucked into her inner breast pocket with a distracted smile. "And ask how he's doing."

"Let's talk in here." Heather led them down the opposite corridor and into the office at the very end. Diana immediately knew it wasn't Heather's office—the distinct scent of Reynard's aftershave was in the air, along with leather and polished wood. There was a jaw-dropping view, a match to the one from Friday's conference room, and from even higher up.

"I've been escaping in here to get space to think," Heather said. "My office is on the other end, and full of people today."

Every surface in the expansive office was pristine except for the desk and the credenza behind it. A stack of file folders threatened to topple off one corner of the desk, but were held in place by the lamp propped against them. Minute dust circles suggested that items on the credenza had been pushed to one side to make room for a laptop currently displaying a stock market ticker. Heather pushed the jumble even further to make room for the file folders in her hand, not seeming to notice that a heavy fountain pen on the other end tumbled onto the floor.

"It's been a rough day," Diana observed.

Heather used both hands to pull her reddish-gold hair into a ponytail for a moment before letting it sweep back into place. "It has. He's still in ICU. The doctor who gave him the electroshock was right. It was sudden cardiac arrest. He was conscious this morning and told me if I wanted him to remain calm I had to get in here and hold down the fort. Our stock was diving. But it stabilized before the close of trading."

"I'm sure in large part to your efforts."

Heather nodded absently, as if the compliment didn't really penetrate. Dressed in a razor-sharp corporate gray suit and a blue poplin shirt open at the neck to display a simple gold cross on an equally plain gold chain, she was not quite the towering presence she had been at the restaurant. Diana realized the degree to which Heather could project a vivid persona and turn it off again, a personality nuance that her father completely lacked.

Diana expected Heather to politely thank them again, then indicate that she had business, and they would just as politely take their leave. Instead, Heather led them to a grouping of chairs around a coffee table, settling into one that faced the door. Lines of worry and fatigue became more obvious.

Paris and Diana sank down into their own chairs almost in unison.

"Would either of you like coffee?" Heather gestured at the sideboard. "There's all kinds."

"We just finished lunch, but thank you," Paris said.

"I'm glad you stopped by. Really, I don't remember much except watching my dad's face and praying. But I know you were there and thank you, it helped."

Paris answered, "Anyone would have done the same. The real heroes were the doctor and her husband."

"Yes. Such incredible luck. They were both so good in the ambulance. I was kind of in shock. They were on their first date in months." She added distractedly, "I made a note somewhere to send them a spa certificate or something."

Diana wasn't sure that Heather wasn't still in shock. "I'm glad they were there."

"Artie brought me dinner at the hospital. It seemed wrong to be hungry."

"The world doesn't stop turning," Paris said. "Don't blame yourself that you can't make it stop."

"Now I remember." Heather's gaze sharpened on Paris, then went to Diana and back to Paris. She thumbed open her phone and tapped in a few characters. She turned it around and set it on the table between them. "I looked you up. This is you, right?"

A younger, smiling Paris gazed out of the phone, a photograph obviously from before the world had kicked her in the teeth. She was relaxed and carefree, with her arm around another woman. Her eyes were full of light and humor. Their matching T-shirts said "Gamers for Equality."

If I'd known her then… Diana had no idea how to finish the thought. All she knew was that she ached to touch that face, and hold that Paris close when the storm hit. And do anything to keep her safe.

Paris let out a half-strangled gasp.

"I had someone dig out the contract this morning," Heather went on. "I always wondered what happened to Paris Ellison and now I know."

Diana's blood chilled in her veins. She had no script for this.

"So the real question is…" Heather picked up the phone and turned to Diana. "*She's* Anita Topaz. So who are you?"

CHAPTER TWENTY-EIGHT

Their ruse had been discovered. That it wasn't a crime didn't change the sirens ripping through the nerves in Paris's stomach and throat. Diana's red suit turned gray. The skies outside went from blue to white. She told herself not to gasp for breath. *Do not have a panic attack. You are not in danger.*

"How did—" It was the most Paris could manage before her throat closed up again.

"I thought I recognized you yesterday. The name wasn't quite right, but it bothered me later when I was desperate for something to think about other than ICU monitors. I pushed hard for our commentators to dig into GamerGate, and you were another casualty. Your social media accounts were gone, but there's always the Wayback Machine." She glanced again at Diana. "So…?"

"I'm what people want to see." Diana's tone was matter-of-fact. "Paris really doesn't want public contact. If you know her story, I'm sure you can understand that. She was feeling very pressured by Reynard House Publishing, with a lot at stake for her."

"So you're like a ghost persona?" Heather sat back in the chair. "That's quite a partnership."

Paris swallowed hard and blew out a carefully controlled breath. "We didn't set out—"

She heard the door behind them open and turned to see a young man in shirtsleeves beckoning.

"I'll be right back," Heather said. After a short conversation, she followed him out of the room.

Paris bolted out of the chair to pace. *Foul word!*

"I think we're okay," Diana said quickly. "She doesn't seem upset."

"I know. That doesn't help right now." *Don't have a panic attack.* She bounced on her toes to bleed more energy as she walked to the far corner of the office where bookcases flanked a smiling Ronald Reynard, then back around the conversation cluster of chairs to the desk in the corner, which enjoyed an amazing vista from the floor-to-ceiling windows. Seeing outside helped. *Deep breath, shake it out.*

She circled the office again, counting the chairs and then the wall hangings to occupy her brain. She was grateful that Diana was being still and quiet. "I need a minute or two. Whatever you do, please don't tell me to calm down."

"I wouldn't—won't. I'm sorry, this was my idea and now we're blown."

"We were blown yesterday, we just didn't know it." Paris did another circuit of the room, forcing herself to move more slowly while she took steady breaths. The sky slowly deepened to blue again and Diana's suit bloomed back to cherry red. "I had no idea Heather recognized me yesterday."

"She seemed very comfortable with you."

"I was comfortable with her. We're both butch, we like gaming..." She stopped at the window again and focused her eyes on the distance while she slowly counted to ten. Her heart rate was settling. Boss Anxiety had set off a flare, that was for certain, but it wasn't going to burn the house down.

She refocused on the window glass and could see Diana in the reflection. She'd picked up a magazine from the coffee table and was idly thumbing through it. It was reassuring to see her calmly sitting there, not wringing her hands or trying to assert that there was nothing to be anxious about.

Another deep breath, possibly the last one she'd need. She smoothed her shirt front and looked down to pick a bit of lint off her trouser leg.

And that's when she saw it.

A signed baseball had rolled almost out of sight under the credenza. Next to it on the floor was a small, framed photo and a Montblanc fountain pen. A diamond cufflink—she glanced and saw its mate still on the credenza. Looking back at the floor she studied again a small hammer not even as long as her shoe. She'd nearly stepped on it.

The bone that formed the handle was a stark white and beautiful against the crudely faceted obsidian that formed the hammer's head.

She realized two things all at once. That Diana wasn't looking for it. She'd been telling the truth about no longer wanting to try to take it. Today's impromptu visit wasn't about that, even though Paris had half thought it must be. Otherwise, why had Diana made such flimsy excuses to make another visit here?

And she could see what Diana was trying to protect. It was delicate and small and didn't belong in this steel-and-glass tower. The idea that someone like Reynard would use it as an accessory to glorify corporate power was repellent.

She glanced into the window glass. Diana was reading or seemed to be.

In one smooth motion, Paris picked up the hammer and tucked it into the long pocket inside her suit jacket. It was heavier than it looked. The obsidian head made a slight bulge in her jacket but otherwise it didn't show.

Diana would know where to send it.

She thought she ought to feel guilty, but she didn't. Perhaps that was why she didn't feel anxious about it either. She returned to the chair she'd vacated, feeling calm given that she had stolen property in her pocket. She had no idea how much it was worth to the people who thought it ought to be for sale.

Diana closed the magazine and set it back onto the coffee table. "Better?"

"Yes. Thank you for letting me be." Paris jumped a little when the door opened again, half expecting security guards who'd seen her pocket the hammer via hidden cameras. But it was only Heather, looking out of sorts. It was time for them to leave, and not only because Paris was starting to worry about hidden cameras and what her mother would have thought.

"I apologize," Heather said. "It's that kind of day."

"We should be going," Diana said. "We've taken too much of your time."

"I have a few more questions, if you don't mind." Heather reclaimed her seat, elbows on her knees. "So you're the face of Anita Topaz. But Paris Ellison does the writing."

Paris nodded. "Is that a problem for you?"

Heather's expression was thoughtful. "It's unorthodox."

Diana said quickly, "My goal was to get her through this meeting and keep the door open on the idea of a feature film. That *was* one of the agenda items."

A sharp knock on the door made Heather snap, "What now?"

The receptionist meekly poked her head in. "I'm sorry Ms. Reynard, but the hospital is trying to reach you."

Going pale, Heather patted her pockets until she found her phone. She glanced at the display and said, "Damn." She appeared to have forgotten anyone else was in the room as she put the phone to her ear.

The conversation was short and Paris knew what the news was before the phone slid out of Heather's hand.

Whatever her feelings about Reynard were, she knew too well what Heather was feeling. The numbness, the desperate wish to turn back the clock, and the unfounded hope that somehow it was all a mistake. They'd called the wrong person, they'd mixed up the patients. Then the splintered acceptance that it was true and irrevocable.

"I have to call Artie," Heather said through stiff lips before dissolving into tears. "Why did he make me come here today?"

"I'm so sorry, Heather. So very sorry." Paris wasn't sure how to offer comfort or if it was even wanted. She snatched a couple of tissues from the box on the coffee table and pressed them into Heather's hands. Heather clasped them to her eyes, but they didn't muffle the keen of grief. She slid out of the chair onto her knees and would have folded into a fetal ball had Paris not offered a shoulder for support.

She heard Diana behind her telling the receptionist to keep people out for a few minutes. Heather was rocking in Paris's arms. Paris pushed back her own memories of grief and focused instead on Heather's labored breathing. She gave every appearance of being a strong woman, but even strong women were once little girls who had loved a parent unconditionally.

It was a few minutes before Heather abruptly collected herself. She pushed Paris away and mopped at her face with fresh tissues. "I'm sorry."

"Don't be."

Heather gathered herself up enough to shakily return to the chair, head in her hands. "I can't believe it. I can't believe I let him talk me into coming here. I wasn't there."

Paris squeezed her hand. "You were doing what he thought mattered. I lost my mom suddenly, but I know it's useless to say now that you'll be able to move on."

"I know that and I don't believe it either." She tried for a smile but it didn't make it to her eyes. Turning her head away she said, "Where's my phone?"

Paris found it on the floor and handed it over. Heather grabbed her hand and held on tight. So she perched on the arm of the chair and tried not to listen, which was impossible. It sounded like a prerecorded greeting.

"What a time to go to voice mail. It's—" Her voice shook as she said after the beep, "It's bad—have a look at the news. Don't call back, just come to my office. As soon as you can."

The door opened to admit an older woman even shorter than Diana. Her short kinked hair was beautifully white against her black skin and she had eyes Paris immediately compared to lasers. She glanced at Diana, then at Heather's hand clutching

Paris's. Her expression said, "Who the hell are you people?" as she approached Heather protectively.

"Is there something I can do for you, Heather?"

Heather swallowed hard. "I guess—our shares are going slam down in the morning. Could you get someone into the press office to set up a twenty-four-seven liaison chain? Priority response to any financial reporter, business as usual, no major changes in store. You know the drill."

"Already done."

"Sorry. Of course it is. Thank you. This is Paris Ellison. She was at lunch with us yesterday." She squeezed Paris's hand but didn't let go. "You know her better as Anita Topaz."

The woman nodded an acknowledgment. "Claudia Lewis, corporate finance."

"Sorry," Heather said again. "I'm not tracking."

"You don't need to. Leave the worry about the stock price and financial news to me. Worry about more important things." Claudia glanced again at Heather's grasp on Paris's hand.

Paris wasn't sure what the long silence meant, then Heather took another tissue and wiped her eyes. "Would you find my assistant and send him in here. And I need you to personally tell security to let Artie into the building. There are…new rules."

"As you say." Claudia's eyes sparkled with sudden tears. "It will be my pleasure."

After the door closed behind Claudia, Heather rested her head against Paris's arm. Her breathing still had a ragged edge. "Huh."

"Did you need something?"

"So this is what freedom feels like."

Paris hadn't a clue what Heather was talking about so she looked to Diana for an explanation.

Diana was gone.

CHAPTER TWENTY-NINE

The genuine need to visit the water closet was primarily why Diana had quietly stepped out of Reynard's office. The hush over the outer office area was immediately noticeable, and a little creepy. The ceaseless chiming, chirping, and buzzing of phones nearly drowned out murmuring voices.

An ashen-faced woman silently pointed her toward the ladies' room where she used the toilet, delaying as she washed her hands, tidied her hair, and added a touch of lipstick. She couldn't make herself leave.

This much was true—Paris was a better person than Diana would ever be. No matter how Paris felt about Reynard, she had offered human comfort to his daughter when Diana had mutely stood there, trying not to show that she didn't care that the man was dead. She hadn't wanted him dead, but she couldn't find a tear to shed about it. He'd pawed her and leered, and used his company as a hunting ground for women. How many other women had found him on the doorstep of their hotel rooms uninvited? What did it say about her as an actress that she couldn't even pretend basic courtesy?

It wasn't as if anyone had looked to her for a response, though. Heather had looked only as far as Paris.

It was that image of Paris and Heather that kept her from going back. They shared some kind of communal world, and had, somehow, recognized each other in a way Diana didn't understand. She could only envy it as she stood outside looking in.

She didn't realize she was crying until the tears spilled down her cheeks. She didn't know why she was crying, either. Was this what desire and affection and attraction meant? Those were supposed to be good things—so why was her heart twisting in her chest?

The mirror was merciless. There was no escaping her increasingly red nose and puffy eyes. Like she had yesterday, after the final realization that she was deeply, wholly attracted to Paris, she searched her face for some kind of recognition.

Anita Topaz stared back at her.

Anita's mascara was starting to run.

There were no witnesses as she worked the Anita Topaz wig off her scalp and scrubbed away the glue. Wouldn't it help to see herself without the mask? Paris would never look in the mirror and not recognize herself, would she? She knew who she was. Heather knew who she was. That funny bartender Lisa absolutely knew who she was. All Diana knew how to do was *pretend* to be other people.

The wig went into the trash, followed by the false eyelashes and blue contact lenses. She scrubbed her face with the rough brown paper towels until her freckles stood out.

Not that she looked any less a stranger when she was done. What on earth did she have to offer Paris? Good sex? Endless anxiety? Sooner or later the former wasn't going to be enough to make the latter worth it. Diana was a trigger Paris should avoid. That didn't add up to anything that could last.

A highlight reel of the numerous activities of last night and this morning ran through her head. She wanted all of that, again. Plus that moment this morning—only this morning—when she'd opened her eyes and saw Paris smiling at her, and smelled coffee, and felt a lingering satisfaction in every tranquil muscle and bone in her body. And thought that she was home, even though it was a strange hotel room in a country not her own.

She's good for me, but I'm not good for her. She was going to end up being another curse that broke Paris's spirit, another shadow in what should have been happy, carefree eyes. What use would Paris ever have for someone who had no training in anything except a sport she could no longer perform? Who dabbled in acting, and stole things because she'd found a way for two wrongs to make a right?

Another long, unhappy look made her turn her back to the mirror. She had no reason to linger. The play was over. The bubble was going to pop now or later.

Now was better for Paris.

She fished out another of the blank note cards they'd bought this morning and found a pen. In the reception area she took a seat long enough to use a magazine as a writing surface. The words were inadequate and so was the *sorry* she added at the end. With the envelope addressed to Paris care of Heather, she gave it to the distracted, frantic receptionist.

"I'd appreciate it—when Ms. Reynard is available. My friend is helping her and I need to leave."

"Surely." Any other day the receptionist might have realized that the woman in the red linen suit didn't look the same, but she hardly glanced at Diana's face.

The big city street was an assault to her ears. This morning she'd felt at home with her Anita Topaz mask providing armor against the furious waves of lorries and cars, buskers and tourists. What had Paris called it? A Storming the Office Building quest? She had nothing left for it now.

By the time she reached the hotel she felt battered and bewildered. This morning's bellman didn't recognize her, but when she offered up the claim tickets he released her bags. She was grateful that ordinary Diana was apparently quite forgettable.

She sat down in the lobby long enough to rifle through her carry-on for her passport and iPhone. She had no reason to care now about anyone being able to track her whereabouts. She thought for a long moment of simply moving uptown to a new hotel and hiding out from the world and herself for a few days. But that would be impossible. Her mother would not forgive her for missing her final dress fitting and the rehearsal dinner. William and Millie didn't deserve her to go No Show. There was a wedding and a life waiting.

A half-life. A life where she spent most of her time plotting out her next adventure. She would leave because staying in one place and getting to know the stranger in the mirror was hard work she didn't want to do.

It was the only life she had to go back to.

She took the train from Penn Station to JFK and searched for a flight to Heathrow. She ignored the days of built-up communications and notifications on her iPhone, eager to update her about events and news. None of it really mattered. There were a couple of shorthand texts from her brother and sister, a typically imperiously loving text from her mother and an email from the trustee of her grandmother's estate wanting a signature at her convenience. She sent a group message to the family that she was on her way home and would see them by morning. Oh, and she was so happy to be joining the pre-wedding fun.

The high, arching terminals at JFK were echoing and cold. At every commotion or sound of hurried footsteps she looked up and of course it was never Paris. It would never be Paris. She'd said she was sorry in the note but Paris wasn't going to forgive her for running away.

She was running away because she was scared and useless and at the end of all her dreams she was never quite worthy of the magic almost in her grasp. She'd been on the edge of glory before and she didn't need the pin in her shoulder to remind her how quickly dreams turned into devastation. Piling on top was the brutal assessment that Paris needed and deserved more— and better—than Diana could ever offer her.

* * *

She had taken the first available seat of any kind, and was hardly unhappy that it was in Business Class. She pushed her seat into sleeping position, turned her back to the cabin and lay awake for the entire flight trying to stop the voice in her head repeating the same questions over and over: She was doing the right thing, so why did it hurt so much?

Clearing customs was simple. She hadn't even found the pecan candy Millie liked, so she had nothing to declare. The private car service the family used was waiting at the usual place. The sun was coming up as they left the parking garage. Paris was probably home by now unless she'd had a reason to stay another night in New York. Maybe Heather had asked her to stay over for moral support—that was really unlikely, but it didn't stop her brain from making it *seem* possible.

If Paris fell into Heather's social circle there would be many eligible women interested in her, starting with Heather. That other women would find Paris attractive—now *that* was wholly plausible. Paris would easily find someone else. Paris would forget all about her. It was for the best.

She was going to arrive home with horribly red eyes at this rate.

Traffic on the M25 gradually thinned. Thankful to be heading away from London during the morning commute, she tried to doze, but instead gazed out the window at passing familiar sights. The signs of spring grasses and plowed rows along the hills of Surrey should have made her glad to be home, but even the thought of real English peas and local Albury carrots didn't lift her mood. She even forgot to press her nose to the window as they passed the turnoff to Maidstone Studios. She always looked, just in case there was someone famous going in or out. The familiar and loved landscape seemed unreal to her and she felt like a tourist in what was supposed to be her real life.

She'd felt this way since the broken shoulder had taken away the Diana she thought she'd been born to be. She'd tried to fill the emptiness with acting and repatriating small artifacts, a life that allowed her to refuse relationships more than a teaspoon deep, as if that lack of depth was a chosen necessity and not who she was.

It wasn't until they took a sharp turn off a roundabout onto the narrow country lane she knew by heart did she finally feel as if she really was home. It would be easy to pretend nothing in New York was real now. She could put on her makeup, don the tweeds and cashmeres of country life, and enjoy luncheons and teas and card games at the club. There would be boating on the Len and all of the wedding preparation.

If she threw herself into the role of dutiful daughter and devoted sister, she could forget Paris.

Gravel crunched under the tires as the driver carefully circumnavigated a tree surgeon's crew taking down a dead dogwood just inside the gates. The meadow garden was full of cowslip in bloom, and the bright yellow clusters moving in the breeze eased some of the knots in her shoulders.

Mote Hall, Diana's home for the nearly twenty-five years since her mother had remarried, was solid and unchanged. The original saltbox estate house had long since expanded to include wings, and her mother had converted the stables to an expansive greenhouse. The solid Georgian brick, always tidy and never changing, was comforting to see. Even the scaffolding that was slowly circling the house to aid in roof repair and structural renovation was a symbol of home.

"Continue around to the back, please. I'll get out there," Diana told the driver. It was much easier to bring in luggage from the back of the house. She really didn't want to go in the front like a visitor. It was quarter past eight, which meant Mrs. Cotton, the housekeeper, would still have some coffee and toast on the sideboard.

As though her thoughts had conjured her up, Mrs. Cotton appeared at the top of the rear steps and was opening Diana's door by the time the car stopped. The carefully coiffed white hair and round apple cheeks were the same as they had been for the five years she'd been the estate's house manager. "Welcome home, Miss. Your mother is still at table and expecting you. The tea is fresh."

Diana kept her red eyes focused on the driver's receipt she was signing. "Thank you, that sounds wonderful. It was a long night."

Knowing that it would have been a simple matter to go upstairs and change out of her crumpled red suit, brush her hair and wash her face, she instead went directly to the breakfast room.

Her mother was reading the morning *Times*. She would turn fifty at the end of the year, Diana realized, which hardly seemed possible. The chestnut hair she proudly kept long and unbraided was lustrous and thick, and her bone-china skin was softer and smoother than Diana's would ever be. Her mother hadn't heard Diana's arrival, or she'd have taken off the reading glasses perched at the end of her narrow, hawkish nose. Whatever she was reading had made her smile. As she had all of Diana's life, she radiated calm and strength.

"Hullo Mum."

The reading glasses were immediately removed and set on the table. "Diana, I thought you'd be along—You look terrible."

She spread her arms in an attempt to shrug. In moments she was wrapped tight in her mother's arms.

"Are you hurt? Are you sick? No? Then it will be all right."

Diana let herself believe it, at least for long enough to be fed and shooed off to bed.

To her surprise, she slept.

CHAPTER THIRTY

Paris lifted her suitcase up the steps to her door not a hundred hours from the time she'd left home on Friday. So much had happened she supposed she ought to feel numb.

She was a long, long way from numb.

Heather's girlfriend Artie had arrived about thirty minutes after Paris had noticed Diana had gone. At the same time the receptionist brought in an envelope for her. Only then had she understood Diana hadn't merely found something else to do. She'd left. She wasn't coming back.

It didn't really matter what Diana's reasoning was. Paris wished she were numb, but instead she was *livid*.

"She probably lied about everything, every word was a lie, and that's why she took off." Still muttering to herself, she thumped her suitcase onto the bed and blindly tossed items into either a laundry pile or a dry cleaning pile.

She could no longer ignore the extra weight in her suit jacket. Using a tissue, she drew out the hammer. It didn't look any worse for its journey in her pocket, and she set it carefully on a clean towel. The white of the bone was almost luminescent. The obsidian hammer's head gleamed in the overhead light.

She'd stolen something from a dead man—it was inconceivable. Not something she would have ever thought to have done. Well, she hadn't known he was dead when she'd taken it. She hadn't felt it in her pocket until she was seated on the train to Boston and now it was really too late to take it back even if she thought she could do so without getting into difficulties with guards and Heather. Heather was not her father, true, and Paris had seen her at her most vulnerable. But there was no guarantee that Reynard Media wouldn't be back wanting to throw Anita Topaz into the media maelstrom. She didn't want to invite their notice in any way at this point.

Plus, she didn't have a state-of-the-art stethoscope or a handy digital *Sissone* or even ordinary lockpicks to make such things easy—that is, if she even knew how to use them.

She could mail it back anonymously. Did she really want to do that? What if the hammer was what Diana said it was—something that belonged to another culture that Reynard never had any business possessing? Maybe Diana hadn't lied about that.

It sure would be nice to ask her, but she couldn't do that, could she? Because Diana had *left*.

She added her rumpled suit to the pile of dry cleaning and took comfort in a faded *Overwatch* T-shirt and well-worn sweatpants. There was nothing for it, though, and she stirred together a half-batch of brownies while her mind clicked back and forth over her decision to take the hammer and the lack of an opportunity to tell Diana what she'd done.

If Diana had known that Paris had the very thing she'd wanted all along, she wouldn't have left.

No, she'd have taken it from you, and then she would have left, Paris told herself viciously. And she wouldn't have received a lovely card as a keepsake.

Parting is such sweet sorrow. I'm sorry. - Diana

No phone number and quoting the most star-crossed lovers of all time. Typical. Just typical.

The pan of chocolatey goodness went into the oven. She set the timer and carried it with her into the bedroom to turn on her computer. If she could calm down enough to edit her last chapter at least the extra day in New York wouldn't have derailed her schedule for the week.

Instead of being furious about Diana, she needed to remember that the trip was a success for Anita Topaz. She was free to write without worrying about publisher demands. Heather Reynard had understood. Wasn't that a kick—honesty had resolved the matter amicably.

She'd achieved exactly what she had steeled herself to do when she'd decided to go to New York, and using the one solution that would have *never* occurred to Diana. Why tell the truth when you can invent a lot of pretty lies?

She pushed away the thought that it might have been a different outcome if Heather Reynard hadn't recognized her and empathized with Paris's plight. And if Heather weren't now in charge of, well, everything. A part of her was aching with sympathetic grief for Heather but she had no illusions about what kind of man Reynard had been. The eulogies were only getting started—"titan of media" and "legendary promoter" would be endless. She'd have her mental image of him in the hotel room doorway, thinking he was about to notch another champagne bottle just as he'd done all his life.

Her shudder of revulsion was about Reynard but she was left wondering if anything that had happened between her and Diana had been any cleaner. She closed her eyes to visualize dancing in Central Park. Diana hadn't been trapped or coerced, and neither had she. Diana might be a liar, and unreliable, and a sneak, but her passion, at least, had seemed genuine. She hadn't tried to use it for her own agenda, at least not in any way that Paris knew.

If what they'd shared had been real, why had Diana run away?

The ding of the timer roused her from a pointless exercise of trying to find the right word to describe the brown of Diana's eyes. She singed her fingertips cutting one brownie to take back to her desk. The miraculous chemistry of butter, sugar, and cocoa sent her taste buds into a swoon. She'd eaten nothing on the train, which meant her last meal had been in that deli, watching Diana eat. Talking with Diana about nothing important. Like two women on a date.

She'd thought Diana was dragging the meal out, as if she didn't want it to end. Paris wanted to believe that, anyway. But she would never know.

Her brain grew less foggy—brownies were medicinal that way—and she decided she was never going to get any peace if she didn't at least try to put some of her uncertainties to rest. How much had Diana lied? Clicking her way to her browser, Paris started with a list of gymnasts representing England. A Google search later she was looking at the name on a list: Diana Beckinsale, Team Great Britain, Artistic Gymnastics, alternate.

Another click and she was looking at a picture of a teenage Diana. She hadn't changed a lot in the ten or so years since. There were more pictures, going back all the way to a pint-sized pixie in a red leotard standing next to a woman likely her mother. Paris quickly found more photos of "Evelyn Countess Weald"—she was very active in civic circles and often photographed. Evelyn looked like the kind of woman who would carefully enunciate the correct form "hashed browns" should she ever order them. It was easy to see where Diana got her eyes and cheekbones.

She's gone. I am abused, and my relief must be to loathe her. Not that Paris had any respect for Othello's choices, but the sentiment for once made sense to her. So Diana hadn't lied about her name, her family, or her competition background. It didn't change the fact that she'd left without a decent word, and without a way to get in touch again.

There were videos, even. Her mouse lingered over the play button. She should let it go. What good would watching Diana-the-Gymnast do?

Her finger slipped—she hadn't meant to click but somehow she did. The first video was in an archive from her gymnastics club and featured a floor exercise from a juniors competition. Diana was a twisting blur as she flipped and spun through a tumbling run.

The next video was a demonstration event and Diana moved confidently the length of the narrow beam, cool and calm at twelve years old, even as she back flipped to a landing she couldn't see.

She fetched another brownie and set the videos to autoplay. Fascinated, she wondered how anyone could do a parallel bar routine without dislocating both shoulders. Diana was really very good at all of it, and had competed at an elite level. At no point did her face ever express anything but certainty that she would succeed. It was an expression Paris recognized from just that afternoon, when Diana had talked her way past the security guard.

Paris thought how nice it must be to be wired that way—that any challenge could be conquered with determination and confidence. It didn't hurt to be beautiful, white, and wealthy either.

The next video began and she didn't immediately realize what she was about to see. Diana ran toward the beam for her opening mount and it all went wrong. Her hands slipped, her shoulder cracked into the beam and she went down on the mat so hard her body bounced. Her hand over her mouth, Paris watched Diana get to her feet, walk back a few steps and attempt to restart the routine. Her shoulder was not in the right place and when she tried to give the beginning signal, one arm moved and the other hung at her side like wet laundry. Diana had looked down then, as if surprised. All at once her legs folded up and she dropped where she stood.

So that was when Diana had fainted. From a broken shoulder. In front of hundreds of people. She hadn't even cried out.

The next video began playing even as Paris took a shaky breath. Diana had spent nearly all of her life in pursuit of a dream and it had ended in a split second. Like the split second it took to press "publish" on a blog. Life as she knew it was over, even if it took years to understand that healed would never be whole. What was lost couldn't be regained. There was only a future to build out of whatever scraps were left from the past.

In a newer video, from someone's wedding, an entourage of bridesmaids in teeth-jarring chartreuse dresses followed a satin-and-lace bride into a garden for photographs. There was a lot of good humor as the women posed and rearranged themselves several times for the camera. It had been recorded not quite four years ago. She could make out snatches of Diana's voice mingling with the others. The camera zoomed in on the faces only once, and Paris paused when it got to Diana's bright smile.

At the time of this video, Paris thought, Diana had probably taken and sent to their homes at least ten artifacts. She had probably been planning another foray into crime while the picture was being taken.

She made herself stop watching. She didn't know that Diana. She knew the Diana who left without saying goodbye.

The addictive nature of editing helped get her mind off the cannonball of hurt in her chest. She picked over sentences she'd written last week, deleted whole paragraphs and decided that Susannah had not expressed anywhere near enough rage at discovering Bryce had betrayed her. At least there was one thing in her life she had the power to fix.

CHAPTER THIRTY-ONE

"It's the walking dead!" Her brother's voice echoed through the sunny breakfast room.

"You're so funny." Diana scratched her nose with her middle finger long enough to be sure William saw it.

His greeting made the small gathering at the far end of the breakfast table turn to look: her mother, whose disapproving gaze went from the clock on the wall to Diana, her soon-to-be sister-in-law Millie who at least looked happy to see her; and the frosty-haired wedding planner who always seemed about to whack someone with her clipboard. Diana only went as far as the sideboard, where she poured herself a cup of tea, and piled toast on a plate.

Before she could leave William's bass voice rang out again. "We're discussing which is more pretentious—using a quail egg, or thinking quail eggs are passé."

Stifling a smile, she faced the gathering. The three women were all looking at her expectantly, and behind them William mouthed, "SAVE ME."

"Care to join us?" Her mother made it sound like a question. It wasn't.

She set down her tea and toast and slid into the chair her mother indicated, knowing her rumpled blouse and jeans hadn't escaped her mother's notice.

"Are you feeling better?" There was sympathy in Millie's blue eyes. She was nicely plump and her simple shirtwaist dress was one of Diana's favorite shades of blue, like a morning sky just before sunrise. Diana thought again that she was happy to have someone who seemed sane, smart, and sweet joining the family.

"Yes. It was some kind of bug." Nothing like an extended crying jag to provide bleary eyes and a stuffy nose as an excuse for taking her dinner last night *en suite*. "What is this about quail eggs?"

"William was being amusing." Her mother had a positive gift for saying something to mean the opposite. She sipped her tea and her heavy diamond wedding ring caught the light with a dazzle that made Diana blink. "We're going over the rehearsal dinner schedule."

"You're rehearsing for the rehearsal?"

Millie crossed her eyes for Diana's benefit, making her laugh into her tea. "There's nothing spontaneous about a wedding."

"Not yet, anyway."

"*Lady* Diana Beckinsale, don't even say that in jest."

"One minute, four seconds," William announced. "That's a record."

She glared at him, thinking that she was going to have to tease him about yet another new beard style, this time trimmed short with precise razor lines and angles that made him look like an animated *Aladdin* bad guy. "What?"

"From arrival to use of full name."

Her mother's lips twitched. "Shall I use your full name as well, young man?"

"Please," Millie said to her. "I need to learn how."

Diana was amazed that her mother actually winked. "We'll practice later. Stops him in his tracks."

Diana grinned into William's what-did-I-do-to-myself face. "I see that being a smartie is working out for you like always."

The wedding planner cleared her throat. It would have been more effective if her tightly wound white bun hadn't reminded Diana of the unintentionally hilarious Deportment of Young Ladies lecturer from when she was at school. "I'm glad you're back, Ms. Beckinsale. As a bridesmaid you'll have some ceremonial duties that begin with the rehearsal dinner which we haven't been able to discuss."

"I'm all ears." She couldn't help herself. "Not literally of course."

Her mother sighed as William went into a fit of his goofy, high-pitched giggles. "Diana, this is serious."

"I know, and I promise that on the day I will be serious." It felt good to be able to laugh though it was an effort. Whenever she came home she slipped into all the familiar patterns—her family's affection made it easy. But none of it was erasing New York. The subsequent discussion of appropriate dinner toasts for the groom's side of the family didn't drown out the many vignettes playing in Diana's head. Some of them were sensual and feverish featuring Paris, but the most prominent were full of recriminations. The word *coward* was blazoned on the inside of her eyelids.

Finally her mother admitted to needing time to get ready for a luncheon. The wedding planner gave the three younger people one last disapproving glance before leaving.

"I'm staying until the weekend," Millie said in response to Diana's query. "Then it's my mum's final fitting and we all check into the inn. Bride and groom on opposite ends of the building, both with chaperones."

Diana laughed at William's loud groan. "Seriously? Propriety at this stage?"

William's unhappy face was in full display. "I have been able to accept all the other edicts, but that one is going to be tough."

"Abstinence is good for the soul, or something like that."

"You're better at that than I am," William said.

A hot flush washed up from Diana's chest until the top of her head felt on fire.

"Get out!" William sat upright. "Is *that* what you sneaked off to do?"

"Sneaking? I wasn't sneak— No. I'm not discussing my sex life with you."

"William," Millie admonished. "She's not going to kiss and tell."

"It was way more than a kiss." William's eyes gleamed with mischief, making Diana wonder why she liked him when he enjoyed tormenting her. "Why the big secret? Some revolutionary bloke that'll make Mum pop a vein?"

"No, it didn't go well. We didn't have any way forward."

"Piff. Is he married or something? Hashtag undesirable?"

"No." Diana shot a glance at Millie. Though she liked her well enough, Diana wasn't sure how much personal revelation a sister-in-law wanted. "We met under really poor circumstances."

"So did Millie and I."

"You met at a wedding. That's totally romantic." Even so, Millie was nodding in agreement with William.

"Mum arranged it. We were a setup. We had a great time and I didn't call her because I didn't want to give Mum the satisfaction. Millie called me."

"You were very lucky I did."

"Best thing that ever happened to me." William smooched her on the cheek while Diana made cat-with-a-hairball noises.

Millie tousled his thick hair. "I felt the same way he did—you know how it is. Constantly being pushed toward matrimony. So your brother and I have agreed that our first date was the one *we* chose to have. Everything started then."

"So," William said as if he'd cured cancer, "have a second date with him."

"Her."

"Oh." They both said in unison.

William blinked. "Well, that's new, isn't it?"

"Very. I'll be the one to tell Mum, okay?"

William nodded. "It's kind of a surprise."

"Tell me about it." Diana pushed her empty plate away.

Millie was smiling at her. "My younger brother—Todd, you met him—he's gay, you know."

"I didn't know."

"It's totally cool with me." Millie hastily added, "Not that you need my approval to be who you are."

William looked half-serious, half-teasing. "So are you bi, or all lesbian, or what?"

"It's not like I think about a guy and want to—" She made the cat-hairball noises again. "I'm just…meh. But now I notice Paris…" Damn, she hadn't meant to name names. "I think about women now and they're beautiful and mysterious and familiar and exotic and wonderful all at once."

William scoffed. "You just figured that out?"

Millie poked him in the arm. "Yes, Mr. Superior Lover Man reinforced in every way all of his life to like girls which worked out well for him because he does, in fact, like girls."

"Girls are awesome." William's salacious grin turned into a gulp as he glanced at Millie. "One girl is awesome. You are awesome. Just you. Awesome."

"You need to work on that," Diana warned him. She sighed. "Girls—*women* are awesome, and so I'm thinking I'm on the all-lesbian all-the-time channel."

Millie pointedly gazed down into her empty teacup and William immediately went about refilling it. "You figured this out in Paris?"

"Paris is a person. A writer in Boston whose mum liked *Romeo and Juliet*."

William laughed. "So much better than Tybalt."

Diana laughed with him. "Exactly what she says."

"Point in her favor I suppose. So why can't you see her? Is she closeted, or a nun or something?"

"No. She—I kind of left without saying goodbye."

Millie's eyebrows shot up as William said, "Wow."

"Yeah."

"That is a daft loser move."

"Newsflash from the Ministry of the Manifestly Obvious."

"You're a walking riot," William said. "So call her up. Send her an email. Snapchat her a naked picture of your jolly bits."

How to explain to anyone that she would only be able to find Paris by going to Boston and hanging out in a bar on certain days of the week between noon and three p.m.? That she'd be going to those lengths after a single night together over a woman she scarcely knew? That she was exactly the kind of person that Paris didn't need in her life because of all the other activities she'd never told her family about? That she'd already looked her up last night and discovered that Paris Ellison didn't exist on the Internet, except in articles about the pushback she'd received about a blog that was also no longer on the Internet. Only the Wayback Machine had a record of her and she'd cried over every picture of that Paris, one she would never know. "It's not that simple. I don't see why she'd forgive me."

"Everybody does stupid things when they're scared. Coming out isn't easy," Millie said quietly. "I know that from Todd's journey. Even with love and acceptance it's scary."

Hours later, tramping around the garden and woods for fresh air, Diana was still asking herself if Millie had been right. Millie thought it was a scared-to-be-gay thing, but that wasn't it. At least Diana didn't think so.

It was more of a scared to be in love thing.

CHAPTER THIRTY-TWO

An indignant meow at the door brought a smile to Paris's face for the first time since she'd arrived home last night. Hobbit, right on time. "Did you miss me?"

Hobbit pointedly sat down next to his empty dish, rigid back to her.

"You did miss me or you wouldn't be pissed." She dumped a small scoop of food into the dish and set down a bowl of fresh water. "Here's your Second Breakfast."

He scarfed up the food and promptly wanted out again. "I get it, the cold shoulder. Fine. Believe me, you're not the first this week. Enjoy Elevenses wherever you're headed next."

Peering out the door after the tabby revealed a bright and cheerful spring morning, one that didn't match Paris's mood. Thankfully, she had Susannah's fictional life to escape to. She would lose herself in a world she'd made where everything turned out the way she intended. So what if the story so far seemed flat and dull and full of sticky, ooey-gooey saccharine ideas about love and sex and relationships that weren't real?

Looking at the garden made her think of flower pots peeking over balconies in New York, and then she was thinking about Diana again. Feeling scattered and unfocused was one of her anxiety triggers, so she finally decided to do yoga, followed by a hot shower. If that didn't help, then a long walk. After coping pretty darned well with everything that had happened in New York, there was no point in losing a battle to Boss Anxiety now over her stupid, romantic proclivities.

She was wrapped in a towel and feeling squeaky clean when she noticed her landlady Adya in the garden, snipping at the aromatic lavender bush as she often did. However, instead of jeans and a work shirt, she was wearing black trousers with a blazer the color of ripe eggplant. A special occasion—and then Paris remembered. *Foul word!* How could she have forgotten about their wedding? She meant to bring them home a gift from New York.

Her brain slipped into hyperdrive, rocketing through the long list of everything she'd lost when the online bullies had stolen her life. A home, a girlfriend, the world of gaming that had been a passion and her livelihood. Hiding herself from discovery had scared her away from travel. From having a smartphone for all the ways it made modern life easier. From signing books for fans. From going to a wedding for two women she really cared about.

The greens of the garden wavered to gray. Too much to think about and a lot of regrets. She wasn't sorry she'd run from San Francisco. Her only goal had been to survive, and she'd done that.

She hadn't just survived, she'd found another way to succeed. She'd just proved in New York that she'd leveled up. *Walk into a Meeting Full of Strangers*—achievement unlocked.

When car doors slammed outside she winced. She was missing out. Again.

She couldn't get Diana back, but if she called for a cab now…

* * *

Boston City Hall was a monolith of concrete slabs arranged in stacks at odd angles. Paris didn't know if it was the deliberate antithesis of the gold-domed, historic statehouse a few blocks away, or if it had been built during a passion for modern design. What it most certainly had were lots of active surveillance cameras.

Though it was not really reasonable to think that any of the a-holes who had wanted to maim and murder her would actively be hacking government video feeds and running facial recognition software, it was a scenario her brain was more than capable of making *seem* possible. The anxiety spike she anticipated was beginning its rise and she focused on taking deep, steady breaths.

She was at least thirty minutes behind the wedding party, but she hadn't had to park a car, tough duty in Boston. With any luck they'd still be finalizing paperwork and paying fees. After needlessly smoothing the slacks of her last clean suit, she squared her shoulders and went through the metal detector queue. *Deep breath. Count to ten.*

The signs for wedding ceremonies were easy to follow in the maze of drab corridors. To her relief she spotted Grace and Adya at one of the counters. She noticed, too, that other people were watching them with indulgent smiles. They would all be looking at her if she joined them. They weren't hostile, she told herself. *Deep breath.*

As she approached the wedding party, however, it was clear that something was wrong. The Kerns, their long-term bridge combatants and friends, were standing with them. Marva Kerns was digging frantically in her handbag while her husband paced.

"Bill can run right home and get it but I don't know that he will get back in time for the cut off," Marva was saying. "I feel like a fool."

"It's all right," Grace said. She was lovely in a silver dress with beading all around the high neck and shoulders, and all the more charming for the silver-spangly Birkenstocks that peeked out at the bottom. "We can come back tomorrow."

"In that case," the weary clerk at the desk said, "I could be helping the next couple in the queue."

Paris startled them all by asking, "What are you missing?"

"Dear, you came? But why?" Grace looked very pleased and yet confused.

Adya, her wild hair combed neatly for the first time since Paris had known her, clasped her hand in greeting. "Isn't this going to overwhelm you?"

"Not today," Paris said firmly. "I would really love to see you get married, if there's room. What's wrong?"

Marva was near tears. "I forgot my ID."

"I have mine," Paris said. "If that's okay with the brides and with you."

"Perfect," the entire wedding party chimed.

"Perfect," the clerk echoed briskly, seizing a document.

Paris passed over her Massachusetts identification card and filled out the portion of the paperwork for Witness #2. Colorful posters against the drab, government-gray walls bleached out in suddenly bright lighting. *Deep breath.* This is an okay reaction to what you're doing, she told herself. It's only the color shift, you know you can deal with that. It's not an anxiety attack. *Deep breath.* She'd been a vapor in the world for five years, and now she was going to be real again. It meant risk, but only a small one, and she could handle it.

She wasn't going to be closed out of life anymore.

Grace and Adya were very grateful and Paris was equally heartened by hugs from both of the Kerns. The process complete, the clerk gave them the next time slot for their ceremony. Grace and Adya held hands as they all walked down the hall to the ceremony waiting area.

The duly authorized representative of the Commonwealth was a kind-faced black woman in a pink blazer. She seemed genuinely touched by the prospect of marrying the two old women.

"You've been waiting for a long time, so let's not linger," she said. "I have a traditional ceremony and one that's been adapted for long-term couples."

"We want that one," Adya said.

"As long as it begins with 'dearly beloved,'" Grace added.

"It does. If the guests would be seated?"

There were four chairs and Paris quelled her urge to fidget away some of her excess energy.

"Dearly beloved..."

She wasn't embarrassed that she cried. Marva, after pressing tissues into the hands of the weeping Grace and Adya, gave one to Paris as well before blowing her own nose. Bill's eyes were gleaming and all three of them clapped when the short ceremony concluded with the traditional kiss.

More signatures and Paris's hand wasn't even shaking. She knew she had to keep herself safe, but this small risk she was taking was in service of love.

And she still believed in it, it seemed.

CHAPTER THIRTY-THREE

The next three days blurred together for Diana. There was the final fitting for yet another bridesmaid dress. At least the gowns were a lush, bearable shiraz in color, and there were no poufy sleeves. The fitting had been followed by a formal tea hosted by Millie's redoubtable mother, and that had been followed by a night of raucous clubbing in London.

The sun was up Saturday morning when the limousine dumped the hen party at the inn in Kent where the wedding guests were staying. Diana found her little sister waiting for her in the room they were to share. The table was littered with texts, notebooks, and study guides.

"You've been having fun," was all Florence said as Diana shut herself in their bathroom and regretted the last Slippery Nipple for about an hour.

When she finally dragged herself to her bed, she mumbled, "Thank goodness there's only the rehearsal dinner to get through today."

Florence looked up from her laptop. Like William, she had thick black hair, dark eyes and smooth golden brown skin inherited from their father, and like Diana, their mother's hawkish nose. Still a teenager, Florence was already adept at looking down it, especially at the sins of her elders. "I will never understand the need to get stinking blotto."

"You're too young to understand," Diana said. "Count your lucky stars."

"William said you had news."

"Damn him."

"He said I couldn't tell Mum. He didn't say anything about Dad or the *Telegraph*."

Diana rolled onto her back, glad the room had stopped spinning. The light from the window was distressingly bright. "I think I'm not going to die now."

"Changing the subject are we?"

"Whose idea was it to let you join Debate?"

In a voice that sounded exactly like their mother's, Florence said, "And still changing the subject."

A cold cloth was settled on her forehead. She opened her eyes.

"You're welcome." Her sister's gaze was slightly worried, but largely disapproving.

It wouldn't help if she told Florence that in this light she looked forty. "Thanks. I truly don't know what I was thinking. Except I was bored and that's no reason to drink."

"It's no reason to do anything." Florence sat down on the edge of the bed. "So? News?"

"I've fallen in love with a woman."

"Oh." Florence frowned. "Is that all? For heaven's sake, I thought you were pregnant, or had to have back surgery or something."

Diana closed her eyes again. "Not everybody is going to be as thrilled as you are."

"If you're here and drinking, I'm thinking there's a story and it's not a good one."

"I'm a complete loser. Ask William."

"He may have said that."

"I think I'm done discussing this with you. Unless you'd like to share details of your love life in return?"

"What details? I have exams in two weeks."

Florence's voice faded to nothing, and what seemed like moments later it was back.

"Wake up. Mum says we shouldn't be late to lunch."

Diana pried open one eye. "Where's that from?"

"What?" Florence followed Diana's squinting gaze. "My T-shirt? Some online shop."

"No—what's on it?"

"It's Link playing the Ocarina of Time. Since when are you interested in *Zelda*?"

"I saw that same shirt recently." She wasn't going to explain that she'd last seen the T-shirt on the floor next to a fainting couch in a New York hotel room.

Florence gave her a suspicious look. "You must have really noticed the shirt, or whoever was wearing it. This woman, she's a gamer?"

For someone who was as adept as she at keeping secrets, she was having spectacularly little success with her family at the moment. "Was."

"Cool. I'm going to shower and try to look like I wasn't up most of the night." Florence nudged the bed and Diana winced. "I recommend you do the same thing."

Lunch was a gracious and elegant event, or at least Diana was certain it must be. She viewed it all through sunglasses, a fact that did not please Evelyn, Countess Weald, one bit. Thankfully, she was not the only one doing so in the inn's dining room—groomsmen and bridesmaids alike had adopted dark glasses and ordered black coffee and little else.

After managing toast and a wedge of cheese, Diana huddled in the common room with the other bridesmaids, yawning into yet more coffee.

Millie was not quite as poorly off as the rest of them. That, or she was putting up a good front. "We'd all feel better if we went for a walk. The grounds are very pretty and peaceful."

"There's a lovely picture window. So bright, letting in all that sun." It was making Diana's eyes water. "I bet that if all of you went into the gardens I would be able to sit right here and wave."

William had slumped into an armchair. "The Best Man now has my permission to strangle the next person who suggests alcohol."

"What if it's the Best Man?"

"Then the Maid of Honor can strangle him."

The Maid of Honor, Carrie or Mary or Quite Contrary—Diana hadn't caught her name—groaned from the window seat where she was prone. "Don't discuss homicide. We're in an English country inn, and that's where all the murders happen."

"Don't give me any ideas," Diana muttered. The way she felt had to be somebody else's fault. She couldn't have brought it on herself.

* * *

By the time the rehearsal dinner began, Diana could look at food again. That turned out to be a good thing, because the menu served in the inn's private dining room was a tribute to William's Punjabi heritage from his father's side. Served family style, the long tables were laden with tureens and platters that left the air steamy with coriander, masala, and fennel. She stuffed herself with fresh rosemary-scented popadoms wrapped around homemade paneer. It was hard to be depressed with her mouth comically puckered from the so-sour-it-hurt fruit pickle.

As hosts, her mother and stepfather were each presiding over a table. Her mother was at the other table and Diana was happy to be seated out of her mother's line of sight.

"Did you pick the menu?" Diana asked her stepfather. "The chana is delicious."

"Your mother did. I'm the father of the groom with no official duties but dancing with my new daughter-in-law tomorrow evening."

Anwar was earth and water to her mother's air and fire. Her three-year-old self had lost her heart completely to him the day they'd met. He'd inquired politely after the health of her ragged Paddington Bear and asked the restaurant to bring another chair so Paddington could dine with them instead of sitting under the table. When her mother had protested that it wasn't exactly what one did at whatever Michelin-starred eatery they'd been in, he had simply said, "When we dine together we show who we are."

Within weeks Diana knew she would never be afraid of Anwar the way even pictures of her birth father made her afraid. An outsider looking in might see only a clinging socialite wisely marrying a wealthy businessman, but Diana appreciated that together they made a whole. It was why she believed in love, and why she'd hoped to experience it even when her body hadn't been interested.

Until Paris.

She'd drifted off in mid-sentence and realized Anwar was looking at her with concern. "Evelyn said you were all quite indulgent last night. Are you well?"

"Well enough, *Pita*. I don't normally drink like that and I'm still paying for it. Your flight was on time this afternoon?"

"On time after a delay in Belgrade. Where have you been visiting? What roles did you play this time?"

She told him about Boston and *Tartuffe*, and found herself mentioning the cozy bar where she'd had lunch and the interesting writer she'd met.

He sounded overly casual when he asked, "Is that Paris?"

"I'm going to kill William."

"Florence told me."

"I'll kill them both. After the wedding, or Mum will have my head."

He smiled at her silliness. "We take notice because it is notable for you to be suffering in this way. I don't want to add to your suffering. You know that my family didn't like that I married your mother. Someone so different from our blood— they were sure it would be a disaster. She would take all the family money. She would put her child first. She would bring shame on us all. They didn't know your mother."

"They've never wanted to either."

"No, which is a waste." He smoothed his neatly trimmed mustache, dark eyes fixed on her. "God is love. God is good. Love always brings us closer to God. Love cannot be a sin."

"Those are the vows you said when you married Mum." She blinked back tears. "I remember that day so well—or at least I think I do. There was a lot of cake."

His smile was full of fond recollection. "You did eat a great deal of cake, and you danced until you dropped."

"I remember that too." She'd stood on Anwar's shoes at first, then learned the steps for herself.

"My heart misled me more than once before I met your mother. But I didn't stop listening to it."

She wanted to say *bah humbug* because it sounded a lot like "the right one will come along" advice. Just like an Anita Topaz novel—and now she was thinking about Paris again. "I made a mess of it. I'm not good for her."

"You know this how?"

She couldn't help her tart tone. "Because I have a brain."

"You are very like your mother." He laughed in Diana's outraged face. "You list the numbers, add them up, take one look at the result, and off you go."

"It's not like anything will change."

"People are not numbers," he observed while dishing out more chana for himself. At Diana's nod, he added another spoonful to her plate. "You know that."

"I'm getting a headache, *Pita*." She had to look away. The faith in his eyes for her good sense was undeserved.

A sharp *ping* poked her hangover back to life and left Diana wincing. Her mother was using her wineglass as a bell, lightly tapping it with a knife.

"Showtime," she muttered to Anwar, who was already rising to his feet.

After Anwar's toast came her mother's, then, as the groom's eldest sibling, Diana raised her glass to the happy couple, carefully schooling the envy out of her voice.

Dinner concluded with a brief moment when she thought her interest in something, anything, might be caught by another bridesmaid. Not the woman, but the earrings she wore. The laborious engravings on the white metal looked distinctly African. Gorgeous little trinkets she'd bought at auction, the woman gushed after Diana asked about them. The catalog had said they had been handed down from a director of the East India Company and the latest heir had put them up for sale, wasn't that lucky? That made them at least 170 years old, Diana estimated, and that meant it was unlikely that the African woman they'd belonged to had given them up voluntarily. A museum curator would call such objects "personal heritage ornaments."

Yes, Diana agreed, they looked wonderful with the tribal geometrics that were all the rage this season.

Diana wanted to care enough to think about how those earrings might find their way home with her help. She wanted to care but she didn't.

CHAPTER THIRTY-FOUR

"So what gives?" Lisa set the bowl of steaming tomato soup on the table.

Paris inhaled the sweet, salty aroma and began her stirring and blowing ritual. "What do you mean?"

"Third day in a row you've come here for lunch. I know the tomato soup is good, but it's not that good."

"Can't I change my habits?"

"Yes." Lisa pulled out the chair opposite Paris and sat down. Bright spring sunlight came in through the window, turning her long blond locks into spun gold. It wasn't like Lisa was even trying. Like Diana, she knew where the best light was by instinct.

Lisa is not the femme you're mad at, she told herself.

"I'm trying to expand my horizons again. I feel like it's safe to go in the water."

Lisa nodded. "Like going on a trip for the first time in five years. Which you said went really well. Except you're here every day now and you look like death."

"Thanks," Paris muttered. Mouth half full of toasted sourdough bread dipped liberally in the soup, she said, "This is her fault."

"Oh, so there is a her. Knew it. Fiona?"

"Her real name is Diana. Fiona was a stage name."

"Really?"

"You were right about the fake fur and the real emeralds. And she's British, not Irish."

"A pretty good actress, then."

"Too good." Paris slurped her first spoonful of soup. She was hopeful Lisa didn't like slurpers and would leave her alone.

Lisa leaned back in the chair, apparently having nothing else to do. Paris noticed then that the place was very quiet, with only a couple of regulars at the bar. "And how is this her fault?"

"She left—not a word. No phone number. I'm lucky to know her real name."

"Aren't those the rules for a one-night stand?"

"It wasn't…" Maybe it was.

"Oh! So you're here hoping she'll turn up."

It didn't help for Lisa to put it into words. Lisa didn't have to know that every morning Paris told herself she wouldn't go, because there was no way Diana was coming back. "No, I want tomato soup."

"Sure." Lisa slowly shook her head. "You got stomped on."

"Well I did." Now she had tears in her eyes and damn it, Lisa could probably tell. "I've turned into a complete cliché, the lovelorn heroine who wonders why she's not happy when she hooks up with people who don't stick around."

"But in all of your books, the disappearing-act frogs turn out to be princes."

Paris blinked. "You've read my books?"

Lisa shrugged. "One or two. Well, maybe all of them. That's beside the point."

"The point is?"

"You're feeling kicked in the teeth right now." She opened her big blue eyes as wide as they would go. "It gets better."

"Nice try."

"I didn't think you'd believe me. But it does, you know. I caught She-Who-Must-Not-Be-Named with an anorexic surfboard waxer. Next thing I know I'm clinging and repressed and judgmental—and sloppy."

"The bitch!"

"I know, right? So then I think I'm going to get some self-esteem back with this totally smokin' hot bartender at this new place I'm working at, but she gives me a huge cold shoulder." She gestured at her bosom. "Doesn't even see this."

"What an idiot."

"She completely is." Lisa brushed her hair over her shoulder with a dismissive gesture. "I forgave her. She's my best friend now."

"That is so lesbian." Paris enjoyed another dunk of bread into the soup, then broke off some of the cheddar. Heaven on a plate. "You said something about having a point."

"So Ms. Cold Shoulder is how I met Tan—"

"The wonder wife who keeps you warm at night. I've heard the rest of the story."

"Spoilsport—it's a good story. I'm just trying to say that Ms. One-Night Stand might lead to something…better."

"Probably not."

"Not if you spend the rest of your life with your eyes on the pavement."

"Are you ever wrong?"

Lisa twisted in her seat. "Hey fellas! Am I ever wrong?"

"No, Lisa," came the answer, in sing-song unison.

"See?"

"The benefits of owning the joint."

"I've always wanted a very small country to run, so this is perfect. You should try it."

"I run fictional countries. That works for me."

"Then bring a laptop and work here if you want. That is, if you intend to camp out waiting for Fiona-Diana to come back. Even if she never does, something better might walk through the door."

Something better, Paris mused as she walked home. What could something better possibly be? A woman who didn't run away, didn't have so many secrets Paris needed a character guide to keep track—that would be a start. Who danced in the park and melted when Paris touched her—also required. Who was brave, laughed easily and never lost her cool.

She paused at the top of the hill above the house to let the sun warm her face. The cloudless sky was criss-crossed with vapor from jets heading toward all points of the compass. White sailboats skimmed the surface of the bay, running ahead of a warming wind blowing in from the south.

It was a beautiful day, yet she was living on the other side of the mirror where blue skies meant rain. At least that was what it felt like.

She trudged down the hill and waved at the newlyweds who were clipping bunches of lilacs from the unruly bush in the front yard. The answering machine was blinking when she opened her door.

It won't be Diana, she told herself, and it wasn't. She was so busy not being disappointed that she missed Finn's opening words.

"—and she's more than happy to take you on. She'd be a fool, otherwise. You need to let RMG know that future contracts and proposals should go to your agent." He rattled off the contact information and told her to expect a representation agreement in the mail, and if she had any questions feel free, et cetera.

She played back the message to make sure she had all the details. An agent was a good thing, a welcome change to how Anita Topaz did business with the world.

Wasn't this what she had wanted? A month ago she would have been happy, and now everywhere she looked she was aware that Diana was gone. She was being a sap. Or a hopeful fool. Not that there was much difference.

The hopeful fool tugged open the kitchen junk drawer, dug toward the back and came up with the slip of paper with the number Diana had given her. She pictured that Diana, with long blond hair, wrapped in fake fur, wearing perfect makeup and glittering jewels. So beautifully fake. Then the Diana who had gasped in frantic pleasure, with freckles and pale lips. Real and alive.

This number won't work, she told herself. But it might, Hopeful Fool insisted. The debate raged back and forth in her head until her phone crackled with the three-tone chime and the snippy voice announced, "The number you have reached is not in service at this time."

She sent Hopeful Fool on her way and sat down at her desk to work. She was going to make progress today, and stop all this nonsensical distraction. The problem was she'd edited and edited, because that was fun and obsessively consuming for her. But she hadn't written a single new paragraph, and it didn't seem likely that she was going to anytime soon.

She wished the phone number had worked. She felt stuck and trapped, and angry with herself for not knowing how to get back to writing. It was an ideal situation for Boss Anxiety to make an appearance, but she visualized swatting away the tiresome creature, and hard enough that she could hear a satisfying *splat*.

And still the words wouldn't come. Her head might believe in love, but her heart was empty.

CHAPTER THIRTY-FIVE

"I am going to build a bonfire and put these shoes on it." Diana dropped the offending footwear on the floor as she eased herself painfully into the nearest chair at the family table, which occupied the bay alcove at the end of the kitchen. Cook had left sandwiches in the refrigerator and her mother was already switching on the kettle.

William and Millie were on the way to Reykjavik for a week of camping out in an ice house under the last of the northern lights for the season. The remainder of the family seemed to have had the strength to dance the rest of the night away. Diana had wanted her shoes off in the worst way, and had spent far too much of the evening evading the erstwhile Evan, who lingered hopefully *everywhere*. She wanted her own bed, and quiet.

"You didn't have to come back with me," Diana said again.

Her mother fetched a small carafe of milk from the nearest refrigerator and added it to the always ready tea tray. "I'm exhausted. I don't think I've slept for the past week."

Diana stopped herself from saying that it was *only* a wedding. The day in truth had been perfectly organized, the setting idyllic and the reception full of enchanting music and food. William and Millie had both seemed to treasure the chance to celebrate with their friends and family all in one place. They'd also kept pace with several of their peers in stipulating that they would accept no gifts, and offering the names of several charities should people wish to make a difference in that way.

That she'd spent most of the day looking for something to grouse about wasn't the fault of the happy couple, or society— or even her mother. "It was a brilliant day, Mum."

Her mother set down the tea tray and met Diana's gaze square on. "Do you really think so?"

Surprised by the vulnerability in her mother's eyes, Diana said, "Of course. It wasn't exactly the wedding I would have, but it was perfect for them."

"What kind of wedding would you have?" The kettle shrilled and her mother hurried to shut it off.

"Have Florence and William been blabbing?"

Her mother turned from the stove, a sharp look in her otherwise weary eyes. "Why? Is there something to blab about?"

"There is *nothing* to blab about."

"Fine."

It wasn't that she feared her mother would be dismayed that Diana's romantic life had taken a turn toward women. It was that her mother fixed things, even when Diana wished she wouldn't try. She'd been grateful when that fearless tendency had secured her one of the best coaches in gymnastics and steamrolled over school objections to the amount of distraction pursuing competitive achievements generated. She was an adult now, and she wanted to be in charge of her own life. One could not ask Mum to help one day and not help the next. Better not to ask at all.

Besides, there was nothing in her so-called love life that could be fixed.

Steeping tea had never smelled so good. She limped to the sink for a glass of water and downed pills for her back. "I'm not wearing high heels for the rest of the year."

"Have you been to the doctor about your back lately?"

"No—nothing's changed. He'll repeat the list of surgical options available if the usual list of symptoms persist. I'll promise not to do the activities that make it hurt. We'll agree that in that case, it's hardly a bother and there's no need to take further action at this time." She rejoined her mother at the table. "There you have it."

"So it's not hurting more?"

"No, I don't think so. I shouldn't wear high heels. Ever. I do and it hurts. I know there's damage, but most of the pain is self-inflicted, for now."

They sipped companionably and Diana helped herself to one of the watercress and cream cheese sandwiches. Her mother sighed deeply and her shoulders relaxed. The last time her mother had seemed so tired was several days after a brutal storm had taken the roof off a local pensioners' care home, and Mote Hall had been filled with temporary beds and two dozen extra mouths to feed.

Thinking they would enjoy a quiet cuppa and then retire, Diana was reminded by her mother's next words that there was really no such thing as an off button for her mother's observant curiosity.

"Am I going to have to bribe your brother and sister to find out what it was they could blab to me, as you put it?"

"There's really nothing."

"And you didn't arrive home in tears and spend twenty-four hours in your room going through two boxes of tissues."

There was no point in further shilly-shallying. Her mother would ferret it out and resisting made it seem as if she were ashamed. "I had an…An experience. With a woman."

Her mother's expression remained curious. "And?"

"You heard the noun correctly?"

"Yes. With a woman." Hurt in her eyes, her mother asked, "Were you expecting me to be homophobic?"

"You've been setting me up with men since forever, Mum."

"If I'd known women would do the trick, I'd have been setting you up with them. I have friends with single lesbian daughters. I wanted you to have—" She looked just over Diana's shoulder. "The joys that I know are part of life. I suppose it's my own guilt I'm really trying to assuage, but truly, I want you to be happy."

Thoroughly confused, Diana asked, "Guilt? About what?"

"Sweetie, you were nine. You didn't know the choices you were making. That's on me."

"What are you talking about?"

"Elite level gymnastics. It's one thing to have a hobby and quite another to practice for three hours a day with the intention of competing. You understood about injuries—you'd sprained wrists and ankles already. But you had no way of comprehending the other risk, the one to your normal development."

"Oh, you mean the delayed puberty. It was kind of a gift—no periods for six extra years." It was the usual cheerful line she told herself, but there had been an undeniable toll. She was definitely getting a late start on life. She knew *now* that sex was really, really fun with the right person. She'd missed out on desire and attraction, which could be as painful as they were glorious. "Did you know, Mum? That delayed puberty was a risk?"

"Yes. I didn't think it a great price to pay. But after your injury I thought you'd catch up in a year, maybe two. Not a decade before you were even drawn to someone."

"Not everybody is meant to pair off."

"If being solitary was your normal state, then fine. But I couldn't know for sure. Was it natural, or was it because I hoped you'd win medals?" The level of anguish in her mother's eyes shocked Diana. "I wondered if you'd ever be able to have children."

She squeezed her mother's hand. "It's not the be-all and end-all for a woman, you know."

"I know that. But to have a choice in the matter versus it taken from you by something I decided for you when you were nine…"

"Water under the bridge, a long time ago." She reached for more tea, then decided against it. She hoped to sleep tonight and more caffeine wouldn't help. "If you'd known I was going to break my shoulder would you have not wanted me to do gymnastics?"

Her mother shook her head. "No. Because of all the times you didn't break your shoulder. You were inspiring to watch. I was so proud of you. You were proud of you. Determined and strong. Competing gave you ambition and drive, and fearlessness."

"So stop being guilty. In the end, I think it gave more than it took. I assure you everything works." She fought down a blush. "It was a great experience."

"Yet here you are."

"I had to come home for the wedding." The lie in her voice was so obvious her mother didn't even have to point it out. "Fine. I ran away."

"Why?"

"Because I'm not the right person for her. She deserves the right person."

Her mother put down her teacup and added a little more milk. "She's welcome here as long as she makes decent conversation. And she's good to you."

Her mother didn't elaborate but Diana would have been surprised if she hadn't been thinking about Diana's father, who hadn't been good for either of them. "That wasn't the reason. She's plenty good enough for me."

"I see."

"Do you?"

"You had a great experience. She's very good for you. Yet you prefer to suffer." Her mother had taken on the most infuriating of her expressions, the one that said she could read Diana's mind and saw through anything Diana might say.

"You can't fix it, Mum. It's not going to work out."

"If you've made up your mind, then of course, it won't work out."

"She has an anxiety disorder. Talking to me triggers her. She has this way of flexing her fingers that releases tension, so I know when it's me making her uncomfortable. We can't get through a conversation without me setting her off."

"Because conversations early in a relationship are notoriously easy for everyone."

"Mum." Diana sighed. "She deserves someone who makes the world…easier. I don't."

"How considerate of you to decide her limitations for her."

Diana swallowed the last bite of her sandwich as her mother's words echoed in her head. "That's not what I did."

"Of course not." Her mother's arch tone eased. "You know that Anwar's parents don't like me."

Diana nodded.

Her mother removed her earrings and set them on the table, then unpinned her hair so that the coil of thick chestnut came loose. "They are always chillingly polite, just as they were tonight. I don't know if it's my skin being a different color than his, our different religions, that he was so rich and I was a hard-up divorcee with a child." Her mother grimaced as a bobby pin tangled and refused to come out.

"Let me do it, Mum." Diana stood behind her mother's chair and gently worked out the knot that had the bobby pin trapped, then found the last few pins to add to the pile on the table.

"Thank you. I was going to sleep with them, but this is better."

"So how did you change your mind and say yes?"

"He asked why I was turning him down and I told him the truth. I was going to cause him pain. It hurt him very badly when I said that. He said I must really not know or love him well enough to think that he was unable to judge for himself what the damage would be if we married. He knew and he was asking me anyway." Her voice was soft with the memory. "I thought about it for several days, about where exactly the line fell between sacrifice and selfishness. I thought it would be too hard for *him*. Did I really mean it would be too hard for me to watch him suffer?"

Diana's hands stilled. "Was it hard?"

"Yes. At times. He has suffered. He loves his parents and the gulf they will not cross hurts him. I do what I can to make it better, but it was his choice and I trust that he is capable of making his own choices."

"While his parents think you're selfish for marrying him."

"That's very true. However, I would rather be the woman Anwar loves than the woman his parents would love."

Lying awake in bed later, hearing all the sounds of the quiet old house settling while a night breeze ruffled at the window curtains, Diana replayed her mother's words again and again.

She'd told herself she was running because Paris was better off without her. Had she run because she didn't want Paris to tell her so? But it was true—she didn't want to be another shadow in Paris's eyes. But was that all she could ever be to Paris—a dark energy? Had she nothing else to offer?

That was the problem, wasn't it? She'd thought she'd sorted out her life. Fun times acting and the thrill of liberating artifacts from the hands of the unsuspecting. She'd vaguely thought that someday a magic spark would happen and she would settle down into happy bliss of some kind. Somehow.

It did feel like magic, the way she felt about Paris. It was inexplicably real and beyond common sense. But instead of a carpet of flowers spreading out at her feet, complete with birds chirping in three-part harmony and skies raining cherry blossoms, she stood on the edge of fear. Any move meant falling.

She'd learned that falling always meant pain.

CHAPTER THIRTY-SIX

It was a leap of logic—several in fact—to blame Lisa. Lisa *had* suggested Paris work in the bar. After a day of frustration at the keyboard that left Susannah still standing on a beach in Italy, Paris took herself to the fancy laptop store and walked out with a featherweight top-of-the-line model. It would work anywhere, they promised, and it talked to the shiny new phone she'd also acquired.

It was hard to blame Lisa for what she decided to do after that, but Paris was going to try. She supposed that Lisa counted as her only friend, and if you couldn't blame a friend for your decisions, what was the point of having one?

New game, new rules. Five years ago she had erased nearly all anxiety triggers from her life, and anything that might lead to them. Knowing how a motivated hacker could trace digital footprints to their source had made her ruthlessly shut the online world out of her life. In the intervening years the twerps and vicious trolls had found new targets, no doubt. She could risk creating a new footprint with reasonable cautions. Still no social media, no gaming, but she could at least take advantage of twenty-first century conveniences.

She could have a panic attack again if triggered—that hadn't changed. What had happened to her would have derailed anyone, let alone someone with an anxiety disorder. She was the hiker who survived a bear attack by playing dead. Now she was finally raising her head to judge how safe it was to move again.

Her passport had three years left on it, and there was no reason not to see if working somewhere else would break her out of the funk. Why not see the Italian Riviera with her own eyes? Writers traveled, or so she'd heard, and she was more fortunate than most to have built up quite a nest egg.

Boss Anxiety was eager to tell her it wasn't safe out there. There were still bears. Being a hermit was wise. She did her best to ignore that ever-present pulse and when necessary she used all her tricks. Deep breathing mode helped, as did the exertion of trundling her suitcase through Logan airport toward the international flights security line. Nothing she was doing was beyond what she could handle. Her name on a flight manifest wouldn't bring death threats.

Just like that she was on a red-eye. The darkened cabin eased her anxiety levels. She could get used to flying first class if that meant being able to sleep. She expected to feel as if she'd been in the air for days, but it seemed like no time at all from takeoff to landing.

Aware that she looked as if she'd slept in her clothes—which she had—she changed her tired, rumpled sweatpants and T-shirt in favor of presentable slacks, shirt, and a tailored blazer. Over her shoulder she slung a slim knapsack she'd dubbed her Bag of Holding. Transformation complete, she felt well armored for this particular adventure. The phone was super handy for ordering a ride out of the airport. She spent the hour's journey peering out the window at landscapes she'd only read about.

The countryside grew lovelier as they drove south. There were trees in bloom and green-mounded hillsides striped with freshly turned earth. The crowded subdivisions near the airport gave way to larger, older houses behind ornate gates, and the farther apart the houses were the narrower the traffic lanes became. Thin trees with vivid green leaves lined the street on each side, their branches joined overhead.

They had just passed a meadow carpeted with yellow flowers when the car turned into a long gravel driveway. For the first time since leaving the airport Paris felt a hard pang of anxiety. The place was much, much larger than she'd expected. The central building was square and solid, and two long wings spread out right and left, dotted with white-framed doors and dormers. The driver rolled to a stop in front of curving marble steps that led to tall double doors.

All she had to do was walk up the stairs, give her name and take it from there.

It had seemed very doable at home. A quest. It wasn't what she expected, and she didn't have to stay if she didn't feel right.

Another deep breath. She worried she might hyperventilate at this rate. Ignoring the driver's curious gaze she squeezed her hands into fists and wrapped her arms tight around her, thinking of her mother. *Count to ten*. Her breathing eased and she finally got out of the car.

She was about halfway up the steps when the left-hand door opened. The tall woman with reddish-brown hair seemed startled to find Paris on her doorstep, but quickly recovered. "Can I help you?"

"Yes, ma'am." Her mouth was too dry to say more. She flexed her fingers and mentally counted to ten.

The woman's gaze had swept over Paris and returned to her face with sharp attention. Was that disapproval? Had she used the wrong form of address?

"You must be Paris."

That was not the greeting she'd predicted. She cleared her throat, hoping to find her voice.

"Come in." The gesture was imperious and Paris quickly obeyed.

A dark-haired teenager carrying a plate of toast and eggs emerged from what seemed like a breakfast room. She paused and looked inquiringly at Paris.

"Florence, this is Paris."

"How—" was all Paris could manage.

The teen's eyebrows went all the way up. "So *you're* Paris."

She nodded, trying to fathom how on earth these people could recognize her.

The teen addressed herself to both of them. "Diana left."

Countess Weald—whose eyes were very like Diana's—gave the teen a narrow look. "What do you mean she left?"

"She's on her way to America. Boston." She glanced meaningfully at Paris. "Isn't that where you're from?"

Paris's brain finally unlocked words. "I decided yesterday to go to the Italian Riviera. For book research. Since I was coming to Europe…"

The Countess's expression softened. "You could hardly pass our doorstep without stopping to say hello."

"Yes," Paris agreed, though it sounded absolutely idiotic. She flexed out her fingers.

Diana's mother was in person as formidable as she'd appeared in pictures. "Please take our guest in to breakfast. She must be famished."

"Just in here." The young woman's brown eyes were several shades darker than Diana's. "Diana said you had a Zelda T-shirt—Link with the Ocarina of Time."

Paris redrew the mental map of the journey she'd undertaken. She'd fallen into some kind of alternate reality, but she didn't know where. She hadn't known what to expect when she showed up with her ridiculous cover story of "I was just passing by," but it hadn't been chatting about a gaming T-shirt in an oak paneled dining room that smelled comfortingly of fresh bread, roses, and furniture polish. "Yes, I have one."

"Me too. I *adore* Zelda. When my exams are over I'm going to binge *Mask of Majora* for a weekend. Have a seat. My brother and his new wife are off on their honeymoon, and my father is taking his parents to the airport. Would you like some eggs? The tomatoes are from our greenhouse. So delicious, and Cook makes super bread. I'm going to gain a stone if I keep this up." She heaped a plate with food as she spoke and set it down at one of the place settings. "Please, do sit down."

"Thank you," Paris said automatically. She carefully hung her Bag of Holding on the back of the chair. She could make out the rise and fall of the Countess's voice, but the words were indistinct. "Did Diana mention me?"

"Yes." Florence opened her mouth to say more, but Diana's mother came in, tucking her phone into her pocket.

"I apologize for my abruptness earlier," she said. "I needed to make a phone call. Is breakfast to your liking?"

"Yes ma'am." Paris had a bite of eggs to prove it.

"Please call me Evelyn. I find that travel makes me ravenous. What takes you to Italy?"

She didn't know what Diana had told them about her. It didn't matter, either. Out of the jumble of all the possibilities and foolish hope that somehow there could be a future she knew this was true: it couldn't be based on lies. Lies crumbled and it was game over.

"I'm a writer and I'm stuck on my current novel. New horizons, actually seeing places I write about seemed like a good idea." The brown bread was fresh, as promised. She spread it with strawberry jam and it was possibly the best thing she'd ever had for breakfast that wasn't the contents of a minibar with Diana to look at.

"This is a perfect time of year to visit Italy. I recommend autumn as well. Might you go from there to France?"

They chatted about must-see destinations. It wasn't a surprise to learn that Evelyn had been everywhere. Florence chimed in with her favorite places. It sounded like she traveled to rock climb, a supposition supported by the whipcord muscles in Florence's forearms.

All the while Paris was wondering if this was politeness to someone who showed up unannounced to see a family member who wasn't there. Would it become clear when her visit was over, and she should get back in the waiting car and go away? Another part of her mind was spinning the fact that Diana had told her sister she was going to Boston. She wanted to hope, desperately, that it meant something good. The phone in her pocket would surely be full of ways to get back to Boston ASAP.

"Let me show you the gardens," Evelyn said a short while later. "They're in bloom right now, and I try to take a walk at this time of day."

Paris slung her knapsack on her shoulder and they toured the impressive greenhouse where the tomatoes from breakfast had been picked, and through an aromatic garden of herbs and lettuces. The meadow of yellow flowers was part of the estate's grounds with several winding paths that led to a central gazebo. The morning was cool and slightly overcast, though sunlight poured through gaps in the clouds and warmed her face. It was so lovely that it was easy to quell the anxiety that nudged at her. Yes, she was in a foreign land and talking to Diana's tall and intimidating mother, but she could handle it.

"I've never thought our meadow could be an enchanted area," Evelyn said in response to a comment from Paris.

"Before books I wrote story lines for video games. The gazebo could hold healing potions or power flowers. The cowslips—that's what you said these were?" At the nod of agreement Paris continued, "They could be home to vicious pixies."

Evelyn stepped into the shade of the gazebo. "And what kind of books do you write?"

Paris inhaled deeply—the gazebo was covered in honeysuckle, her favorite scent. "Have you heard of Anita Topaz? That's my pen name."

"I'm sorry, but I haven't."

"If you're not a romance novel fan, then you won't have heard of me. Fame is contextual."

"That it is." Evelyn smiled and Paris recognized the twist of the lips slightly to the right. Diana had her mother's strong frame, but was eight or nine inches shorter. "Your books are popular, I take it."

"Popular enough, in the US. I like smart women who have dreams of their own."

The change that came over Evelyn was so subtle that Paris almost missed it. The intimidating distance and reserve faded away, and was replaced by humor and warmth. "You have excellent taste."

Paris's cheeks flooded with heat. "I was talking about characters in my books."

"Of course. Excuse me a moment." She pulled her phone from her pocket, flipped through a few screens and put it away. "There's something I left in the house. I'll be right back. Please enjoy the garden."

She watched Evelyn leave the meadow by the most direct path to the back of the house. Quiet descended. Paris fished her phone out of her knapsack to text the driver she could see leaning against his black sedan. He texted back that he could wait as long as she needed him to. That anxiety taken care of, she studied offers of flights back to Boston.

A delivery van came into view as it turned off the road onto the long gravel driveway. A moment later a plain black sedan followed it and both disappeared around the house. A gardening truck eased onto the verge just outside the gate and moments later a leaf blower roared into use.

There weren't any flights leaving today, none that the app could find at least. She wasn't going to change her flight to Italy tonight until she had a reason to. She wondered if Florence would give her Diana's phone number—she ought to have thought of that earlier. Should she go back to the house to ask? Would that be rude? Sitting in a garden was pleasant enough, but it wasn't getting her any closer to Diana.

CHAPTER THIRTY-SEVEN

"Diana, this is your mother. Please come back with the car. Immediately."

Diana groaned loudly as she deleted the voice mail and thought hard about throwing her phone out the window of the car taking her to Heathrow.

She could pretend she'd never heard the message—and now her phone was playing her mother's ring tone again. "Mum, I'll miss my flight."

"This is urgent, Diana. Come back."

"I'm going to kill Florence. All of you are very bad at keeping secrets."

"That can hardly be a character flaw on our part. Are you turning around?"

"Mum!" But the call had already gone dead.

So much for her hope that, taking into account the time difference, she'd be able to turn up at Mona Lisa's bar somewhere around lunchtime today. She didn't care if she had to wait every day for a month. Even if Paris couldn't forgive her for leaving, at least she could say she was sorry in person and take her lumps. They could part more cleanly.

She would get a few more minutes with Paris. They might not be good minutes, but better than none, surely.

But now she'd never make the plane and her mother didn't care. Might even not want her to, though she'd thought after their heart-to-heart last night that her mother was okay with Diana's choices.

This was her mother being her mother. Her blood pressure wasn't helped when the car fell in behind a delivery van that apparently didn't have a working accelerator. She wanted to bite something, hard.

When the car finally stopped behind the house, there was no sign of her mother. Stomping up the stairs she felt completely justified at using every bit of her ability to project her voice as she yelled, "I'm back!"

"There's no need to shout," her mother said from behind her.

"Mum! This is so—"

"Go out to the gazebo."

"What the buggery—"

"*Lady* Diana Beckinsale! For once in your life do as you're told."

"I always do as I'm told!"

"Never the first time. It's always the second or third time with you." Her mother pointed at the door. "Go."

"I'm twenty-seven, Mother, and you can't order me around like a toddler."

Her mother closed her eyes for a moment. Her expression softened to a smile. "She likes smart women with dreams. You might start there."

To Diana's aggravation, her mother went into her study without another word and shut the door.

"Thou art all ice! Thy kindness freezes, Mother," Diana shouted through the door.

"Don't be childish," came the muffled reply.

"It's not childish. It's Shakespeare," Diana muttered. She drew back her leg to kick the study door, but thought better of it.

Even as she swore to herself that she would not do what her mother wanted she peeked at the gazebo from the withdrawing room. Someone was pacing in the small structure.

She made her way through the kitchen and mudroom and out into the root vegetable garden. The gate at the end opened onto a path into the meadow. The visitor's back was to her. She would have called out, but the gardener's leaf blower was too loud for her to be heard.

Ten paces from the gazebo she realized who it was. She halted, her feet rooted to the spot.

Everything her mother had said last night was still running through her head. She shouldn't make decisions about what Paris could and couldn't handle—that was up to Paris. And yet she didn't want to cause Paris pain. Was love always like this? Knowing that happiness came with a price? What if only one of you paid?

Diana didn't know if she could handle that kind of debt. She didn't know if she had her mother's backbone. Did she believe in love or didn't she?

She was *not* ready for this conversation. She'd planned to rehearse all the possible dialogue on the flight, and while she sat nursing a beer, possibly day after day, hoping to see Paris again.

She'd been so eager to get back on a plane that she hadn't taken the time for makeup, and had planned to put on something other than slacks and a T-shirt when she landed. Her hair was a mess. She was going to cry and her eyes already felt red.

For a moment she hated and loved her mother in equal measures. Paris was within her reach and she couldn't make herself move.

CHAPTER THIRTY-EIGHT

Wondering why Evelyn didn't return, and frustrated with the lack of flights back to Boston suggested by her supposedly best-thing-ever phone, Paris tried to cast off the accompanying anxiety as the sun came out again. The warmth bathed her face and she inhaled the scent of the honeysuckle blossoms. This place could easily be enchanted, she thought, and any gesture could make magic happen. If she searched carefully, she might find a portal. A portal that would lead her to her heart's desire, even.

Half laughing at her foolish hopes, she turned in place.

Her heart's desire was standing right there.

She blinked. Those charming freckles were still there, as were the shining brown eyes gazing at her.

The sun went behind the clouds again and Diana's eyes went cold. Diana crossed her arms and glared at Paris. "Why are you here?"

"Looking for you."

"I don't know why. I would have thought my note was clear."

Paris wasn't sure why she had thought it would be helpful to hear Diana say that the note was, in fact, her final word. It was as if Diana had stabbed her in the heart and now she was begging her to rip off the stitches, just for good measure. She flexed out her fingers. "It was. Brutally so."

Diana's expression hardened. "I realize that our time together was intimate and special, but it's over now. We're not a combination that works."

"Are you afraid to be out—to be with a woman? Is that it?" I can handle it, if that's the case, Paris thought.

Diana's eyes widened in genuine surprise at the idea. "No. Of course not."

"There's no 'of course not' in this world for women like us. We're not safe—not yet. I understand if you're scared."

"That's not it." Diana's irritation was obvious.

Paris bounced lightly on her toes. "But something is. I'm pretty sure that was your first time."

"It was that bad, was it?" There was finally something in Diana's expression that wasn't cold reserve. Hurt, perhaps?

"That's not what I meant. It's okay if you're feeling weird in your own skin. I was scared when I realized that on top of everything else that made me different I was also gay. It felt like the universe was piling on."

Diana was staring at her feet. "That's not it."

"So what is it? Tell me and I'll go."

Diana swayed slightly. This is it, Paris thought. Magic happens or she breaks us both. She shook her arms slightly, visualized anxiety dripping from her fingertips. The yellow flowers went gray. She couldn't help herself—she was holding her breath.

"It's that," Diana said. She pointed at Paris. "All those things you do because you're anxious."

She exhaled as if Diana had punched her in the stomach. Sharp-edged anguish sent a spasm of pain down her spine. "I don't believe you."

"You can hardly tolerate being near me."

Her throat was so tight she could hardly force out the words. "These things—all the compensations I do, they're not about you."

"Aren't they? How many times just since we met have you nearly had a panic attack?"

"You can trigger me. Anybody can. I choose whether to expose myself. That's up to me."

Much of the coldness in Diana's face had been replaced by a kind of desperation. "I trigger you."

"I'm the way I am. I'll be this way whether you're around or not." She swallowed hard, and put the truth into words. "If you can't handle being with someone like me, fine. I thought it was because I'm a woman, which I can't change. But it's really because I'm neurally different than you, which I can't change." She managed to shrug. "Same thing."

It didn't feel the same. It hurt much, much worse.

"I'm a thief." Diana's lips were hard and firm. "Sometimes. I don't want to give up who I am."

"I'm not asking you to. I am interested in who you are, right now. The risks you take make me anxious, of course they do. I choose to be near you anyway. If you'll let me. I can handle who you are, believe me, or I wouldn't be here. I *couldn't* be here."

Diana glanced over shoulder, as if she heard her mother's voice. "It's my turn to say that I don't believe you."

Paris reached into her Bag of Holding. She hadn't been sure she would find Diana, but had held out hope. "Then why were you going to Boston?"

"Who says I was going to Boston?"

"Florence."

"She doesn't know my plans."

A kind of calm unexpectedly settled on Paris. She wasn't sure why for a moment, then she had to smile. "I think you should know that I can tell when you're trying to lie to me."

Diana finally moved, taking a step closer, but still outside the gazebo. Paris sat down on the bench and opened the plastic bag she'd taken out of her knapsack. Diana craned to see what it was.

"I used acid-free cotton to protect it. It has signs of having been kept in too dry an environment," Paris said conversationally. She extracted the bundle from the plastic bag and held it out. "I didn't know what to do with it after that. I had two reasons for coming to see you."

Like a feral cat wary of any offering of food, Diana came close enough to her to take the wrapped object. "What is it?"

Paris didn't answer.

Diana unwound the cotton strips, her gaze going back and forth from the object in her hands and Paris's face. The moment a corner of dark obsidian came into sight Diana dropped onto the bench next to Paris. "It can't be."

"It is."

"But how—"

"Because I could. Because it wants to go home."

Diana wiped her eyes with one hand. "I don't know what to say."

"Gobsmacked would work, maybe?"

"I never expected you to do anything, take a risk like this, that was never the plan." Diana finally—finally—looked into Paris's eyes. "I don't want to put you in that position. I never meant to unleash anything on you."

"I took it when Heather left us alone. You left before I could tell you."

Diana was silent for a long time, the hammer on her lap. She stirred finally. "It should be in California. The Chumash still exist."

"Can you get it back to them?"

"Yes, of course," she said distractedly. "You said there were two reasons you came to see me."

"Isn't the other obvious?"

"Yes." A smile broke through a suddenly watery smile. "I'm going to make you say it."

"I'm pretty sure I fell for you the moment we met. I'd like to find out for sure. However we might make that work."

Diana carefully set the hammer to one side.

"We could try traveling together. You could spend time with me. I think you'd like my landladies. And I could spend time here with you. Your mother seems to—"

Diana kissed her. Hard, breathless, quick. "Stop talking for a minute."

The next kiss was like fire and Paris's head filled with the scent of Diana, mingling with honeysuckle and sunshine. There was no other choice that made sense except to hold her close. Tomorrow was forever away, and right now she was whole.

They kissed until they were both laughing. Limp with relief and exhilaration, Paris drew back enough to study Diana's beautiful face.

"I was going to Boston to tell you how sorry I was." Diana's eyes were glowing. "And hopefully to sleep with you again."

Paris sucked in a deep breath.

"I'm trying out the honesty thing." Diana raised her eyebrows suggestively. "You know all my secrets so why invent new ones?"

She filled her hands with Diana's hair. A warm breeze stirred the honeysuckle blossoms and the leaf blower had stopped. There was only the sound of her heart thrumming in her ears and their breathless whispers.

Diana glanced toward the house before kissing Paris again. "We don't have to solve anything right now. It's important not to ignore that there are still issues…We need to talk it through. The things…problems…" The speech had sounded better in her head when she'd rehearsed it in the car. "We don't want to end up like Romeo and Juliet. If they'd had twenty seconds of conversation—"

"Double suicide becomes wedding instead." Paris couldn't help herself. Her hand slipped behind Diana's neck and they kissed until her lips felt swollen.

Diana brushed her cheek against Paris's, soft as a hummingbird. "There's also that I don't know how to be gay."

"You could have fooled me." She bit softly on Diana's lower lip, enjoying the responsive shiver.

"I'm not afraid to be with you and for the world to know it. I'm not used to it. Not the way you and Heather seem to be. Like you spoke another language."

"We didn't start out so awesome." Paris leaned away so she could see Diana's eyes. With a gesture at herself she said, "I don't know about her, but this took practice."

"It showed, the practice."

She gave Diana a Spock eyebrow lift. "I trust that you enjoyed it."

"I did."

"Serious question." Thinking was increasingly difficult. "Tell me honestly, was that your first time? Ever?"

"Why do you think so?"

"You seemed surprised that it felt as good as it did." The passion and satisfaction on Diana's face were memories Paris wanted to add to.

"I *was* surprised." For the first time Paris saw uncertainty in Diana's face. "It was scary, but scary good. Really good. Which made it more scary."

"I'm not sure that makes sense."

Diana quoted primly, "Reason and love keep little company together."

"Show off—which play?"

Diana poked her in the chest. "*Midsummer*! What kind of Shakespeare geek are you?"

"I'm not in your league. I got lucky is all."

She meant so much more than Shakespeare, and would have kissed Diana again if the sound of approaching footsteps hadn't intruded. They both quickly tidied clothing that had somehow gone askew.

Their visitor wasn't the Countess, at least, but Florence, whose eyes were very large with curiosity. "Mother would like to know if Paris is staying to lunch and if Mrs. Cotton should prepare a room for her."

Diana looked at Paris for an answer, her face alight with an inviting smile.

"I have a flight to Italy this evening." Diana's expression faltered slightly and Paris quickly said, "Come with me."

"Oh."

"If you want to. If you have no other plans."

"The wedding celebration was over yesterday," Florence offered. Her innocent tone took on a faint quality of mischief. "She went on a bender during the hen party, but the hangover is gone."

"Go away, brat!" Diana ordered. "Don't you have to go back to school today?"

Unperturbed, Florence nodded. "Yes. I'm leaving in a bit. Shall I tell Mother that lunch is yes, room is no?"

"No comment."

Paris studied the grounds and buildings again as Florence took a meandering path back to the house. Diana's home was much larger than she had thought it would be. As they'd talked there had been a steady increase in the number of people going about various duties. She wanted to go back to kissing Diana, but privacy wasn't going to be easy even in a house this size.

Diana may have reached the same conclusion because she squeezed Paris's hand and let go. "Let's go in the house and talk."

"Sounds dull."

"We'll adjourn to my room."

"That doesn't sound dull."

Diana pulled her to her feet. "It will not be—and step, two, three. You can kiss me—and step, two, three."

Paris laughed and they fell into easy, mutual rhythm. It was a magic meadow after all.

CHAPTER THIRTY-NINE

"Do you think they like me?" Diana cuddled into Paris's side in spite of the heat. Boston's muggy night air threatened to turn her Vera Wang cocktail dress into damp rags. At least she wasn't wearing a wig.

"Of course they do," Paris said. "Grace and Adya think you're charming."

"I think they're adorable." The past three months had been a whirlwind, with far too much time spent on airplanes. Finally meeting Paris's landladies had been grounding, but Diana still felt on probation. They didn't seem to mind that their tenant had only been there for a handful of days until the past week, but they weren't keen that Paris was leaving in a few days for Toronto. "I'm on probation though, I know it."

"We're coming back here after Toronto and they'll love you even more," Paris predicted.

A black sedan made a U-turn a few doors down and pulled up in front of them.

"Right on time." Diana slithered into the backseat while Paris confirmed with the driver that after he'd dropped them he would return and wait for Grace and Adya who were still getting ready.

It was a short drive to Mona Lisa's, but Diana had pointed out that while she was happy to walk there, not when she was wearing party clothes. "Tonight should be fun. If it's not, we can leave."

"I'll be fine." Paris tucked Diana's arm under hers. "Sweetie, don't anticipate my stress for me. There's no reason for both of us to feel it. Trust me to say something."

"I'm learning." She felt Paris's anxiety and didn't think that would ever stop. What she was learning was how to cope with its effect on her.

"I love you for that." She kissed the top of Diana's head. "And for a few of your other special talents."

Diana was deeply pleased that Paris was wearing the Pierre Cardin cologne she'd given her for their two-month anniversary. "Glad to know you're not bored yet."

"I'm not. But I noticed you were looking through an auction catalog this morning."

"I was."

"Do you have your eye on something?"

"I think so. The catalog is from two years ago. I need to track down a few of the items. Find out where they ended up."

Paris's fingers moved lightly on her slacks. "Okay."

"You have a deadline. Doing this will keep me busy." Diana put her head on Paris's shoulder. They'd done a lot of talking, but not found a magic wand that fixed everything. Given that they could afford to travel between their homes, and that Anita Topaz was suddenly a very busy woman, picking one place to live over the other hadn't been crucial. As long as they kept talking, it seemed to work. They had agreed to one thing, though: neither of them would be someone they weren't to make the relationship work.

The car arrived at Mona Lisa's and Diana led the way into the bar. It wasn't crowded yet because the official invites were for half-seven, and that was twenty minutes away. Even so, a raucous cheer greeted them.

"You look amazing," she told Lisa, and it was an understatement. The red velvet dress had a retro-fifties silhouette. The chunky heels and bright beaded jewelry turned Lisa into one hundred percent pinup.

"So do you—putting the va in va-voom."

"Thanks. Can't go wrong with a little black dress." The high waist made her look taller as did the Steve Madden CFM pumps that she was going to take off at the soonest possible moment.

"Is that your real accent this time? You sound like a royal."

"I actually do talk like this. Prep school and all that."

Lisa was smiling benignly as she watched Paris chat with the regular barflies. "You should be aware," she said to Diana conversationally, "that my best friend knows how to bury unwanted things under glaciers."

"How inter—wait, what?"

Lisa gave her a bland look.

"You're quite frightening."

"You think so?" The curve of her lips was worthy of Lady Macbeth, "Good. Because I get very, very unhappy when things I care about are damaged."

"Duly noted," Diana managed. She groped for Paris's hand while giving Lisa a bright smile. So she was on probation with Lisa too? Well, she was happy that Paris had such staunch friends, wasn't she?

As Paris turned away from her conversation Lisa gestured at the TVs, all tuned to the same channel and presently on mute. "We'll be ready to roll when the bigwigs show up."

Paris seemed content to hold hands and stay close. It was the first time they were giving their agreement a try. Choosing the warm, familiar surroundings of the bar had seemed like their best foot forward. Diana had already spotted the reporter. She nodded in that direction to Paris who was finishing a long, steadying breath. "Ready?"

"As I'll ever be."

Diana put on her best party face and led the way. "Betty Johns? From *The Globe*?"

"You must be Anita." The slender blond shook hands and then looked curiously at Paris.

"Actually," Diana said, "*we* are Anita Topaz."

"We're a team," Paris added.

"I think I have my first question already," Johns said as she scribbled a note on her tablet. "Reynard Media said there would be some surprises."

"We'll try to keep it interesting." Diana took the chair closest to the reporter and waited until Paris had settled next to her to continue. "Ellis does the writing and I do the rest. We play to our mutual strengths."

Paris's hand patting the arm of her chair was out of the reporter's sight. "I'm camera shy. Whatever you think that means, times a million."

"Are you fielding a lot of media these days?"

Diana answered smoothly, "Definitely. We're thrilled that Reynard Media is willing to take a chance on a romantic comedy."

"The box office can be unpredictable."

"We believe that *Hands Off the Merchandise* has everything rom com fans could want, and plenty of intrigue." Diana had all the lines down, following the RMG talking points item by item. "We're going to Toronto next week to meet with the screenwriter."

Johns leaned forward, her gaze taking in Paris's suit and tie. "You can answer this off the record if you want. But is the writer of the Anita Topaz romances a lesbian?"

"It's not off the record," Paris said. "The answer is yes."

Johns scribbled a note. "Why do you write straight romances?"

"It didn't occur to me I had other choices. Not when I developed Anita Topaz's voice and story style."

"Is there a message behind the fact that the recent press releases don't call them bodice rippers?"

"It was always meant ironically," Diana answered. "We quite like the 'Smart is the New Sexy' campaign for the next novel and the movie."

Paris chimed in once or twice, and they'd covered all the important topics by the time the bar grew too loud for them to hear each other without shouting.

A commotion at the door was probably the VIPs—bigwigs, as Lisa had called them.

"Is that them?" the reporter asked Paris, who had stood up to see.

"Yes."

"I'm on it. Thank you both." With that Johns grabbed her notebook and recorder and sliced her way through the crowd toward Heather Reynard. Newly confirmed as the CEO of Reynard Media Group, Heather was newsworthy and then some. Some people said she was now one of the most powerful women in the world—and she'd introduced the world to her partner of a decade by way of announcing their wedding plans.

Diana spared a kind thought for her mother. By removing Diana from her father's influence, Diana had never been in Heather's position of enforced conformity and divided loyalties. What a life it must have been. Paris had told her that Heather's partner hadn't even been allowed in the corporate headquarters. Plenty of people were saying that Heather should have given her father the finger and come out years ago. None of them had stood to lose hundreds of millions of dollars and the position that Heather now held. Heather had sent a gracious thank-you note to Paris for being there when the news came. After an obsessively perky marketing intern had left another message asking Paris to make a personal appearance, Paris had written back. Heather had listened, proposed a compromise—and here they were.

Paris put her arms around Diana and they relaxed into each other.

Lisa arrived with a drink in each hand. "Iced tea," she said. "This one has Grey Goose Citron in it."

"I'll take that," Diana said.

"I thought you would. So how did it go?"

"Pretty well," Paris said. "I never got to say how good Diana is at challenging my storyboards and making me work harder for a better story. The reporter didn't ask many questions about the writing itself."

"So I knew most of the answers," Diana finished.

"Gotta go. Looks like showtime." Lisa merged with the crowd. A few moments later she was sitting on the bar facing the televisions.

It was amazing—the place fell silent. The woman knew how to hold a room, Diana thought. She kicked off her shoes and Paris helped her up onto her chair so she could see.

"We all know why you're here. Free drinks. Let's all say thank you to Reynard Media Group for a swell party that's just getting started."

"Thank you Reynard Media," the crowd echoed.

"Let's also say thank you to our own Anita Topaz for making it happen."

"Domestic drinks only," Diana called out. "Nothing imported."

Amid laughter, the crowded chanted, "Thank you Anita Topaz."

From her high position Diana could now see how crowded the bar was. It looked as if Heather had brought the RMG publicist who had video chatted with them last week and several other people as well. She waved eagerly at Grace and Adya who had found the seats that Paris had asked Lisa to hold for them.

"Pipe down in the back." Lisa winked at Diana. "So now you're going to listen politely to our VIP guest, Heather Reynard."

The crowd did exactly as instructed, and Heather—wisely—kept it brief.

She was one of the tallest people in the bar and her voice carried easily. "Fresh from our production team, you're about to see what no one else has. It's the first trailer of *Hands Off the Merchandise* based on the book by Anita Topaz, and it reveals the star who will play Demi Moran. Let's roll it."

The TVs exploded with techno runway music. Diana was so excited she forgot she was standing on a chair and had to clutch Paris's shoulder to keep steady. They both cheered with everyone else when the fresh-faced local girl who'd grabbed a supporting actress Oscar last year appeared. She would make an excellent Demi, Diana thought.

Heather was eventually free of the reporters and edging toward them. She paused to answer a few questions for the local gay newspaper. Diana was only beginning to appreciate how much the community resembled an iceberg. Parts of it were visible to anyone, but a lot remained hidden from a casual glance. Now that she'd learned to see it, Diana saw how far and wide it spread.

Diana felt Paris jump when a flash went off. It was no longer possible to hide her from cameras. That was the trade-off of a high profile event like a movie deal. The RMG publicist had assured them that once actors were named, no one would care about the writers. For Paris's sake, Diana hoped that was true. It was also true that she didn't invite the limelight for herself either.

Heather had finally reached them. "How are you holding up?"

"Okay," Paris said. "On the phone you said you had more personal news."

"I do. Legal backtracked through some of the email you had saved. Too many women are still terrified out of their careers and silenced on social platforms that hide behind a pretense at neutrality. There's no moral neutral ground about rape and death threats. Several of the accounts that sent you threats led to real people. If you want to sue for damages they can be made an example of—no financial outlay for you. RMG has very, very deep pockets. Vivid examples of not getting away with brutalizing women online are needed."

Paris took a deep breath. "Can I think about it? It's—a walk in a cesspool."

"I understand." Diana believed that Heather actually did understand. "Can you get back to me in a week? The attack dogs are ready."

Paris nodded. "How are *you* holding up?"

Diana was surprised to see a glitter in Heather's eyes. "The father I could respect and the man he was can't be the same person. But they are. I don't know that I'll ever reconcile that." Her jaw tightened and for a moment she looked like Diana's mother when she'd decided something needed fixing. "I can run a different company with a different culture."

When Heather and her entourage left the bar, Paris muttered, "I feel a little bit guilty about it."

"By 'it' do you mean an antiquity now in California being authenticated and restored?"

"Yeah. I think given time, if someone asked her, Heather would have donated it."

"You could be right." Diana squeezed her arm. "But it's a long, weary job, waiting for some people to do the right thing."

Paris kissed her and Diana went back for seconds. A satisfying minute later Paris asked, "Why don't we blow this Popsicle stand?"

"What are you offering?"

"I might be convinced to make brownies for breakfast."

"Nothing I'd like better. For breakfast." She tugged Paris in the direction of the door. "If we start thanking everyone now we might be home by midnight."

It was at least an hour before they made their way out to the street. "Gosh, it has not cooled off out here. I'm glad the car is on its way." Diana regarded Paris, her smart, brave, delectable Paris, with a proud smile. "You must be floating."

"I am. It was an out-of-body experience." Paris mopped at her brow. "It's actually real. It's going to happen."

"Thank your agent—she's a dynamo."

"Thank you." Paris pulled her close. "You were terrific. I think the partnership is going to work out."

Diana looked into Paris's eyes and saw a shimmering reflection of herself, brown hair, brown eyes, freckles and all. Nakedly herself and wrapped safe in her lover's arms. "You do?"

Paris was cast in green and orange neon from the bar's signs. Her cocky haircut had been refreshed and she wore the suit and tie like a second skin. Diana realized that there was very little left of the woman who had reminded her of a wary dog, certain that every hand was an enemy. "I do."

"So do I."

She relaxed into Paris's arms. Home.

Bella Books, Inc.

Women. Books. Even Better Together.

P.O. Box 10543
Tallahassee, FL 32302

Phone: 800-729-4992
www.bellabooks.com